The Soldier of Virginia

The Soldier of Virginia

A Novel on George Washington

Marjorie Bowen

INHERITANCE PUBLICATIONS
NEERLANDIA, ALBERTA, CANADA
PELLA, IOWA, U.S.A.

Canadian Cataloguing in Publication Data
Bowen, Marjorie.
The soldier of Virginia

ISBN 0-921100-99-X

1. Washington, George, 1732-1799—Fiction. 2. United States—History—Revolution, 1775-1783—Fiction. I. Title.
PR6003.O676S66 1997 823'.912 C97-910884-5

Library of Congress Cataloging-in-Publication Data
Bowen, Marjorie, 1888-1952.
The soldier of Virginia : a novel on George Washington / Marjorie Bowen.
p. cm.
ISBN 0-921100-99-X (pb)
1. Washington, George, 1732-1799—Fiction. 2. Virginia—History—Colonial period, ca. 1600-1775—Fiction. 3. United States—History—Revolution, 1775-1783—Fiction. 4. United States—History—1783-1815—Fiction. 5. Presidents—United States—Fiction. 6. Generals—United States—Fiction. I. Title.
PR6003.O676S65 1997
823'.912—dc21 97-32035
CIP
AC

Cover Painting (detail): Emanuel Leutze, *Washington Rallying the Troops at Monmouth.* University of California, Berkeley Art Museum; gift of Mrs. Mark Hopkins.

Box 154, Neerlandia, Alberta Canada T0G 1R0 Tel. & Fax (403) 674 3949
e-mail: inhpubl@telusplanet.net
Website: http://www.telusplanet.net/public/inhpubl/webip/ip.htm

Published simultaneously in U.S.A. by Inheritance Publications
Box 366, Pella, Iowa 50219

Available in Australia from Inheritance Publications
Box 1122, Kelmscott, W.A. 6111 Tel. & Fax (09) 390 4940

Printed in Canada

Contents

PART ONE

MR. WASHINGTON

PART TWO

THE CAUSE OF LIBERTY

PART THREE

THE CAUSE WON

George Washington (1732-1799)

PART ONE
MR. WASHINGTON

"Your good health and fortune are the toast at every table."
Colonel Fairfax to Washington.

Mount Vernon

PROLOGUE

GOVERNOR DINWIDDIE'S ENVOY

"Mr. Washington — and who is Mr. Washington?"

"It is the Governor of Virginia's envoy, Monsieur — bearing a letter from his Excellency."

St. Pierre gave his inferior officer a quick glance; two things occurred to him: the first was that Dinwiddie must be serious if he had sent a messenger in such weather; the second was that it would have been more courteous if the envoy had been a man of some rank. He remarked on neither of these things, but quietly requested that Mr. Washington should be brought into his presence.

The scene was St. Pierre's room in the newly erected Fort le Bœuf; December cold filled the apartment despite the huge fire of logs that roared on the hearth; and the view from the window was of a frozen lake, great trees against a drab sky, and the steady falling of snowflakes.

Monsieur St. Pierre moved his chair so that it faced the entrance, and thoughtfully beat a little tattoo on the arm of it. When the door was opened he raised his head, still with a thoughtful air, and rose with a deliberate kind of courtesy.

The man who entered and the man awaiting him looked at each other for a full, intent moment.

The newcomer saw a plain, rude apartment hung with skins over the rough walls, carpetless, and furnished with the simplicity to be looked for in one holding an outpost in a little known corner of the New World. Yet here and there were evidences of the old civilization — in some beautiful glasses on a side table, in an elaborate, gilt ormolu clock, hanging in one corner, in a shelf of books bound in rich leather, and in the person of Monsieur St. Pierre himself, who was very much of the old world, and of those flowers of the old world — Paris and Versailles.

He was a man of middle age, fair-faced and slender; he wore his blue uniform and his sword; his hair was powdered and tied with a great bow of sapphire ribbon, his expression alert, intelligent, and perfectly composed. The young Virginian had an impression of a smooth, clever officer, well suited to his post.

Monsieur St. Pierre, on his side, was summing up Governor Dinwiddie's messenger with equal swiftness and acumen. He saw a man very young, unusually tall and unusually graceful, wrapped in furs to the chin, with a cap pulled down to his ears and soft riding-boots drawn to his knees. Before he spoke, the young man took off his cap with a winning air of courtesy and disclosed a quantity of heavy brown hair that framed an aristocratic, charming face, the most attractive feature of which was a pair of gray eyes very ardent, brilliant and beautiful.

"I am Mr. Washington," he said gravely.

St. Pierre answered in the same language, English. "I do not know the family, Monsieur."

The Virginian replied with unaltered gravity. "Of the Washingtons of Stafford County, Sir; my brother was Captain Lawrence Washington of Mount Vernon, and I was formerly land surveyor to my Lord Fairfax of Belvoir. Recently I have joined the colonial army. Governor Dinwiddie charged me with this mission, which is to deliver, personally, to you, this letter."

He unbuttoned his fur coat, showing a glimpse of scarlet and heavy lace, and drew from his bosom a letter sealed with the seal of the governor of Virginia. As he handed this with his proud, fearless, youthful gravity to St. Pierre, the Frenchman was delicately aware of an atmosphere of great strength that the young man gave out with the cold air he had brought in with him from the freezing forest.

He put the letter in his pocket and said politely and carelessly, "Will you not be seated, Mr. Washington?" He resumed his own chair. "You must have had a difficult journey," he added.

"It took nineteen days, Sir," answered the Virginian. "The snow delayed us a great deal." He removed his heavy gloves and his furs, revealing his claret-colored coat flourished in gold, and his scarlet waistcoat embroidered with manifold wreaths of silk flowers.

"You are not alone?" asked the Frenchman, regarding him with a close and yet easy scrutiny.

"I have one Christopher Gist with me, Sir, who came exploring here three years past, and who serves as guide; and my friend, Van Brahm; also four fellows well used to the woods."

"Were you not, with such a poor escort, afraid of an attack from the Indians?" The glance of the two men crossed.

"No," answered the Virginian quietly. "I found them of friendly leanings, and have even a small retinue of those who elected to follow me, including several notable sachems."

St. Pierre smiled. "Yet your expedition, in such weather, required some courage, Monsieur."

Mr. Washington slowly flushed. "I hope," he said, "that Governor Dinwiddie would not have sent me on any expedition that did not require courage," and he smiled also, in a gentle yet absolutely proud manner.

Now that he was free of his furs, his extreme youth was very apparent; he could not have been more than twenty-two or twenty-three. The Frenchman, on a sudden impulse it seemed, asked abruptly, "You know what is in this letter?" — he touched his breast.

"Yes."

"You are to wait for an answer, Mr. Washington?"

"Yes." There was a slight flash in the beautiful gray eyes of the Virginian.

"Ah!" exclaimed Monsieur St. Pierre swiftly. "I see I speak not only to the envoy but to the confidant."

Mr. Washington rose and bowed grandly. "You may take it so if you please, Sir," he said.

"We may discuss this matter after supper," answered the Frenchman.

"We may discuss it now," answered the Virginian. "I have been so long delayed on the way that I would be as brief as possible on this matter that I may return as soon as may be to Richmond."

The Frenchman answered smoothly. "I have not yet read your letter, Mr. Washington — give me grace till after supper."

He rose, and the Virginian was about to answer, when a melody broke the frosty air, a melody at variance with the rough walls and the bitter prospect from the rude window, but in keeping with the beautiful glasses, the gilt clock, the elegant books, the figure of Monsieur St. Pierre — the music of the old world, the music of courts.

"My daughter will entertain you," said the Frenchman.

Mr. Washington rose without a word and followed his host to an inner door which St. Pierre opened on to a smaller room, furnished more like the homes of Richmond than the outer apartment. The furniture was elegant, though worn, and the best room in the best house of the old trading station had been skillfully enough transformed into a lady's chamber.

A beautiful clavichord, gilt and painted with hunting scenes, stood opposite the great fire, and before the keys a fair creature was seated who seemed, despite the ruby glow of the flames, of an ethereal pallor and brightness. She wore a white muslin gown, an overskirt of mauve taffeta frilled with violet silk, and a mantle of the white furs from the north, fastened on her bosom by a sparkling clasp of brilliants. Her pale gold hair slipped over her fichu in love locks and was carelessly arranged in a fashion which emphasized the youthful melancholy of her appearance.

Near her was seated a young officer wearing the same uniform as Monsieur St. Pierre, a man of a thin, hawk-like face and an air of pleasant authority. Monsieur St. Pierre presented them.

"My daughter, Mademoiselle Hortense — Monsieur de Beaujeu — this is Mr. Washington, the envoy of the governor of Virginia."

The lady rose and curtsied; the officer bowed; Monsieur St. Pierre left them.

The lady indicated a chair near the fire. "You are welcome," she said, in a pretty, halting English. "Have you come a long way?"

"From Richmond, in Virginia, Madam; it is near to two hundred miles."

"Ah!" said Monsieur de Beaujeu. "Then you know the forests and the Indians."

"It is the first time, Sir, that I have left Virginia."

The Frenchman looked at him narrowly. "You risked a great deal," he remarked.

"Only my life. I carried no secrets," answered Mr. Washington gravely; he seated himself opposite the young officer and turned his deep eyes on the lady. "Have you ever been to Virginia, Madam?"

"Oh, no, no further than this." She gave a shudder and a sigh. "It is terrible, this exile, is it not, Monsieur?"

"Exile!" he echoed.

"We are exiled from France, as you are from England," she answered. "And we long for Paris as you long for London."

"I — I am not English, Mademoiselle, save by allegiance." He smiled. "My family left England nearly a hundred years ago. I am Virginian."

She looked bewildered; her graceful hand made a slight gesture toward the frozen prospect beyond the window. "Then this is — home to you?" she asked.

He was still smiling, but his voice was grave. "Virginia, Mademoiselle, is very much *home*" — the word was stressed beautifully — "to me."

"Ah!" she exclaimed. "Canada is to me — exile — the saddest!"

"Hortense," said Monsieur de Beaujeu in a reserved manner, "has the foolish idea that she will never see France again."

A little pause of silence fell, seemed to descend with the encroaching dusk and drive speech and light away together. The young Virginian fixed his serene soft eyes on the frail foreign beauty, who sat so mournfully by the gorgeous clavichord. He compared her in his mind to all things white and delicate that he had ever seen: to white violets, to flowers of frost lying in frozen grass, to the long beams of crystal moonlight he had often watched quiver in the waves of the Potomac, to the snow-wreaths he had seen glimmering untouched on the branches of the great trees in the virgin forests, above and beyond the hand of man. There was color on her amber locks, in her hazel eyes, in her sweet face, and in the slender throat that rose above the white fur, but color misted and refined by this cold look of purity, like the colors of blossoms in moonlight.

"Will you not continue your playing, Mademoiselle?" he asked, gently disturbing the silence.

Her fine fingers fell to the ivory and ebony keys; she began playing a formal gavotte, looking the while out of the window at the winter evening darkening above the waters of Lake le Bœuf.

Under cover of the melody Monsieur de Beaujeu spoke. "Is this your first stop, Monsieur?"

The Virginian straightened at once. "No, Sir, I stopped at Venango, where I was entertained by three of your countrymen, who delayed me by putting dissension among my Indians."

He spoke quietly, almost gently, but always with that reserved and perfectly fearless air that conveyed great strength.

"Is your mission a secret?" asked Monsieur de Beaujeu.

"Not in the least."

"May I hear?"

The gray eyes steadily returned the challenge of the brown. "Oh, yes. I come with a message from Governor Dinwiddie requesting the removal of the three forts — Venango, Fort le Bœuf, and Presqu'isle, that you have built on British soil."

"British soil . . ." repeated the Frenchman slowly.

"British soil," said Mr. Washington. "The valley of the Ohio and Lake Erie, Sir, belong to England."

"These frontier questions . . ." began Monsieur de Beaujeu.

"This is no question at all, but a matter of established fact," returned Mr. Washington serenely. "You have built three forts on British ground and you must at once retire or . . ."

The Frenchman caught him up. "Or — a threat from Virginia?"

"Or — I shall come a second time, not with Governor Dinwiddie's letters, but with Governor Dinwiddie's men."

Monsieur de Beaujeu rose abruptly; the young Virginian regarded him with a slow scrutiny in his magnificent eyes.

The gavotte came to an end; Mademoiselle Hortense turned to her guest. "Are you fond of music?"

"Yes, Mademoiselle."

"Do you play?"

"Sometimes, Mademoiselle."

He crossed over to the clavichord and she marked his full, splendid height and the great strength of his make, and shrank a little, as if he overwhelmed her.

"Will you play now?" she asked, leaving her seat.

He took the place with a little laugh.

"I will light the candles."

"No, I can play in the dark." He smiled up at her slender radiance. Monsieur de Beaujeu was watching him thoughtfully and intently.

Mr. Washington touched the keys; he played well — well enough for the salons of Paris; too well for a man, Monsieur de Beaujeu thought.

"What is that?" asked Hortense.

"An English song . . ." he stopped abruptly, and broke into another measure. "This is an English song, too — very old-fashioned, Madam — *Lillibulero* they called it."

"Ah, I know. It was composed against the French, was it not?"

"Against the enemies of England, Madam," he replied serenely.

"It sounds defiant — triumphant."

"Oh, they conquered, you know," smiled Mr. Washington. "We always do . . ."

"There was Fontenoy," said Monsieur de Beaujeu.

"You may count that as a German defeat," answered the Virginian composedly.

Hortense sighed; she moved past him, a white shadow in the deepening gloom. "You hate my nation, Monsieur," she remarked reproachfully.

He ceased playing. "You are of no nation," he said gravely; "any more than the snow-flowers or the spring blossoms are of one particular country, Madam."

"But you hate the French?" challenged Monsieur de Beaujeu.

"I think, Sir, I hate the French policy in Canada," answered Mr. Washington calmly. He rose from the music-stool and looked at the Frenchman whom he topped by nearly a head. "Your Indians and your Jesuits, Sir, must remain on the other side of the frontier."

Hortense's fair hand touched her countryman's sleeve. "Does this mean war?" she asked with a dim fear.

"Perhaps," said Monsieur de Beaujeu.

"I thought," remarked the Virginian softly, "it would so be taken; the three Frenchmen at Venango told me they meant to keep the Ohio valley."

"So we do," assented Monsieur de Beaujeu.

The Virginian slightly lifted his splendid head. "I'm glad," he said simply. "There is no way but war to settle this dispute."

As he spoke, the bearskin curtain in front of the door was pulled aside and St. Pierre entered. He sharply asked for candles and his gentle daughter began lighting them, on the mantelpiece, on the clavichord, and on the round tulip table with blue satin pockets filled with lace and muslin needlework.

St. Pierre came to the fireplace which was a cavern of red-gold light, crossed by the spectral forms of glowing logs; he held Dinwiddie's letter in his hand, and looked at Mr. Washington. "This is an arbitrary demand," he said.

"Yours was an arbitrary action," replied the Virginian. "Canada to the French and America to the English. You, Sir, have provoked this in crossing the borders."

St. Pierre was looking at him with a hard intentness. "Is England behind this?"

"Virginia is," said Mr. Washington.

"But England?"

"Governor Dinwiddie has full authority from His Majesty's Government," answered the Virginian. "But we and the other States know well enough how to act without advice from Britain — at present, Sir, you deal with us. May I ask for your answer to Virginia?"

The Frenchman smiled. "I requested some delay, but then I did not know the brusque contents of this letter; my answer is that I can do nothing but forward your request to Monsieur Duquesne, Governor of Canada."

Mr. Washington smiled; his vivid personality seemed to flash out swiftly as if he had suddenly declared himself in loud tones; but he answered very quietly, "What reply will Monsieur Duquesne make?"

"I know, and you know also, Monsieur," said St. Pierre, slightly flushing, "that what France has once taken up she does not lightly lay down."

"And what England has once possessed," flashed Mr. Washington, "she does not easily relinquish. You will know what to expect from Virginia."

"Monsieur Duquesne's reply shall be sent to Governor Dinwiddie," said the Frenchman, very stately.

"Then I think my audience is ended," replied the Virginian.

"Will you not share our supper?" suggested Hortense timidly.

He turned to her with a swift smile. "Madam, I must go back to Richmond without delay; gentlemen" — he included the two officers in a little bow — "I will no longer detain you."

Monsieur de Beaujeu laughed, and Monsieur St. Pierre spoke gravely, "That must be as you wish, Monsieur."

His daughter shuddered. "This means war, I think," she said.

Mr. Washington stooped to kiss the hand she offered him. "Do not hate me for the errand on which I come," he said. "Adieu."

He smiled frankly at Monsieur de Beaujeu, who laughed again, and followed the elder man into the outer room, where his coat, cap, and gloves lay over one of the worn chairs of the trading-station. He threw on these furs; he seemed elated and pleased; yet, indeed, his bearing was inscrutable.

Monsieur St. Pierre accompanied him to the door. "God protect us from a bloody war," he said.

"God protect us," answered Mr. Washington, "from a weak peace." He descended the rough dark stairs. Below, in the passage, waited a man with a weary, enthusiastic face, who swung his bear-skin gloves by long scarlet tassels.

"Mr. Gist — Christopher Gist," said the Virginian in a low, excited voice, "they have refused! We are riding home at once, Mr. Gist!"

The door was opened for them by the French servant; Mr. Washington looked back at St. Pierre, who stood at the head of the first flight of stairs, and raised his cap, then stepped out into the bitter, colorless, fading evening.

The Indians and the horses with their saddle-bags were soon ready in the little courtyard of the former trading-station that now served as a French fort. The young Virginian, his guide, Van Brahm, his old fencing master, his four attendants and the escort of Indians, mounted and turned their backs on Fort le Bœuf.

Against the immense sweep of gray sky rose the immense trees, some bare, some clothed in somber foliage wreathed with snow; the air was full, too, of this sense of immensity; the wind was powerfully icy, fragrant with the pure breath of untouched snow. Above the dark distance of the lake rose a flight of wild fowl, darker yet, and swiftly disappearing into the shadows of the night.

Christopher Gist turned up his collar; neither he nor any member of the party made any comment on the fact of their leader's wilful leaving of shelter as night was falling; the Indians, indeed, were glad; they did not understand an armed truce and, looking on the French as enemies, they wished to take no favors at their hands, but come straight to the decision of the tomahawks.

The beautiful horses were turned toward the huge forests that only Gist and the Redskins knew how to track. A few flakes of snow fluttered slowly from the darkening heavens; after the brief sunset interval the storm was beginning again.

"Shall we fight Canada?" asked Van Brahm.

Mr. Washington's eyes sparkled as brightly as the brilliant brooch that clasped his cravat and glimmered through the opening of his fur collar. "If it rests with me, we shall," he said.

CHAPTER I

WILLIAMSBURG

Two ladies were buying taffeta in a shop opposite the old State House in Williamsburg. The low shop, surrounded with straight shelves and divided by a long counter, polished by much use, was cool and fragrantly dim, but beyond the diamond-paned window the street lay in bright, early spring sunshine which glowed on the red brick houses in the Dutch style, with white lines of mortaring, and on the State House and the cupola surmounted by an elaborate lion weathercock.

The muslin gowns and satin coats of the ladies fell in delicate folds over their high stools. Bales of taffeta — mauve, pink, white, and flowered — covered the counter between them, but they were not looking at the stuffs, but, very earnestly, at the old merchant, and the two fair faces under the chip hats and the withered face under the white wig wore the same expression of interest, excitement, and anxiety.

"I heard today, Madam," said the silk mercer, addressing the younger of the two ladies, "that Mr. Fry and Mr. Washington were to be sent to the Ohio valley to build a fort — with orders to resist anyone who opposed them — and that, Madam, in my opinion, means war."

"Ah, no," answered the fair customer, shaking her golden head. "I can't believe it, I won't believe it!"

The other lady spoke. "I think it will be war, Sarah, if Mr. Washington goes."

"Do you know him, Madam?" asked the shopman.

"I have met him," she answered, "at the Government House. I am sure he is very resolute."

"But why should he want war, Martha?" persisted Sarah Mildmay.

"Because war is the only honorable way," replied her companion. "The French defy us — you may read in the newsletters the high behavior of Governor Duquesne."

"Yes, Madam," put in the old man, "but Governor Dinwiddie is equal to them, of a surety. He wrote to the Carolinas, to Maryland, to New York, and only this morning I saw the volunteers from Maryland marching through the town, four hundred of them, Madam."

"But they start on a peaceable expedition," urged Mistress Mildmay.

"Mr. Washington is to occupy the trading-station at Mills Creek," smiled Martha Dandridge, "and all the outposts on the Allegheny. I think such an expedition can scarce be peaceable."

"La, Martha, but one would think that you want war," exclaimed the other reproachfully, "and hordes of Indians and Jesuits overrunning Virginia."

"It is to prevent such a misfortune that Governor Dinwiddie sends this force," smiled Martha. She had a lovely smile that dimpled a cheek as soft and delicate as a blossom of the redbud bush.

"Mr. Washington should be the head of this same expedition," remarked the mercer, smoothing with absent fingers the bale of mauve taffeta before him, "not Mr. Joshua Fry; Mr. Washington's family is better thought of than any in Virginia."

"But he is such a youth," protested Sarah Mildmay.

"No," answered Martha with a sparkle in her eyes and a kind of sparkle, too, in her voice. "Say Mr. Fry is English and University trained, and you have a truer reason; we have that prejudice here to honor the English above our own."

"That has a disloyal sound," laughed Mistress Mildmay.

"Indeed not, but it is hard to be ever deferring to those so far away." She bent over the stuffs, perhaps to disguise the color that had mounted into her cheeks and control the feeling that had crept into her voice. "But we must choose your gown," she added. "Politics had put it out of my head, and here I am wasting Mr. Saunders' time and yours."

Mistress Mildmay turned her blue eyes on the pile of stuffs. "After all," she said, "there is nothing so serious as to distract one long from the choice of a silk!" With her delicate, white lace-mittened hands she held up a fine taffeta, yellow of a primrose tint, embroidered in wreaths of blue and pink flowers.

"It has come straight from Paris, Madam," said the old merchant with a touch of pride, "and I have heard that the queen had a sacque of such a stuff when last she went to the opera."

"But it is a swinging price?" questioned Sarah doubtfully.

"Two pistoles a yard, Madam, and it would be more in Paris."

"I think it is inexpensive enough," said Martha Dandridge, "but over-bright for a maiden's dress, Sarah. There would be more eyes gazing at the gown than at Mistress Mildmay."

Sarah agreed demurely. "What is right for the Queen of France, Mr. Saunders, is too fine for me. I could fancy a blue and pink interchangeable, like you sold Mrs. Capel last week; it was a mighty pretty piece and looked as if it would wear like a tabaret."

"It was a sarcenet, Madam; the interchangeable taffetas are not being sold this season but the mantua makers do say that this hangs in more elegant folds."

"It is excellent for frilling," said Martha. "I should advise it, Sarah — with flouncings of silvered silk and a Dresden apron."

Mistress Mildmay considered.

"It is but a pistole a yard," remarked Mr. Saunders, shaking out the gleaming lengths of the sarcenet the watchful apprentice had brought forward.

"Eighteen yards at the most," said Martha, with a practical air, "*and* two for the hat — it's a bargain, my dear."

"Well, you may put me down for that, Mr. Saunders," answered Sarah.

The silk merchant bowed over his counter. "And has Mistress Dandridge any orders?" he asked.

"I wish to dispose of a few pistoles, Sir, on some silk, of a wearing quality, for a capuchin — some sober color, Mr. Saunders, such as I might wear in Richmond town."

At a whispered word from the old man a lad neatly dressed in gray cleared away the taffetas and brought down several rolls of silk; after a little earnest consultation, Martha, with a grave deliberation, chose a puce-colored silk for the capuchin, and a white for the lining.

This accomplished, the two ladies sighed with satisfaction, and at another whisper, the apprentice brought a bottle of wine, two fine glasses, and some sweet macaroons, which Mr. Saunders offered with much courtesy to his customers.

Sarah Mildmay, sipping the Syracuse, referred again to the threatened war with Canada. Mr. Saunders, directing with a jealous eye the folding up and putting away of the bales of costly silk, sarcenet, taffetas, and satin, answered with a slightly distracted air, "We can't afford a war, Madam."

"As well as Canada or France!" exclaimed Martha Dandridge, rising. "There is sometimes a peace, Mr Saunders, as costly as any wars." Then, with a smile of great sweetness, she bowed to the old merchant, and, slipping her hand through Sarah Mildmay's arm, left the shop with her companion.

A number of people were leaving the State House, which contained the News Room, the Post Office, and the chambers of the burgesses of Virginia, and most of these knew and saluted the ladies who, as they crossed the street, looked like two bouquets of delicate flowers in the faint bright hues of their muslin gowns.

Two gentlemen in particular showed a most gallant greeting and seemed wishful of speaking, but Martha Dandridge passed on, and would not look back. But Mistress Mildmay glanced at the two tall gentlemen on the steps of the State House, standing bare-headed and smiling, with sunlight in their hair.

"It is Mr. Conway and Mr. Custis," she said, "two proper gentlemen!"

"Is their properness a reason that we must stop and speak to them?" smiled Martha.

Sarah answered demurely. "As good a reason as any you will find, dear heart."

"Had it been Mr. Washington . . ." Martha interrupted. "Mr. Washington has qualities . . ." Her color heightened.

"He is not so rich as Mr. Custis," — Sarah pursed her lips — "though I think he has a good property in Stafford County."

"Oh, for shame!" cried Martha. "What is that?"

"A great deal," replied Sarah with an air of wisdom. "Have you seen him since he returned from Fort le Bœuf?" she added.

The elder lady answered rather hurriedly. "Twice at Belvoir, my Lord Fairfax's place; then — before you came to Williamsburg we went out to Captain Lawrence's plantation on the Potomac, where they used to live with their mother — so sweet she is! Captain Lawrence is a fighting man; he was a volunteer with Admiral Vernon in the late Spanish War, and it's from him he calls his plantation Mount Vernon."

"Ah," said Sarah, not vastly interested. "And will you see him before he leaves Virginia again?"

"See who?"

"Why, what a simpleton you are, to be sure — see who? Why, Mr. *George* Washington."

Martha answered with attempted lightness, yet unsteadily. "Of course not. I think they start tomorrow, and we have a very slight acquaintance."

"Oh," cried Sarah.

A retired square composed of flat, dark red houses in the Dutch fashion, approached by double flights of short stone steps, was the home of Martha Dandridge.

Some trees had been transplanted from the woods and induced to shed their beauty over the quiet, pleasant town, and here, between the dark, upright houses, grew the buttonwood, still bare of leaves, the shellbark hickory, and the red maple, already beginning to burst into its purplish flowers that herald the leaves.

Such an air of leisure, of peace, of elegant refinement, dwelt in the little square. The houses with their green shutters and porticoed doors conveyed such a gentle austerity that the rudest hushed their voices, the happiest stilled their laughter, the most self-assured stepped more lightly on entering this domain of almost cloistral quietness. It was very near the end of the town, and full of the holy fragrance the wind blew daily from the great spaces of wood and plain. Now, with the first unutterable throb of the spring, this sensation of the near presence of the beautiful wild, pulsed in the stillness almost unbearably.

A mockingbird was in one of the red maples. Martha Dandridge shivered as she ascended the winged steps to her home; an inexplicable and bittersweet longing stirred her heart. The golden silence seemed at once too exquisite and too melancholy to endure. Sarah Mildmay noticed, too, the beautiful piece of the square, the houses, the budding trees, and the great arc of blue, glimmering with soft light.

"It is so pleasant in Williamsburg now, that I shall be sorry to return to Dumfries," she said as they entered the house.

Her young hostess smiled, but did not answer. The mansion was very still, everyone seemed abroad.

The two ladies stepped into the dining room that opened off the hall; it was shuttered from the sun and cool with a drowsy shade.

"How silent you are!" exclaimed Sarah curiously.

Martha started and flushed. "Would you have one chattering all the time?" she answered lightly.

There was a tap on the door and a maidservant entered. "Madam," she said to Martha, "there is a gentleman above, waiting to see you."

Martha turned very pale. "No, it was to see my father," she corrected.

"Madam, to see you — he came here an hour since and would not be denied."

Martha flushed now, then paled again. "You should not have suffered him," she answered.

"Why do you not ask his name?" inquired Sarah slyly. "Ah, dear heart?"

"Of course," said Mistress Dandridge, confused. "Who is it, Ann?"

"It is Mr. Washington, Madam, Mr. George Washington — maybe one should say General now, as he is to fight the French."

"Here is another fire-eater," cried Sarah. "Ann is ready to see them all coming home with scalps at their belts. It is not war yet, you naughty maid, and we are all still praying for peace."

Then, seeing Martha's still figure and pale face, she said in sudden tenderness, "Why do you not go up to him, sweet?"

Martha put her hand to her heart. "I never expected this. Ought I to go — should I? Will you come, too, Sarah?"

"No, I will not."

Martha Dandridge turned her fine eyes on Ann. "Tell Mr. Washington," she said, "that I am coming up."

CHAPTER II

THE PRIDE OF MARTHA DANDRIDGE

Martha entered the withdrawingroom with a delicate slowness; she closed the door behind her softly. "Good afternoon, Mr. Washington," she said formally.

He was standing by the window looking out on the boughs of the red maple, and it flashed across her composure that when she had glanced up at the purple flowers she might, by raising her eyes a little higher, have seen him; and instantly, after this thought came another, that she had known all the time, by some terrifying magic she had learned of late, that he was there, waiting for her coming.

She seated herself on a striped settee and folded her hands in her lap; the many frills of her white muslin skirts flowed over the polished wooden floor, and the gleaming pink of her satin coat was thrown up against the warm darkness of the polished paneled walls. Behind her hung an oval mirror which reflected the long dusky ringlets, confined by the soft bondage of violet velvet ribbons, and the crimson silk roses in her wide straw hat.

Mr. Washington turned from the window and looked at her, resting his hand on the back of an old gilt chair, the brocade seat of which was cut from the weddinggown of Martha's grandmother, which had been woven in Italy and sold at the Exchange in London at five guineas a yard.

Martha looked at this hand, at the fall of white lace at the wrist, at the dark blue cuff with crystal buttons, and never raised her eyes to his face.

"Won't you be seated?" she said. There was an extraordinary stillness about her pose, voice, and expression.

"I wish to stand, Mistress Dandridge," he answered. "I can, I think, speak better so."

She was silent; her eyes were still on his slack, fine right hand.

"Governor Dinwiddie," he continued in his soft, slow voice, "has appointed me second to Captain Joshua Fry in this expedition to build, and hold, forts in the Ohio Valley."

"I know," she said. "Sir, I congratulate you."

"It is a chance," he answered simply. "I know the country a little now; I may be useful."

She raised her eyes to his face, then dropped them instantly; though she perfectly remembered his face, yet every time she saw him she had a sense of something strange in him, as if she met him for the first time;

her instant's glance had remarked keenly the little things to which she was so quiveringly alive in this man, the bright blue color of his neck ribbon, the pattern of lace he wore, the powder in his curled hair.

"You have come to say goodbye, I suppose," she said. "It is very courteous of you, Mr. Washington."

"We start tomorrow for Mills Creek," he replied, with an evasion of a direct answer. He crossed to the mantelpiece, where early wood lilies stood in a great jar of black pottery from China. "I wished above all things," he added, "to see you before I left Williamsburg. I rode over from my lodging this morning, hoping to see you."

Her heart gave a jerk at the changed sound of his voice, at his nearer approach.

"Believe me," he continued, "I could not have left in peace without seeing you again." She looked down at the floor, pale, unsmiling.

"But now," he went on, with a note of fierceness in that new voice at whose bidding all her pulses were beating, "I wish I had not come."

She lifted her head, but kept her eyes veiled, for she could not bear to look full at him. "Have I given you so poor a welcome?" she asked in trembling tones.

Even though he had his back to the light and she was gazing at him through her lashes, she could not help seeing that his eyes were marvelously dark and bright and shining.

"I should not have come," he said, with a gloomy glance at the lilies, "if I had been sure of returning."

She drew a long breath and looked straight ahead of her, out of the window, at the view of the house opposite with a lead weathercock shining from the borrowed glory of the sun against the vivid blue, and in front the maple blooming with flowers like wet balls of blood.

"Yes," she said, "we may never see you in Richmond again. But death that way is better than inaction, Mr. Washington."

"I was not made for that — inaction," he answered simply; then swiftly, "why do you never look at me, Mistress Dandridge?"

The blood rushed over her throat and face, the muslin of her gown quivered; she lifted her face proudly. "I? Oh — I am looking at you now," she stammered. She opened her large eyes on him bravely, and he was faced full with her unconscious beauty, her transparent sweetness, even as she was forced to face his dark handsomeness, his dangerous, passionate composure. "What made you say that?" she asked, struggling for her dignity. "It was a strange remark, Mr. Washington."

For all her pride, her eyes were overborne again by his, and sought once more the refuge of the blue sky without.

"Forgive me," he said, slightly unsteadily. "Only — I shall like to remember it — but I had no right — nor any right to be here, taking your time, Madam."

"Have I complained?" she asked faintly.

"You have always been gracious to me," he responded, "and I fear that I have taken advantage of it — both in coming here and speaking as I have spoken, Miss Dandridge."

"You have not displeased me," she answered even more faintly.

"Your goodness," he murmured, "makes it more difficult."

He moved nearer to her and she shivered; it seemed as if he would take the place on the sofa beside her. There was something impelling, masterful, in his quick forward step; a feeling of utter confusion and fear crushed Martha Dandridge.

"Mr. Washington," she said, "will you open the window — it's so mighty close . . ."

Her swift glance saw him flush from his Malines neckband to his pomaded curls.

"Forgive me," he said, and withdrew instantly.

"No, the window, please," she repeated, anxious to justify her excuse.

He crossed and set the casement open on the fragrant peace and light of the square. When he turned again into the room the color was still in his face. "You must think ill of me," he said, with a proud humility, "for this intrusion. I came to ask your good wishes on the venture on which I start tomorrow. Before you dismiss me utterly, will you give them to me?"

"Yes — sincerely," she murmured.

He bowed very low. "Long after you have forgotten this afternoon, Mistress Dandridge, I shall be remembering those words, with great gratitude."

She said nothing; she rose and gave him a formal curtsey of farewell; she sank onto the settee again, still silent, and would not look at him.

She let him go to the door and open it, conscious that she was sitting lifeless as a doll, that she had been like a doll ever since she had entered the room, that she had said nothing of what was raging in her heart, that she was letting him go in a miserable fashion, that he might never return . . .

The mockingbird gave a queer low call; Martha rose suddenly. "Mr. Washington!" she cried. "Mr. Washington — come back!"

He turned instantly and shut the door; a wave of cowardice shook Martha, but the thought of the lifetime of regret to be lived through if she let him go like this and he never came back nerved her.

"I should like to tell you," she forced her voice to some steadiness, "that my sincere wishes, my earnest thoughts, will be with you — in —

in this venture." Scorn at her own weakness and folly swept over her, giving her strength. Why should she be so shamefaced at saying what was next her heart? "It is a splendid chance for you — for Virginia; I am glad that we are acting like this; I am glad we are going to keep our own territory free; I think you mean that there shall be war — do you not?"

He was looking at her very earnestly. "I do," he said.

There was a little pause of silence, during which she walked to the hearth with drooping head, the wide shade of her hat over her eyes and the wood lilies a background for her lace-covered shoulders.

Mr. Washington spoke again. "War is the only way — we must have Canada."

"Governor Dinwiddie sends so few men!" answered Martha.

"Yes, we have a small force, but the British Government is not over-generous, and we dare not empty Virginia of men."

She marked with a thrill the "we" he used so unconsciously, as if he was already one of the rulers of the land, one of the makers of the destinies of the future.

"I envy you," she said.

He came nearer to her and stood by the settee on which she had been seated. "I am nothing," he answered in a restrained voice. "I have all to do . . ."

Martha turned and pulled one of the wood lilies from the black bowl. "The doing must be — splendid," she answered thoughtfully.

He replied with a kind of passionate gravity. "Yes, but one might fail, or one might succeed only to find the reward one hoped for — vanished."

Martha trembled and kept her eyes on the wood lily. "What reward are you thinking of?" she asked.

"That I may not tell you — yet."

The white fingers closed round the green stalk till it was bruised, and the lily-head bent and rested against the stormily heaving breast, as Martha Dandridge turned her eyes on the ardent face of the man by the settee.

Strange and magic scents wafted in through the open casement, strange and magic sounds of whisperings of birds, of leaves in the bud, of even more subtle murmurs like the music of the passing fairy clouds that floated behind the old lead weathercock opposite, filled the room as completely as the soft gold light that gleamed on wall, ceiling, floor, and the figure of the lady with her hands crushed on the lily she held above the black velvet bow on her breast, the ends of which fell over the fine frills of muslin that rippled from her waist to her ankles.

"You may tell me what this reward is — please tell me," she said. She saw him pale and quiver.

"I am nothing," he repeated, and his voice was hoarse.

She still looked at him, though his figure began to swim before her eyes in mists of extraordinary gold. "I am nothing, too," she answered.

He gazed at her with his changeful hazel eyes darkened to near black. "You mean?" he questioned, and stood in an attitude of arrested motion, with his hand on his heart.

"That I call you back, Mr. Washington," she answered very faintly.

For one fatal instant he did not move nor speak, and Martha Dandridge plunged into an abyss of shame, a blackness of humiliation, from which rose, grimly, the one support of a bitter pride.

"I called you back," she said in another voice; "you must forgive me — that was what I wanted to ask you — to forgive me for my whim . . ."

"Your whim?" he echoed.

"Yes," she answered with deadly coldness. "For what should I have to say to you, Mr. Washington?" He was very pale indeed now, and in the strong revulsion of her agony of shame she rejoiced cruelly in the wounded anger that sparkled in his eyes.

"It was kind of you to come," she continued, with the easy fluency of the lips that often comes to the aid and concealment of a great emotion. "My father should have been in to see you. Will you take some refreshments?"

"No," he said; then, in a tone as contained as her own, "Farewell, Mistress Dandridge."

"Farewell," she answered, and was vaguely surprised at the complete indifference of her tone.

He went to the door for the second time and opened it; then spoke, looking back at her, "You gave me your good wishes, did you not?"

She faced him with a meaningless smile. "My good wishes go with the Virginians, of a surety, Mr. Washington." The door closed; he was gone.

The lily fell from Martha's fingers and her hands went up to her throat. She turned swiftly and instantly to the window; all her emotions were suspended, she had only one thought — to see him again — to watch him out of sight. She heard the front door shut; a second more of unutterable tension, and she saw the tall figure in the dark blue mantle cross the square, pass under the light shadow of the trees and walk rapidly away.

Another moment (scarcely that, measured by the time the gilt bracket clock was ticking out on the wall) and he was gone completely, and the square was as empty as the house, as her heart and life were and would be. It was over: he had gone like this; she had done violence to her own heart to speak to him — to give him his chance, and the incredibly horrible had happened. He had *not* responded, he had *not* spoken.

Her deeply hurt pride saw herself as something offered and rejected. Struggling with her wild regret, her wild sense of loss, was another emotion: "Did I deceive him? Did he think I did not care? Ah, heart, heart, what did I do to make him believe I did not care?"

She saw the lily on the hearth and almost mechanically picked it up and restored it to the bowl. As she did so she noticed the bruised stem and blushed fiercely; the flower seemed symbolic of herself; she, too, had been bruised and cast down by a careless hand. Would someone put her back again among her comrades, where she might hide her wound as the lily concealed the bent stalk among the leaves?

She crossed to the red lacquer desk by the window, still in a mood of proud self-containment, drew out a sheet of gold-edged notepaper and wrote a letter.

CHAPTER III

CONFESSIONS

Toward the next dawn Sarah Mildmay woke up suddenly and shivered, watching the cold creeping light in her pleasant room and wondering what had roused her. She listened and her sense of discomfort and slight terror increased, for she heard the distinct sounds of sobbing. After a moment she connected this sobbing with Martha, who had been flushed and blithe the previous evening, and carelessly reserved about that unlooked for visit of Mr. Washington that had so interested Sarah.

Mistress Mildmay, with her curiosity and pity aroused in equal parts, leaped out of bed, put on her blue muslin hat and a pair of white doeskin slippers, beautifully embroidered by Indian hands in a design of beads, and crept out of her room and knocked at the door next to her own. There was no answer to this timid rap, and Sarah turned the handle and entered.

Martha's bedroom faced the front of the house, which looked east, and as Sarah opened the door she was startled by the supernatural effect of the blue light that flooded the chamber from the two windows which had been set wide open on the early air. This effect of silver-azure light was increased by a lamp burning yellowly on a table at the foot of the bed with the white hangings and tumbled sheets. This lamp was like amber and opal against the blue of the dawn, the flame being shielded by a drawn silk shade, on which was painted a circle of Chinese figures in black and gray.

Close beside it sat Martha, the radiant beams tangled in her brown loose hair, in her violet sarcenet robe; she was sitting limply in a low, chintz-covered chair, which was wreathed with blooming roses. Her hands had fallen into her lap, and she faced the dawn spreading slowly above the housetops opposite.

"Oh, Martha!" exclaimed Sarah slowly.

Martha started, stood up and pressed a wet twist of handkerchief to her pallid lips.

The bright young blonde beauty was pale, too, as she crept closer. "Oh, Martha, oh, love," she murmured; "I heard you crying."

"Please go away," was the faint answer. "I am perfectly well." She tried to turn away her tear-stained face, but Sarah had come close and was looking at her.

"You are not well," declared that lady, snatching her hand. "You have been crying all night — and for Mr. Washington!"

"How dare you!" cried Martha; she sank into the chair again and hid her eyes in the soaked handkerchief.

Sarah slipped to her knees and pressed the hands she held captive to her cheek. "Can't you talk of it to me, dear heart? Won't you tell me, my sweet, my dear? What has he done? Is he a wretch? Oh, I hate him already!"

Martha would not be wooed from the entrenchments of silence, but she did not withdraw her hand, which Sarah caressed with passionate kisses.

"Beloved — tell me — why did he come yesterday? What happened?" she pleaded. "It will help you to tell me."

Martha raised misty eyes unutterably sad, and gazed forlornly out at the blue beyond the long open window. She seemed too utterly crushed for pride or resentment.

"You have it in three words," she said hoarsely and forlornly. "I love him — there you are, you child — I love the creature!"

Sarah opened her blue eyes wide. "But I knew that," she said ingenuously.

Martha turned to her in a kind of bitter desperation. "There! I suppose all the city knew it — I suppose, like a poor fool, I had it written in my face for everyone to see! Oh, I am indeed humiliated!"

Sarah caught hold of her strongly, for, indeed, it seemed as if she would rise and rush away. "No — but who should tell it if not I, Martha, who love you so dearly?"

"I have been in a bewilderment, a confusion. These tears are a tribute to a dead folly — dead, yes, dead indeed!"

"He will come back." urged Sarah.

"Not to me — never to me — to some other woman, perhaps — never to me! Don't you understand?" She wrenched herself from Sarah and placed her two hands on the other's shoulders, while she gazed wildly down into the blue eyes. "Don't you understand?" she repeated. "He does not care!"

"Oh!" gasped Sarah; then sincerely, with warm loyalty, "but that is not possible. This is one of those hideous mistakes we read of in the romances, dear."

Martha shook her head. "It is not a mistake. Believe me, I know. I did not believe it possible to be so utterly humiliated as I have been; I thought it was to be — I thought I knew him." The proud fair head sank. "I thought he came yesterday to tell me that . . . that . . . he wanted me . . . he did not speak . . ." The proud head sank lower. "*I called him back*!" Her long fingers twisted in an agony on her lap.

"I said," she continued in a low voice, " 'Come back.' I said, 'You may speak to me.' I *looked* at him and he at me. I gave him my face to read; I was holding out my heart in my hands . . ."

She paused a moment and struck her breast. Lower still went the proud head.

". . . and he stood silent — never moved nor spoke. And he must have *known*, he must *know* now — though I thank my pride I did what I could — I hope I hurt him; he went — perhaps to laugh at me — at Martha Dandridge, who offered herself to him!"

"No, no," cried Sarah in great distress. "You have misapprehended this. It is not possible. Why, I have seen the man's eyes on you; one cannot be deceived. He did not dare — remember who you are and what he is."

"Yes, what I am," answered Martha swiftly. "I put too high a value on myself, without a doubt — women generally do — what am I, indeed?"

"Martha, Martha, you are distracted. Look at it clearly, as everyone else looks at it — as *he* looks at it; you are one of the richest heiresses in Williamsburg — you are known to be coveted by Mr. Custis, a very wealthy man — and he is a younger son — who has a mere fine plantation on the Potomac — just my Lord Fairfax's former land surveyor."

"It is the man of all others," said Martha with sparkling eyes, "whom Governor Dinwiddie selected for this mission to Fort le Bœuf."

"Oh, dearest, no need to defend him. I know what he seems to you; you *must* think him a hero, but try to imagine what he appears in his own eyes. Think what your father would have said had this young man asked for your hand."

"But had he *cared*," said Martha unsteadily, "he would not have thought of any of that."

"But men do," answered Sarah, half sadly. "I think that is the great difference, dear. If a woman loves she has no more pride at all — nothing matters, either what people say or what they think — and she finds it difficult to understand how a man's pride can still be so acute, no, more acute, than it ever was before. She doesn't want it like that, I know, dear; she wants to help, to be one with him in his struggles, to believe in him when no one else does, to champion him, to give everything for nothing; but he — he is different: he wants to come crowned, successful, admired, rich. He wants to say: 'here I am — this is what I am — this is what I own — this is what I can do; and you, pretty, useless thing, can come and share all these glories that I have achieved!' "

Martha raised her head and fixed her tired, tear-stained eyes on the dawn that was beginning to flush from opal blue to gleaming pink behind the motionless lead weathercock opposite.

Sarah rose softly and turned out the now useless lamp. "I think," she said under her breath, "that Mr. Washington feels like that, Martha. I think he is waiting."

Martha stirred in her chair wearily. "No," she said in a lifeless voice, "no, no . . ."

"Wait till he returns," urged Sarah, "successful, Governor Dinwiddie's favorite."

"He may never return," answered Martha, "and he will not return to me, as I told you." She rose and glanced at the china timepiece on the mantlepiece.

"They will be just marching out of Williamsburg now, Sarah," she said faintly, and crushed the long pink ribbons of her gown under her heart. "Leaving Williamsburg — leaving Virginia, marching away — away! Oh, that I was a man and marching with them!"

Sarah got up from her knees and put her arms around the slender figure; the two women clung together in the steadily brightening, almost awful light of the dawn which was fast breaking in golden-rosy fire.

"You must never speak of this, even to me," said Martha, with her face hidden on the other's shoulder. "Never — never! It's dead with the night fast dying now — dead, indeed. Before the sun is up it must be buried deep in our hearts — yours and mine. Promise me, beloved."

"Until he returns," whispered Sarah.

Martha shuddered. "No — no, you do not understand. It has happened; it is over. If ever I see him again, it will be as a stranger. Promise me," she insisted.

"Dear love, why?"

"You know."

"No, because you are wrong; I am sure you are wrong; you are weaving unhappiness for yourself."

Martha disengaged herself from her friend's tender arms. "I know what I am about," she answered almost sternly. "I am resolved what to do and I am right. If you had not chanced to come here tonight, you would never have guessed my secret. Now you must promise not to betray me, even to myself — if you can, to forget."

"Well, if I must," sighed Sarah. She looked forlornly around the room. "I shall be back in Dumfries soon, and under no temptation to speak to you — but may I not write about him?"

"No."

"Oh, Martha — are you angry with me? Surely not, dearest?"

"No, not angry." The tears welled again in Martha's eyes and she cast herself into the rose-wreathed chair. "There is something else I must tell you," she added with an effort.

"Oh!" exclaimed Sarah dismayed.

"To show you how utterly forgotten, dead, and buried this must be . . ." went on Martha; she shook back her hair, against the shadows of which her face showed pallid and wan.

The first beams of the sun rose above the housetops and penetrated the soft obscurity of the delicate chamber.

"I wrote yesterday to Mr. Custis," continued Martha firmly, "promising to be his wife."

CHAPTER IV
GREAT MEADOWS

It was late in May. Forty Virginians had been sent to build a fort at the juncture of the Ohio and the Allegheny; the French artillery had advanced on them and forced them to surrender, after which the French commander raised a fort on the spot that he named Fort Duquesne, after the Governor of Canada.

Setting his teeth at this affront, Mr. Washington — Captain Washington now — of the colonial forces, pushed on from Alexandria, where Joshua Fry was waiting for the gathering of his composite force that had been raised, not only in Virginia, but in New York, New Jersey, Pennsylvania, Maryland, both the Carolinas, and Massachusetts, and which was maintained at the expense of the British Crown.

Captain Washington, with a hundred and fifty men and a party of friendly Indians, marched on the same route he had traversed a few months before, on his mission to Fort le Bœuf; and toward the end of May reached Great Meadows, on the Youghiougany, close to the frontier of Canada. There he encamped and waited.

He expected to be challenged, if not attacked, and he had very little hope of reinforcements, or indeed of any prompt action from Fry, whom he had left a sick man on the banks of the lower Potomac; but, small as was his number, and isolated as was his position, he resolved to accept any challenge that might be offered him, and, if possible, to provoke a war that should only end in the conquest of Canada.

The young land surveyor who had had no military training, who had never been under fire nor seen a battle, yet who quietly conceived and steadfastly maintained these visions of a limitless ambition, fortified his encampment at Great Meadows after the Indian fashion, and sent a message to Christopher Gist, now settled in these regions, asking him what news he had of the movement of the French, who hitherto had given no sign of their existence.

The day after this messenger had departed, Mr. Washington rode up and down his little encampment with a thoughtful air.

Though he was not a hundred miles from Richmond, and only half as far as Fort le Bœuf, he was in an untouched wilderness of virgin forest and untracked plains and valleys that probably only two white men, he and Christopher Gist, had looked upon. The white oak, the black walnut, pines, sycamores, catalpas, and maple grew over the slopes and plains in huge forests, through which only a Redskin could find his way. Now, in the height of spring, the yellowish-green flowers of the tall sugar maple, the red blossoms of the white maple, the marvelous fiery young leaves of the oak, the deep color of the pines combined in a glory of color beneath the blue heavens; and the ground beneath the trees and the open spaces, the valleys and the meadows, was covered with wood lilies and colored lilies, strange creepers, mosses and long-leaved plants, the exquisite dogwood with its heart-shaped leaf and white flower, and the frail blossoms of the red bud, while the gooseberry and whortleberry bushes, thrusting up through the bare brambles on which the whippoorwill, the jay, and the mockingbird perched, showed sharp green leaves among their thorns.

The pure air was full of a thousand scents, from the aromatic odor of the bruised leaves of the black walnut to the delicate perfume of stretches of wood lilies nodding together in the shade.

It was a country worth fighting for; at least, George Washington, looking steadily over the prospect with his large, resolute, gray eyes, thought so. He was riding an Indian horse with a hair-rope bridle and a deer-skin saddle stuffed with grass.

His dress was something in the Indian style, too: a loose leather tunic, belted with scarlet, and high, close riding tops fringed at the knee; his hair was unpowdered, confined by a simple ribbon, and he wore a large sombrero hat without a feather.

Two very fine pistols were in his holster and a third in his belt, as well as the sword that hung from the gold and scarlet sword belt worked by his mother's fingers at Mount Vernon.

At his second circling of the encampment he met an officer of the Virginian militia. They saluted.

"Any news from Alexandria, Captain Washington?"

"None at all. Nor is there like to be. We must manage our affair, here, I think, Sir."

"Well, there is nothing to manage yet."

"No," smiled George Washington, "but there will be as soon as the French find out we are here."

"They may never discover us," returned the Virginian, with an air of disappointment.

"Then," returned Captain Washington, "we will go and discover them."

He glanced round at his minute army of a hundred and fifty, represented by the Indian wigwams scattered over the exquisite meadows and the horses picketed by the distant stream that ran out of the wood to Youghiougany.

"This is a fine game," smiled the other man.

"Yes," said the young commander, and he smiled, too, charmingly. "And it will be something more than a game before it is done."

Still with a thoughtful air he turned back to his tent and dismounted there, giving his horse to the waiting militiaman. He seated himself on the fresh trunk of a tree that had recently been felled for firewood, and reflectively lit and smoked a long clay pipe filled with Virginian leaf.

He was thinking of Williamsburg, of a certain face that had held an expression of cold pride and aversion and an unaccountable fear, when last he had seen it: a face that was often before his sleeping and waking dreams.

Well, if he succeeded, if he came back as he hoped to come back, if he won the success that he hoped to win, the success that seemed, to his ardent young ambition, so easy to grasp and wear, he would force that fair gentle face to change that inscrutable look to one of open dismissal or — to that expression that he had mused and dreamed of as radiant, heavenly . . . illumining that one particular countenance, of all other exquisite countenances in the world.

Behind him a great wave of honeysuckle swept over some low, thorny bushes and filled the air with honey sweetness; a trail of the long-fingered flowers lay near his feet. He looked down at it and remembered the wood lilies in the black bowl and the blossom she had held in her hands and the snapped stem that had sent the flower head lying on her breast.

He rose up slowly, with a lazy air, and wandered away into the forest, on the edge of which the camp was placed. He stepped, still slowly, under the trees that were so high and tightly interlaced that the sunlight rested on the highest branches, and here below it was cool and mysterious and beautifully dark.

Down a little slope grew the wood lilies, making a white light in the green gloom: a cloud of trembling silver, a haze of glimmering radiance. Mr. Washington went toward them, treading carefully so as not to step on them.

He took his pipe from his mouth and his face grew very grave; in the subdued, cool light his expression seemed shadowed and mournful. Presently he went on one knee and put out his slender right hand over the lilies, but he did not pick any, and slowly turned back out of the forest toward the camp.

Before his tent a graceful Indian lad was springing from an unshod mustang flecked with foam. Mr. Washington was alert instantly; he hastened to the messenger, who drew a letter from the leather and bead pouch at his side. The young commander blushed and broke the seal. He knew it was the answer from Christopher Gist.

At the news it contained his eyes sparkled and he smiled. A French force was advancing from the Ohio, and was now within proximity to Great Meadows. They had, Gist declared, orders to demand the withdrawal of any English whom they might meet. Mr. Washington questioned the young Indian.

"Do you know where the French are?"

"They advance from the juncture of the Allegheny and the Monongahela," replied the youth. "They have many tribes with them: the Uncas, the Chingachgooks, the Chippewayos; they have many great guns, too; they have passed the settlement of Christopher Gist, and they are perhaps two days, perhaps one day, from here."

The young Virginian looked into the passive face of his ally. "Have you seen them?"

"Yes."

"Could you guide me through the forest to them?"

"Yes. They are sending out parties of forty, fifty, or a hundred, to see what forts you are building and how far you are coming."

A dark, joyous flash sprang into Mr. Washington's great eyes. "We will go and meet them," he said; he took off his hat and waved it toward the mysterious stretches of forests that concealed his enemy. "Gentlemen!" he cried, "I think that this means war!"

CHAPTER V

THE FIRST SHOT

Mr. Washington, with forty men and a number of Indian allies and guides, pushed on through the forests from the camp at Great Meadows, starting in the pitch darkness and in heavy rain.

Early on the second day he received news from an Indian scout of the near advance of a detachment of French under Coulon de Jumonville, and toward evening, having emerged from a forest, through which they had been obliged to make slow progress, leading their horses, they came out into an open valley not far from where the French had just built Fort Duquesne, having now left Maryland for Pennsylvania.

There the Virginians halted, waiting the return of a party of Indians who had been sent to reconnoiter.

When these returned they reported that De Jumonville and his force had been close on the track of the Virginians all day, and were now endeavoring to slip away through the forest unperceived, doubtless with the idea of bringing a larger force from Fort Duquesne to utterly overwhelm the few men Mr. Washington led.

But the woodcraft of the friendly Indians was as skillful as that of their Canadian rivals; they conducted the colonists in single file through a great plantation of beech and oak, and brought them out in a little glade across which the French were bound to pass on their return to the valley of the Ohio.

Nor had they long to wait. From their concealment behind the huge trunks they presently beheld the enemy, one by one, ride out from the scattered trees opposite and, with a light swiftness, down the green slope that was flooded with the strong purple-gold light of the setting sun. Mr. Washington sprang silently into the saddle, and rode forward into the open.

Remembering the elegant officers at Venango and Fort le Bœuf, he looked eagerly for some similar figure, to whom, as the leader of the troop, he could address himself. But all these men were Indians, in Indian array, riding the wild Indian horses — unshod, with flowing tails and manes, and equipped only with hair-rope bridles and skin saddles.

A magnificent warrior, in full battle array, appeared to be the leader. At sight of Mr. Washington he drew up his splendid white horse, and his keen eye swept the gleam of the muskets showing in the ambush of the trees behind the young commander.

He appeared to recognize that evasion or flight was useless, for he gave a signal to his followers (who by now had all emerged from the wood and were even less in number than the Americans) and they halted behind him.

Mr. Washington waited.

Slowly, in silence and in a very stately fashion, the little troop of Indians advanced down the slope and up again, till they were in easy speaking distance of the men waiting for them, indeed, no more than a few yards away. Mr. Washington looked closely at the leader, who appeared a brave of high rank. He was a man of great height and powerful figure, crowned with a huge coronal of eagle's feathers, and painted on breast, arms and face with red, blue, and yellow in a grotesque pattern; round his waist was a silk sash of many colors, and his leather trousers with their long fringes were ornamented with glittering beads; several Indian weapons hung at his deer-skin saddle and at his waist; in his right hand he carried a long elegant musket.

Mr. Washington touched his hat. "Which are you?" he asked, in his clear young voice. "England or France?"

"France!" came the answer, in good English. "And you, messieurs?"

Mr. Washington started. The voice, the accent, the manner of speaking betrayed the European; that the resplendent chief was a Frenchman, as were at least half his stained and painted followers, became evident.

"British," said the Virginian. "I am George Washington, holding a commission from the governor of Virginia to build and hold forts in the Ohio Valley."

The other smiled and threw up his head, shaking the long eagle feathers.

"I am Coulon de Jumonville, holding the commission of the Governor of Canada to demand the withdrawal of all Americans and their allies from the Ohio Valley."

The two young men eyed each other in silence, each sitting very erect, very alert; each with his followers silent and watchful behind him.

The inexperienced land surveyor who represented England was not unmindful of the importance this moment might have in history. In the swift instant of silence that followed the answer of De Jumonville, he visualized perfectly clearly the significance of this meeting and the effect it might have, one way or another, on the history of two nations. He was aware that the decision of peace or war between two of the greatest countries in the world did not rest in the hands of the famous politicians at Westminster and Versailles, nor even in the hands of Dinwiddie at Williamsburg, or Duquesne at Montreal; but with him — and the Frenchman in paint and feathers.

All the issues that had hung long and vaguely between France and England might now reach their culmination or be again evaded, again postponed — that was to be decided not in any councils nor in the consultations of any statesmen, but here, in the wild open, in the midst of untracked country, in an obscure part of the world, between two unknown men.

Even as this thought swept over George Washington, he knew what use to make of his opportunity. His clear eyes narrowed and fixed in a penetrating way on De Jumonville; was that man prudent, was he cautious? — but the Virginian read, in the flashing glance the Frenchman returned him, a reckless spirit with the same purpose as his own.

He rode a little further from the trees where his men waited.

"In the name of His Majesty King George," he said, "I command you to withdraw from British territory."

Coulon de Jumonville laughed. At the sound of it Mr. Washington laughed, too — laughed at the sheer joy of the approaching conflict, at his own strength and courage that he felt surging up within him, triumphantly, to meet the moment, at the feel of the pure west wind on his face, and all the glorious prospect of wood and land that glimmered away before his eyes to the flaming sunset — all seemed so much more beautiful, magnificent, and proud than it had ever seemed before; and he represented the power that owned this land — that would defend it.

"Were you sent to defy us?" he asked.

"I was not sent to welcome you," smiled Coulon de Jumonville.

"Will you retire?" demanded Mr. Washington.

The Frenchman raised his hand and let it fall. "Will you surrender?" he asked, and the Virginian saw that he was being covered by the French muskets, on the gleaming bores of which the sun sparkled red. "Will you surrender?" repeated De Jumonville.

For answer Mr. Washington took his commission from his breast with his left hand, and with his right raised his hat from his bright hair as he proceeded to read the King's commands to the loyal colonies to prevent and expel the French from the British frontier.

He was the unprotected target for over thirty marksmen, French and Indian, who leaned forward from their motionless horses, ready to fire.

"I give you five minutes," said De Jumonville.

The Virginian's young voice continued unshaken, unmoved.

"I warn you," said De Jumonville; he drew a toy-like watch, strangely out of keeping with his savage attire, from his belt and glanced at it.

The Virginians behind the trees were waiting, watching the erect figure of Mr. Washington for orders.

He serenely finished reading his commission, restored it to his pocket, and replaced his hat.

"Now, Sir, do you propose to withdraw?" he asked courteously, as if he did not even see the array of guns pointed at him from behind De Jumonville.

The Frenchman looked at his watch again; it gleamed in his dark hand a second. "You are very foolhardy!" he exclaimed.

"Will you withdraw?" repeated Mr. Washington.

"No!" thundered De Jumonville. "No, Monsieur!"

"Fire!" said Mr. Washington, looking over his shoulder at his men.

Instantly the musketry cracked in front of him and behind him; the glade was full of smoke and flashes of flame. He put his hand to the pistol in his holster and rode at De Jumonville, feeling the bullets on his saddle, passing his cheek, and thudding on the ground near him.

The French officer's white horse reared through the smoke; his rider let go the long hair-rope bridle and flung up his bare painted arms as if he saluted the setting sun; the tawny eagle feathers nodded against the sky, the ornaments of beads and fringes tossed as the horse sprang to one side. Then Coulon de Jumonville fell backward from the saddle, the horse dashed wildly free down the glade, and Mr. Washington was bending from the saddle looking down into the dying face of the Frenchman.

He had two bullets in his bare breast, and the scarlet blood was trickling through the scarlet paint and the collar of purple beads.

"So it was your chance, not mine," he smiled, looking up. "*Ah, mon Dieu, ayez pitié de moi, un pêcheur . . .*"

He turned over and buried his face in the long, soft, pure grass.

"I am sorry," said Mr. Washington. He was rather pale; his color had not changed at the contemplation of his own danger, for personal fear never occurred to him; but he felt a generous regret at this sudden ending of another gallant life.

The little affray was soon over. When the smoke cleared it was found that ten French had been killed and two Americans. The rest of De Jumonville's little force was captured and disarmed. It was ended before the sun was set: the first shot fired, the first blood shed, the first prisoners taken — war made inevitable.

Mr. Washington's mind flew again to London and Paris. Those men were committed now: these few minutes and these two young unknown men — one already dead and never to be known now — had decided the policies of two great nations.

The Virginian looked at the trampled grass, red not only with the sun glints, but with bedabbled blood, at the silent captives, at the dead, at his own men flushed, excited, reloading with wad, bullet, and powder.

He became very pale indeed: the sense of what he had put his hand to was almost overwhelming; The swift translation of thought and resolve into action and fact was almost terrifying: he was very young for such a responsibility, and his quick imagination flew wide and foresaw all the possible consequences of his action in the years to come.

He gave his orders to return to the camp at Great Meadows; but, as the dark was fast falling, and there was no moon, he commanded that they should wait till dawn and bury the dead before they started.

He watched with wide, inscrutable eyes of youthful gravity, as Coulon de Jumonville was lifted up and carried between two Virginians into the dark shade of the trees; then he followed, dismounted, wrapped himself in his cloak and lit his pipe. As he smoked he gazed thoughtfully at the long streaks of red between the tree trunks that marked the setting of the sun.

CHAPTER VI
THE GRAVE OF COULON DE JUMONVILLE

As it was beginning to grow light in the wood, Christopher Gist and an Indian came upon them.

The settler found his way through the isolated groups of men, some sleeping, some digging, and some guarded by others armed and ready, to where Mr. Washington sat with his back against a huge white oak.

"Good morning," said Christopher Gist.

The young man looked up; he was bareheaded and his hair waved free on his shoulders. His hands were busy with something, the light was too uncertain for the settler, at the first glance, to see what.

"Ah, Mr. Gist, Christopher Gist," he said gravely. "So you have come to join us."

Mr. Gist seated himself nearby. "So the first shot has been fired, Captain Washington?"

"Yes," came the answer, "and I think it will echo through all Europe."

"And your name, too," said the other quietly. "Your name, Sir."

As he spoke he looked curiously and closely at Mr. Washington's hands and saw that he was occupied in cutting and binding two boughs of wood into the form of a cross. The leaves he had stripped away lay in a little pile on the messy ground, and the peculiar aromatic odor of them crept into the nostrils of Christopher Gist; they were the leaves of the black walnut. "Are you returning to Great Meadows?" he asked.

"I must, to await the orders of Mr. Fry. I fear he will be too sick a man to leave Alexandria for some while yet."

Mr. Gist kept his enthusiastic, quiet eyes on the dark outlines of the still figure with the busy hands. The dawn, slipping round the trunk of the great oak, showed palely luminous behind the noble lines of wide shoulders, bent head, and the loose locks of falling hair.

"They will be proud of you in Virginia," said the older man; then he added, "have you had news from Richmond?"

"Not since I left. I expected none."

"Perhaps you will be sorry to return," suggested Christopher Gist, "sorry to leave the woods."

"I was sorry to leave Virginia," was the slow answer. "No — I shall not regret returning — if I may do so with honor."

Mr. Washington put down the cross, which he appeared to have finished, and clasped his hands round his raised knee.

"I could never endure a town again," said Christopher Gist simply.

The younger man made no answer; the sacred silence of the woodland dawn was broken by the tremulous stir of waking birds and the noise of the men with the spades concealed in the recesses of the forest.

The shadows were lifting, like a veil, from all the fragrant, softly quivering life of tree and plant. A swimming haze of gold-flecked opal began to float between the fine boughs and clustering leaves, and to rest hesitatingly, as if half afraid, on the stretches of grass and moss and flowers.

Elusive scents rose and faded: the honeysuckle, the jasmine, the fine breath of the lilies, the pungent perfume of the mint, and that strong aroma of the bruised walnut leaves. The great square leaves of a catalpa tree nearby began to be outlined against a sky turning rosy silver, and a bird darting through the undergrowth took on a magic color of indescribable blue, vivid as sunlight on a sword.

Mr. Washington turned to his companion; the light was quivering over his shoulder and showed his handsome face, startling in its earnestness, in its pallor and look of arrested passion.

"Twelve men died yesterday," he said, with what seemed to Christopher Gist curious irrelevancy.

"The French officer in command among them?"

"Yes. A young man — not above my age."

"Well, he died in a pleasant way."

Mr. Washington unclasped his right hand from his knee and drew his fingers through the little pile of green walnut leaves. "Where is he now, Mr. Gist? It is a strange thing — death. He was splendid, too. Coulon de Jumonville they called him." He looked on the ground a while, then added in a low and extraordinarily gentle voice, "I wonder if there is a lady somewhere who will weep for him, Mr. Gist!"

"Maybe. All these things — all the *great* things are hard on women."

"On us, too, perhaps."

"No — we get the *glory*. That youth wished to die in that fashion — we all do; to be young and fearless and to die finely in the open, a free thing, is very magnificent — but I doubt if it is so magnificent for the women who wait at home for news." He laughed a little. "There is no woman waiting for news of me, and that is sorrow and joy, too. I'm free as the red fox."

The dawn was now so strong that Mr. Washington's face was clearly to be seen, though he sat with his back to the east; it was utterly pale, and his eyes were dark and had a shrouded look of pain.

"There is a lady in Williamsburg . . ." he said, putting back the hair from his brow, "a creature of such beauty that I cannot help thinking of her night and day — yes, she rides at my side, this woman, and follows me into the remotest places of the forest, sits in my tent with me, grows with the dawn and with the dusk — yet the last look I saw on her face was a scornful one, and she has no manner of regard for me; so I am not free and yet have not the delights of love's captivity, for I languish in the bonds of a jailor who knows not she holds me."

He looked away gravely, down the long slopes filled with a light that was steadily turning into a deeper and more fiery hue of gold.

"You wonder that I should speak of this — and now," he continued. "But there is an intolerable anguish, Mr. Gist, in long separation from one so dear and so indifferent; and sometimes I wish I had been even as this young foreigner, left cold and alone in the forest before ever I had seen her lovely face!"

"This is a rare mood for you," said Christopher Gist. "I did not think any lovely face could have disturbed your peace." He smiled and looked round him at the great trees. "There is so much else in the world," he added wisely.

"All those things," replied Mr. Washington, "I can get for myself — not this. It seems as if this came straight from God and that He withheld it."

Mr. Gist looked at him curiously. "What can you get for yourself?" he asked.

"The — other things. All there is in the world. Achievement — you know" — he touched his breast lightly — "it is here, the power to do — what I will." He spoke with extraordinary power and extraordinary modesty. "Sometimes I feel as if I could make a nation — and control it when it is made. And there are so many chances, here — in the new world — so much to do — so much that might he done. And I have had already great opportunities."

"Yes," answered Christopher Gist grimly. "And you took one yesterday when you made war inevitable."

"America will not regret that action of mine, no, nor England," said Mr. Washington quietly.

Mr. Gist glanced at his pale handsomeness, over which the sun was sparkling now in the first radiance of its pristine glory.

"And to go back to the lovely face," he said. "Who is the lady?"

Mr. Washington flushed swiftly. "A little creature, very fair, who lives at Baltimore," he said, with a kind of lightness. "I only saw her twice and have forgotten her name."

Mr. Gist glanced at him keenly, suspecting subterfuge. "Well, you can win and wear her if you wish to," he answered. "It is no more difficult, after all," he smiled dryly, "than making nations and ruling them, or even than making wars and conducting them, Mr. Washington."

"Have you ever tried it?" asked the young man abruptly.

"I have not tried making a nation," evaded Mr. Gist.

George Washington rose to his great height and stretched himself, drawing a deep breath that was not quite like a sigh.

"Nor have I, yet," he said simply. "Nor have I attempted the lady, neither, Mr. Gist, for at present I am nothing; but when I am armed with some success, some achievement, I will essay that enterprise."

He picked up the cross, and with a thoughtful face straightened the arms of it, which he had skillfully bound together with long twists of grass. With his slow, graceful step and a grave air he crossed to where his men were eating their breakfasts and making ready their horses.

In a sleepy voice he asked one to point out Coulon de Jumonville's grave. The man sprang up and showed him a row of rough hillocks in a little space between two rows of beech trees.

All the dead had been laid facing east, ready for the resurrection.

"God," said Mr. Washington, "give them patience till then; it is a long time for brave men to be inactive."

He bent over the spot where they told him the French officer slept in his war paint, and thrust the walnut-wood cross deep into the soft, upturned soil.

"It must be strange," he said, half to himself and half to Christopher Gist, who had followed him, "to lie there quiet, shut away from the sun. How many will lie so before this war is ended? Next spring they will be hid in flowers, but one traveling this way may see the cross and know a Christian lies here albeit not in consecrated ground."

Mr. Gist looked in a kind of amazement at the marvel of this young man, with his unconscious beauty, his unconscious strength and pride, his limitless ambitions, his ardent resolves, his tenderness, and his dreams.

Coulon de Jumonville had been such as he yesterday, and the young Virginian might be as Coulon de Jumonville was now, fallen asleep till the Judgment Day, with virgin earth on his cold heart, tomorrow.

Or the seeds of greatness in him might be cherished, might spread and grow into wonderful fruition. After all, as he had said, there were chances in this magnificent new world that the old world hardly yet knew of nor reckoned with: there was a nation to be formed in this great continent — the youngest nation, perhaps the strongest, the most splendid and most glorious.

And perhaps the man to make and guide this fresh and vigorous nation might be the beautiful young Virginian who was standing in the full rays of early morning, holding the rich, heavy hair back from his brow and gazing with unfathomable eyes at his enemy's grave.

Christopher Gist, from the experience of his difficult, adventurous life, that had taken him often out into the wilderness, never into great places, felt a strange yearning over this youth whom he had learned to love last winter on that long journey to Fort le Bœuf, this youth who stood so calmly and serenely at the beginning of life and spoke so gravely of making, shaping, and guiding nations.

Mr. Washington seemed to have been deeply musing, too. He turned with a start, as if suddenly aware of the scrutiny of Christopher Gist, colored and moved abruptly away to his little army.

An officer of the Maryland Free Company with a couple of Indian guides had just come up. He had, it seemed, started directly after Mr. Washington had left Great Meadows, but had lost track of him, and the Indians had only with difficulty found the trail.

He carried letters that had been brought from the camp on the Lower Potomac to Great Meadows — and unexpected news.

Joshua Fry was dead at Alexandria, and George Washington was now commander of the entire colonial forces, at this moment marching up to Great Meadows to put themselves under his orders.

CHAPTER VII
GOVERNOR DINWIDDIE'S BALL

"Mr. Washington has not a chance," said Mr. Conway.

He was speaking to Martha Dandridge at Governor Dinwiddie's ball; they were seated near an open window, over the balcony of which grew the purple clusters of the wistaria, now in full bloom, and jasmine, showing white even in the darkness of the night. Above this scented weight of flowers sparkled and glittered the large summer stars.

"How — no chance?" asked the lady, her full pink skirts, her bare throat, her powdered locks, the large lace and ivory fan she held, the pink hyacinth and white prairie roses at her bosom, the fine lace — a pattern of cobweb and lilies — that flowed over her shoulders and bosom, one and all glowing and glorious in the light from the pure wax candles that shone on a sconce before an oval mirror behind her delicate head.

"The French are advancing on him, and they are three to one."

"Numbers do not always give the victory," returned the lady coldly.

Mr. Conway smiled. "And young Washington has no experience," he said.

Her soft eyes looked absently round the room — which was pleasant with all the gentlefolk of Virginia. Her young and very exquisite face held a mingled look of strength and pain and a controlled coldness, pitiful to see. "Mr. Washington," she said, in a reserved voice, "seems, so far, to have done well enough."

"By the death of Coulon de Jumonville he made war inevitable," replied Mr. Conway, lifting his fine brows; "he will not find it so easy to make war successful."

"That will not rest wholly with Mr. Washington," said Martha Dandridge, "but with the home government — and the assemblies here."

"Dinwiddie is very martial," remarked Mr. Conway, with a deepening of his not wholly pleasant smile; "but I think he will not be able to get the colonies to act together in this matter. I hear that the Independent Company from South Carolina refused to take the pay that contents the Virginians."

Mistress Dandridge brought her ardent eyes suddenly on his dark, powerful face. "Why do you," she asked, leaning forward a little, "why do you speak as if you wished the war to come to disaster for us?"

He flushed a little, but answered lightly. "Why, Madam, I did not wish war at all."

"I always thought it was the only way for us," she said proudly.

"Perhaps," he answered, "you do not understand what it means. There is no one belonging to you with Washington at Great Meadows!"

The betrothed of Mr. Custis slowly waved her fan to and fro; for the rest, she was as motionless and as pallid as the fainting roses at her breast.

"You think me very selfish," she replied, in a still voice. "If I had someone dear to me with our troops I should still think as I do — which is as every loyalist thinks."

Mr. Conway laughed. "I wonder what every loyalist will think when Washington and all his followers are wiped out."

She was silent, gazing away down the shining vista of the ballroom.

"He has named the fort he has built at Great Meadows, Fort Necessity," Mr. Conway continued, "and his last letters state that he has no bread and but little ammunition."

"You always disliked Mr. Washington," she said, with cold directness. "It seems as if you would be pleased to see him unfortunate."

Mr. Conway answered calmly, "No — I never liked him."

The violins began; their melody rose above the laughter, the talk, the swish of skirt and coat, the sound of high-heeled shoes and the delicate click of sword scabbards.

Martha saw Mr. Custis coming through the press, looking for her. Before he had seen her she had risen, regally dismissed Mr. Conway and stepped into the quiet, the dark, the blossoming fragrance of the balcony.

As soon as she was free from the black eyes of the man whose every word had been an agony, she gave a little sobbing cry under her breath and stumbled forward through the jasmine and wistaria, catching at the iron railings for support.

They were cold to her fingers, but no colder than the awful chill that seemed to strike deeper every moment into her heart: a sense of such misery, such anguish possessed her that it seemed that she was shouting it aloud, that everyone must know, must see. She looked up at the sky, and her face was almost lifeless in the sudden pallor that had fallen on it. The stars seemed to melt and reform before her eyes — sparkle together in one blinding mass of light, divide and subdivide.

"This is wrong," she found herself saying. "I should be with him now — I should have been with him since the first moment we met. That was what was meant, and this is the worst agony in the world. There is everything in the world between us — space and honor and duty and indifference, yet I must bridge that space — or die."

She felt her limbs weak beneath her; she crushed the jasmine in her stiff hands and felt the perfume sting her nostrils.

"What are you doing now?" her sad lips murmured. "I ought to be there — you are mine . . . *mine* . . . God could never have meant a harmless creature to suffer as I am suffering — ah, I wish my heart could break, break — then I should feel no more!"

Behind her was the mockery of the dim lights, the sparkling music, the light voices; before her was the mockery of the blue mysterious night and the throbbing stars, that once had seemed so near, so tender, and so beautiful, and now were so distant, so cruel, so horrible — as if they rejoiced in her anguish.

If he would only return. If she could only know that he was at Mount Vernon or in Richmond it would be so much easier to bear. She did not want to see him again, no, never — but she felt that if she could only have been sure that he was safe, successful, and triumphant, she could endure peaceably and face the life she had undertaken to live.

In one instant she scorned, hated, and pitied herself; in one instant she loved, hated, and pitied him. She pictured him in his feeble fort — Fort Necessity! — without bread, with little ammunition, with few men, and half of those discontented; while up from the Ohio marched a gathering force of French and Indians, merciless enemies, commanded by the brother of the man whose death had made war inevitable, Coulon de Villiers, brother of Coulon de Jumonville.

"Why don't these people here do something?" she muttered to herself. She could bear the soft darkness no longer, but passed through the swaying jasmine sprays back into the ballroom. Governor Dinwiddie, in his black velvet, white lace, and court sword, was standing apart, alone, and watching the dancers. Martha Dandridge crossed over to him.

"Sir," she said, "do you feel anxious?"

He turned to her quickly in his abrupt, animated manner. "About the war, you mean, Madam?" He smiled kindly into her fair, pale face.

"Yes." She clasped her fan so tightly that the sticks crushed and broke.

"I have great trust in Mr. Washington," he answered, "but the truth is, Mistress Dandridge, that there is very little chance for him if he is cornered at Great Meadows — and has very little chance for us if His Majesty's governors do not act together with more harmony and patriotism than they have shown hitherto."

"Yes, and the assemblies also show a faint idea of their duty," he added, with a little lift of his head. "And Virginia cannot do everything."

Martha looked at him curiously; his self-centered point of view maddened her: his quarrels with the assembly, the burdens put upon Virginia. What were these things compared to that young man awaiting an overwhelming foe at Great Meadows?

"Mr. Washington has had a vast responsibility put on him," she said, and was surprised at the calmness of her own voice.

Governor Dinwiddie entirely misunderstood her.

"Yes," he answered; "of course I never meant to stake all on one so inexperienced, but the death of Fry was a thing not to be reckoned on."

She could not answer that. She could not say: I was not thinking of you, of Virginia — but of him; what right had she to champion George Washington?

"Are you not dancing?" asked the governor kindly, noticing her silence.

"Not tonight," she answered. "Believe me, I feel this — about the war."

He was gratified, and showed his pleasure. "Spirit such as yours," he said, "should go far to make us successful; when the ladies will put their country before the homage of the ballroom what may we not expect of the men?"

She crimsoned with shame at this praise, yet it was not undeserved, for she would have died for Virginia.

Governor Dinwiddie continued, "Even if this campaign ends in defeat, as it must, I fear, yet it will rouse the other colonies as to the danger. There is to be a Conference at Albany soon, and there I hope to press the point of our mutual arming, our mutual resolute action against the French."

"Surely you will have no difficulty," she said mechanically; if George Washington was slain at Great Meadows, what would she care whether or not Dinwiddie blew this spark into a great war?

"I am sorry for George Washington," said the governor suddenly. "He has hardly had a chance; I was speaking to his brother yesterday, and Mr. Lawrence said that his letters had been so hopeful. That is a splendid thing, Madam, the hopefulness of youth."

"All great men have been hopeful," she answered, in a sudden warm flash of feeling.

"All *great* men?" he looked at her curiously.

She crimsoned again, but stood her ground. "Yes," she cried. "I think young Mr. Washington has the makings of a great man."

"Ah," answered Governor Dinwiddie musingly. "I think so, too."

Her heart beat fast with pride and pleasure; it was unbelievably sweet to hear him so spoken of.

"We likely need a great man in British America in the years to come," added the governor.

The dance came to an end; the musicians put their violins and flutes down; the shining floor cleared; others claimed the attention of the governor, and Martha hastened to the alcove where Sarah Mildmay's blithe and sparkling beauty was reflected three times in the long beveled mirrors, one either side of her and one behind. She looked at Martha, and the forbidden name was in her loving blue eyes.

"Any news from Great Meadows?" she asked.

Martha fingered the crushed fan, and kept her head erect on her long slender neck. "How should I know, dear?" she asked steadily.

"I saw you talking to the governor," answered Sarah. "And Mr. Conway was telling me that any moment we might get news . . ."

"Mr. Conway," interrupted Martha, with a flash in her eyes, "might do better to join the Free Companies than *talk* so much of them. I think he has a spite against all the world, that man . . ."

"No," said Sarah demurely, "only against one or two people."

Martha's white-satin clad foot tapped the ground impatiently. Another *contredanse* had begun; almost everyone else was dancing, and under cover of this general absorption and the music Mistress Mildmay spoke with sudden seriousness.

"Don't do it, dearest," she said; she leaned forward and seized Martha's fine white wrist; "don't do it, beloved — I must speak — for you are doing wrong — just out of pride."

"Be silent," breathed Martha, very pale. "I will not listen to you — let me go."

"No," answered Sarah, in great agitation. "You shall hear me — *he* is coming back, successful or not, and you are going to be married in a week — don't do it!"

"Do you think," whispered Martha coldly and very proudly, "that Mr. Custis will have cause to complain of me as his wife? Do you not suppose that I have told him that . . ."

She abruptly paused.

". . . that you don't love him," finished Sarah bluntly.

Martha colored violently. ". . . that I think respect the proper foundation for a happy union," she said, with a piteous unsteadiness in the stilted words.

"You don't!" said Sarah. "You know you don't! No one does."

But Martha's stately pride of voice, look, and gesture overruled the bright young beauty's earnestness. "You must not speak to me so; I have never given you occasion — because . . . because you heard me say things that night, that I should never have said, that I did not mean — no, do not look at me so," she said firmly. "I repeat, Sarah, that I did not mean — just because of this, I say, you have no right to speak as you do, as I must beg you not to speak again." She looked at the dancers as she spoke, and her glance was calm and steady.

"But you don't deceive me," answered Sarah. "Not in the least. And you cannot prevent me, my dear, from repeating, as one who loves you, that you are making a false step and an error, and doing a prideful thing and a wrong thing and a thing of which I don't approve at all."

Flushed into a pretty rosiness with the effort and earnestness of this speech, Mistress Mildmay rose, shook out her taffeta skirts, and with slightly trembling fingers adjusted the narrow band of black velvet that confined her fair soft throat; as she did so, she turned her back on Martha, to face the mirror at her side.

Martha sat motionless; her eyes were fixed on Governor Dinwiddie, who was standing against the amber-colored paneling by the door, reading a letter that had just been brought him by a Negro servant.

The air seemed suddenly to grow tense with excitement; most of the gentlemen present gathered round the governor.

Sarah saw this in the mirror. "News from Great Meadows," she said, without looking round. "Aren't you interested?"

Martha was silent; she saw Mr. Conway coming toward them. She braced herself by thinking of him and how she hated him; it gave her a curious courage, that feeling of hatred for this man who hated Mr. Washington.

He gave his news briefly with a polite air of regret; she heard him without stirring or speaking, and with no change in the haughty young face she kept turned toward him.

"Washington and all his force have surrendered to Coulon de Villiers at Great Meadows."

CHAPTER VIII
THE AMERICAN

The ailanthus and catalpa were in full leaf in the squares and avenues of Williamsburg, and the new green on the oaks in the forest had entirely replaced the old dead foliage which had braved the winter snows when George Washington returned from the campaign that had ended in defeat.

On an afternoon of a fiery heat he sat in the governor's cabinet and gazed with his peculiar steady and serene gaze at the great spaces of these trees, ailanthus and catalpa that grew so near the governor's house that they pressed their weight of leaves against the gables and darkened the spacious rooms with a cool, slightly melancholy shade.

He had just been telling Robert Dinwiddie something of the difficulties he had had to struggle against during his short experience as commander of the colonial forces, and giving an account (which he occasionally verified from a neat and copious journal he had brought with him) of that day at Fort Necessity when, after an exchange of shots lasting twenty-four rainy hours, Coulon de Villiers had offered better terms than could have been hoped for from his overwhelming superiority of numbers and the feebleness of the fort; and they, leaving their arms and ammunition in the hands of the victors, had returned to Richmond in fulfilment of De Villiers' conditions.

The loss of the enemy had been as great as their own, and the only really disastrous thing about a reverse that had been unavoidable was the tremendous loss of prestige it meant in the eyes of the Indian allies, who had already been dangerously impressed by the superior discipline, artillery, and united action of the French.

Mr. Washington showed himself well aware of this lamentable effect of his defeat and made no attempt to gloss it over; no, he pointed out that it was a real misfortune that the credit and reputation of the English colonists should be damaged in the capricious eyes of the savages so early in the struggle, and urged the governor to take the first opportunity of striking firmly so as to secure the renewed admiration and allegiance of the Indians.

In all he said he was curiously impartial, and spoke with a detached air and a complete repression of his own views, his own achievements, his own personality.

Yet it was this very personality that the governor found himself interested in, beyond anything that had been said, and studying, to the exclusion of the great and important matters on his mind. And these matters on Robert Dinwiddie's mind were really great and really important — such as the coming Conference at Albany, the probability of help arriving from England, and the attitude of the other governors with regard to the war, his own quarrel with the burgesses of Virginia and their slackness in subscribing the necessary funds for the operations in the Ohio Valley. Yet all these things, much as they weighed on his ardent, patriotic, and shrewd spirit, seemed to the governor of Virginia curiously trivial compared to the personality of the handsome, quiet young gentleman who had just returned defeated from his first attempt at soldiering.

He had had this impression before, and very strongly, when he had selected George Washington as his envoy to the French at Fort le Bœuf, and again when he had interviewed him before giving him the command under Fry, and he had it now, with a feeling of absolute conviction — the impression that neither the governors, the Indians, nor the home government were going to matter so much to the colonies of North America as this young man.

It was an absurd feeling, perhaps; the shrewd Dinwiddie himself half felt it so, but it was a feeling that could not be easily dismissed.

At this pause, when Mr. Washington had finished his modest account and laid his neat journal on the smooth, shining, round table, Robert Dinwiddie looked very closely and keenly at the young Virginian whose presence had this effect on him.

George Washington, though in his proper complexion pale, had been turned to the deep hue of the outdoor liver by the months he had spent in the open, and this had somewhat changed his appearance; otherwise he was the same: serene, rather proud, with a look of passion restrained in his face and an air of swift motion restrained in his figure.

He wore a dark blue watered silk and his hair unpowdered; his dress was very elegant, even fashionable; he had a fine diamond in the Bruges lace of his cravat; his hair clasp and his shoe buckles were sparkling paste. Except for the extreme handsomeness of his appearance, his high-born aristocratic look, the perfection of his bearing, his movements, there was nothing remarkable about him that Governor Dinwiddie could find to justify his own secret estimate. For, noticeable as were this physical beauty and nobility, they were not rare things to find among the gentlemen of Virginia; there were many men in Richmond nearly as handsome as Mr. Washington whom the governor had never looked at twice. In this man, he argued to himself, there must be something more, some latent mental superiority, some subconsciousness of power, some inner forces, some splendid qualities, only waiting to be revealed, and tested to be triumphant.

So far he had shown himself courageous, capable, wise, for twenty-three, an exceptional youth who remained calm under both success and failure — secretly Dinwiddie thought that an almost infallible sign of the truly great — but the man scrutinizing him was looking for, expecting, something more than that, something that might change the face of the world.

Yet the beautiful eyes were singularly modest and open in expression, and the whole charming personality was fragrant with a simple unconsciousness. He was as unaware of the dominating effect his spirit had on that of the governor as he was unaware of the effect his beautiful face had on the hearts of women.

Robert Dinwiddie, struggling with a slight sense of bewilderment and confusion, strove, by gentle probing into the mystery of this reserved soul, to explain the influence that the youth had over him.

"Are you ambitious, Mr. Washington?" he asked abruptly.

The young man turned slowly from his contemplation of the swaying green of the great fresh leaves against the diamond panes of the window. "Of course, Sir," he answered.

"In what way?"

Mr. Washington smiled in a fashion that seemed to make the governor's question foolish. "How could one live if one were not ambitious?" he answered. He picked up his journal and began putting straight some loose leaves in it. Robert Dinwiddie had the impression that he was not pleased at this attempt to get within his guard, and that he wished to fall again to the formal business relations. But the governor was not to be rejected so easily.

"Very many people are not ambitious, Mr. Washington."

The young man looked at him quickly and seemed half amused. "It is not a good occasion for me to be speaking of my ambitions, Sir," he answered, "when I return unsuccessful from my first venture."

"No matter for that," returned the governor. "You did all that anyone could, and I should not have been pleased if you had been cut to pieces instead of surrendering. I am satisfied with your conduct."

"Thank you," said Mr. Washington courteously, but not as if he had been very anxious for the good will of the governor or anyone else; it was this serenity, this poise, that Robert Dinwiddie was so eager to fathom.

He kept his eyes fixed keenly on the composed face against the dark background of the black furniture and the black walls of the somber room.

"Do you wish to remain in the militia?" he asked.

"Yes, Sir. I suppose you will be sending another expedition to the Ohio?"

"When General Braddock arrives from England, yes."

He thought that as he spoke a slight shade passed over the countenance he was studying, a shade of deepened pride, even of annoyance or anger. He pressed the point.

"Of course it will all be in the hands of General Braddock. I believe it is his intention to hold a council at Alexandria."

The look of resentment and anger on the face of the young man was now unmistakable.

"You seem displeased," smiled Governor Dinwiddie.

"Sir," answered Mr. Washington, with a little stir of passion in his voice, "these Britishers are almost like foreigners, and I have a fancy that we could manage our own affairs."

"General Braddock is an experienced soldier."

"On the banks of the Rhine, perhaps — what does he know of the banks of the Potomac?"

"That sounds disloyal," said the governor keenly.

"Disloyal to whom, Sir?"

"To His Majesty."

Mr. Washington answered slowly. "It seems as if it might be difficult to be loyal both to His Majesty and to the colonies — to ourselves, Sir. I have nothing more to say, of course. I hope General Braddock will have success, but it is difficult to conceive how he will be able to conduct warfare of a kind to which he is wholly unused in a continent that he has never seen, and has probably but a faint conception of."

There was so much good sense in this, and it was expressed with such moderation and such quiet energy, that the governor felt his impression of the speaker's innate power deepen.

"I hope to gather a large colonial force, and I believe and trust that General Braddock will have the intelligence to take the advice and help of the Colonies, especially in the matter of the Indians."

Mr. Washington was silent; he seemed deeply entrenched in his reserve again; it struck the governor that his attitude was that of a man who will lead or do nothing, who will be in the forefront of every action or retire altogether, a man who could go his own way and disdain every kind of prominence, but one who would never play a secondary part on any stage.

Robert Dinwiddie frowned; if this was the solution of this young man's character he was like to be difficult material to deal with. Good lieutenants are more easily placed, and — to the mediocre man — more useful than brilliant generals.

"I am sorry," said the governor, "that you should have this dislike of General Braddock. I hoped that you would serve under him."

Mr. Washington lowered his eyes; his look might have been that of a prince offered a menial post, but he answered quietly and respectfully.

"Of course, Sir, I should be pleased to go out in this next campaign." And his face was so instantly serene and composed that the flash of pride might easily have been, the governor thought, in his own fancy.

"There is one thing I must tell you, Mr. Washington," he said, "and that is something that may not be agreeable to you."

The young man waited patiently and with a slight smile.

"All the colonial officers will have lower rank than those who hold direct commissions from His Majesty."

A steady color rose and beat in Mr. Washington's cheeks; his eyes changed swiftly to a dark kind of steel blue. "No, Sir, it is not agreeable to me," he said steadily; "and I doubt if it will be agreeable to anyone in Virginia."

Robert Dinwiddie felt he had got within his guard at last; intense pride and intense ambition were evidently, despite his modest demeanor, the ruling factors in this young man's character.

"Anything else is impossible," he said dryly; he was the representative of England, of the King, and the fact caused him to feel a slight sensation of antagonism to the young Virginian.

And it was to the representative of England that Mr. Washington now spoke. "In what way," he asked, "are we inferior to the British, that we should be put beneath them?"

"You are colonial militia," was the answer. "And they belong to His Majesty's standing army."

"We are in our own country."

"Your own country?"

"Yes, Sir. That is something that, I think, they forget in England. Something that you, too, perhaps forget — that we are — a nation."

The governor was silent; he wanted the young American to further explain himself.

Mr. Washington continued, "We are a nation and to be treated as such. We began this war, and I do not doubt that we can end it — successfully. If the British come over to help us let them come as equals, not as superiors — not as masters."

The governor smiled. "You talk very boldly, Mr. Washington."

"No, for how can there be boldness when there is no cause for fear?"

"You have a republican spirit."

"Perhaps I have, Sir. It is difficult to feel loyal to a king one has never seen, and to a constitution made for another country, another people — so many thousands of miles away. But I am no politician. I could not speak on these matters."

He rose, and his great height and proud carriage seemed to dwarf the somber little room.

"About the officers . . ." began the governor.

"Ah, about that," said Mr. Washington calmly. "I resign my commission, Sir."

Dinwiddie was plainly startled. "Do you mean that?" he asked sharply.

"I mean that I do not choose to be second to the English officers — yes. I must ask you to accept my resignation, Sir."

His eyes were calm with an unutterable resolution; if he had talked eloquently for an hour he could not have convinced Dinwiddie more of his unmovable decision.

The governor rose angrily. "I think this unpatriotic, disloyal, Mr. Washington — it is a spirit I had not looked for in you . . ."

The young man interrupted, "You forget, Sir. You speak as if I were English. I am American."

CHAPTER IX
THE RING

Mr. Washington left the governor's house and stood a moment under the catalpa trees. He was reflecting on the unpleasant task he had before him — that of breaking to his mother and his friends that he had on an instant's impulse abandoned what had seemed likely to be a brilliant career.

He was sorry about this, but the rest of the matter, the personal aspect of it, did not trouble him. He had an unconquerable calm in his spirit; he believed that he should eventually do what he was meant to do, despite Governor Dinwiddie and despite General Braddock, and he did not in the least regret that he had resigned his commission.

As he stood thoughtfully under the thick fresh leaves, through which sparkles of sunlight glimmered fitfully, he saw, on the other side of the brilliantly sunny street, a lady in a white gown who carried a blue sunshade with a long silk fringe.

He went rather pale. A sense of his failure at Great Meadows rushed over him more strongly than it had done yet; he felt, swiftly and acutely, that he was — for the moment at least — no longer in the theater of great events. But there was something in the sunshine that caused these feelings to lift and vanish.

He stepped quickly and confidently across the street.

"Mr. Washington!" Martha turned slowly to face him; they were quite alone in the empty street, in the noonday heat. The air was full of the rustling of the catalpa leaves and the waving of the ailanthus crowns of fresh foliage.

"You knew I was back?" he asked, standing before her with his hat in his hand.

"Yes, I knew," she answered; a white scarf with a gold border that she wore floated over her shoulder like a forlorn banner, delicate against the dark, precise brickwork of the house behind her; she wore in her fichu a spray of wistaria, drooping with the heat. "I am going to call on Mistress Driscoll," she added, and made to move on.

This, and her reserve of face and manner, fired him. "So am I," he said, in a masterful tone. "May I walk with you?"

"Of course," she replied, with almost mechanical coldness.

He glanced at her profile; she caught the truant scarf back to her breast and twisted the end of it round her left mittened hand, almost as if she had hurt her fingers.

Neither spoke until they reached a large, pleasant house off the main street; she never made any comment at his accompanying her, which piqued and stung Mr. Washington. He looked at her often, and had a feeling of triumph when he saw that she kept her eyes down.

Mistress Driscoll was out.

"We will wait," said Mr. Washington.

Martha looked at him in a kind of mute protest, but lowered her eyes again and said nothing.

They were shown into the great cool withdrawingroom, where the air was heavy with the perfume of potpourri and the windows were closed against the sun.

As soon as the lackey had gone Mr. Washington spoke.

"Are you angry," he said, "that I should esquire you through Williamsburg?"

She sank into a dark polished chair and looked up at him. Her dress seemed almost luminous against the dull rose brocade cushions; she held her parasol across her knees, and the long fringe of it shook with her trembling.

"Strange that you also should want to see Agnes Driscoll," she murmured.

"I do not," he answered, rather haughtily. "I wished to see you, Mistress Dandridge."

He wondered at the shudder she gave, when he used her name, he thought, and at the way in which the last tinge of color left her already pale face, as if he had struck or insulted her. Confused by this shrinking white look of hers, he paused and frowned, and remembered rather bitterly the coldness of her farewell to him.

"Does it annoy you," he asked gloomily, "that I should wish to speak to you?"

"Oh, no," she answered childishly; "why should it?"

He took no notice of this reply that he knew came not from her heart, but was the mere feeble dallying of her lips.

"You are not dealing sincerely with me," he said, rather angrily.

He went to the window, and stood by the portion that was open, shutter and glass, and looked into the brilliant glamour of the street.

As soon as his back was turned she rose, as if a spell had been moved from her and, giving him a wild look, said, "I must be going home, Mr. Washington — Agnes would never expect me to wait for her."

He looked over his shoulder. "You wish to avoid me," he remarked fiercely, and her desperate glance showed her that he was flushed from his muslin cravat to his dark waving hair. She dropped helpless into her seat again; she had the air of one utterly overwhelmed. Something in this crushed sad demeanor of hers fired him almost to madness. He was silent a moment to gain control of himself.

"I return a defeated man," he said at last.

A little color tinged her face. "No," she answered, "not that — you did the best you could."

"Then," he said swiftly, "you were grieved to hear I had surrendered?"

"I knew that you would not have done so if it had not been inevitable."

His eyes flashed. "I have resigned my commission," he said, and watched her keenly.

"You — have?" She rose and turned to face him. And sat down. And rose again. "You have resigned, Mr. Washington?"

"Yes. A few moments before I met you I informed Governor Dinwiddie of my decision."

"Oh!" she exclaimed; her stiff pallor had left her and she was quite rosy and animated and sparkling with a palpitating life and eagerness. "The pity of it, the waste and pity of that, Mr. Washington!"

"Do you think so?" he asked.

The meaning way in which he spoke seemed to bring her up short again; the expression of confusion and distress that he could not understand again passed over her face. She stood quite still, her hands before her, the left one still wrapped in the end of her white scarf.

"Yes," she answered, with an effort, lowering her eyes. "I think it is a pity that anyone should take his hand from that to which he has set it."

"I have not done so," said Mr. Washington. "I have, as an American, refused to serve under the English officers. You may believe that I was not thinking of my own value, Madam, but of my country's repute."

"What are you going to do, then?" she asked, still without looking up.

"I suppose," he answered, with a little catch in his breath, "one waits."

"Yes," she said; "yes."

"I suppose," he continued, "that if one has some consciousness of — of — any power, any strong resolve or firm purpose — it is not so difficult to wait."

"Men are like that," she said, with sudden force. "It does not matter to them if they wait — years."

"And women," he interposed quickly, "cannot women wait, also?"

"Women are — different."

"I had not thought so," he answered, very gravely.

"Perhaps," said Martha coldly, "you do not know much of women."

"That is true enough," he admitted. "But I know that they can be very constant."

She laughed. "I believe so. And I must be leaving, Mr. Washington. It is vastly foolish for us to remain here, when Mistress Driscoll may not be back inside of hours." With a light swish of her skirts she turned to the door.

But he stepped before her; she had the impression that he was very angry.

"You know," he said, "that you cannot expect me to take this from you, Madam."

She gave him an inscrutable glance, and remained motionless with her right hand outstretched toward the door handle.

"What other behavior do you expect from me, Sir?" she asked, with a chilly courtesy.

A look of pain and doubt clouded his face. "Do you not understand me?" he asked gloomily.

"Not at all. Not in the very least," she smiled coldly. "I do not know what I ever said or did to make you think that I should — understand you. Was there anything?" she challenged.

"Oh — several things."

The color fled even from her lips, but her eyes sparkled with a hard light. "You have a lively fancy," she said, and turned the door handle.

"You shall not dismiss me a second time so haughtily," he said, in a masterful tone. "The memory of your last farewell to me was no pleasant thing for me to carry about with me during those weeks I was away — and now a second time you put scorn between us."

"There is nothing between us," she interrupted in a fiery tone, "and I put nothing — the whole thing is — nothing!"

He looked at her, amazed, startled, and breathing heavily.

"Why, I think you *hate* me!" he exclaimed.

She lifted her eyes bravely to his. "Why do you use such great words? Do I not tell you that the whole thing is nothing?"

"I think you hate me," he repeated heavily.

"Why should I have ever thought enough of you to hate you?" she demanded proudly. "We are scarcely acquaintances, Mr. Washington."

"Then I mistook," he said bitterly, "mistook, indeed."

She opened the door. "Good day," she said, with a hard little smile.

"One moment. May I not see you — soon? May I not wait on you at your father's house? I wish to speak to you — believe me that I do . . ."

The bitterness had left his voice, and he spoke with eagerness and tenderness, and a passion fast breaking restraints.

"You will not find me at my father's house," she replied.

He stopped as he was about to speak again, and put his hand up to his heart. The shock drove the color out of his face; he even trembled a little.

"Not at your father's house?" he repeated, in a changed voice.

"No." She, as pale as he, and shivering, unwound the white silk scarf from her left hand and held it out toward him.

He looked at it, saw a heavy wedding ring there on her fine finger, and stepped back from her two paces.

"So you did not know?" she said. "I thought that you must have heard."

He stood against the wall and pressed his handkerchief to his lips. "No, I did not know," he repeated dully.

She pulled the door open wider and drew her skirts together. "I am married to Mr. Custis," she said. "I doubt not that he would be pleased to see you if you would wait on him. Again, goodbye, Mr. Washington." She went out and was absorbed into the stillness of the quiet old house.

CHAPTER X
THE ENGLISH GENERAL

George Washington was now again "Mr. Washington," a private gentleman and a prosperous planter.

After the first blaze of indignation his quick temper had been roused to by the governor's concession to the claims of the English officers, he did not find it difficult to retire from a public life.

He loved Hunting Creek of which he was now master since his brother's recent death after that fruitless voyage to the West Indies in search of health; he felt very strongly his duty to his brother's child and to his mother, he was intensely interested in agriculture and very proud of his plantations, which he intended to make a model to the whole country.

He liked the long days in the saddle, the gallops after the fox with old Lord Fairfax, the tours of inspection around the cotton and tobacco fields, the shooting and fishing excursions, the pleasant evenings in the beloved old farm, the dear company of those belonging to him, and the constant exchange of pleasant visits with friends and neighbors.

When Lawrence Washington, shortly before his last lingering illness, had resigned his commission in the colonial army and secured a rank in it for his younger brother, George had for the first time turned his attention toward the theater of large events.

When Captain Washington died, George, having then the management of his estates as well as of Ferry Farm and the guardianship of his brother's daughter, had felt himself obliged to resign his occupation of land surveyor, congenial, and prosperous as that business had been.

Then had followed rapidly the events that had placed the young Virginian prominently before the eyes of the colonies; his appointment as adjutant general, his expedition to Fort le Bœuf on the failure of Captain Trant, his command under Joshua Fry, his impatient daring in the affair of Great Meadows, his brief exultation, his inevitable defeat, the news of the sending of a force from England, his proud resignation when he heard that the colonies were to be slighted in the persons of their officers — and his return to the banks of the Potomac a regular citizen.

No jealousy nor bitterness marred the peace into which he had retired. He was anxious to know more of war; he was eager to serve Virginia, but he felt that he had performed no action of any value, that he was neither missed nor wanted, and in his integral modesty he was quite prepared to never more come forward in his country's service, but to remain merely an ardently interested spectator of the policies that he had for so short a time mingled in.

He was not wholly happy, but the secret sorrow that colored a life which was in itself all that his heart desired had not any connection with war nor statecraft; and if he never went near Williamsburg or seldom further than the prospering village of Richmond on the St. James' Falls, it was not from any morbid fear of meeting those who had admired him when he was in the governor's confidence and flattered him when he had seemed a rising man and might ignore him now, but from a deep and not to be conquered dread that he might see or hear of the beautiful Martha Custis.

No one guessed the unexpressed, the thwarted passion that had now been condemned to utter silence forever; no one knew the reason why the handsome young planter, so robust and full of life, would listen to no suggestion of taking a wife, nor why he was so cold, even haughty, with ladies to whose company he began to discover an increasing aversion. Those who had watched the young Virginian's sudden rise to a position of favor and trust, those who had seen his qualities of daring, courage, fortitude, and modesty, could not believe that he would be content to sink himself in tending his plantation on the Potomac, in riding about Mount Vernon, in hunting with Lord Fairfax or reading in the library at Belvoir. For in no way did George Washington seem to be fitted for a life so secluded, so regular, so uneventful.

From his brothers, particularly from Lawrence, he had learned the finished manners, the polished address, the lofty code that they had been taught in England, during their education in the home country. His delicate sense of what was becoming in a man and necessary to a gentleman had never been blunted by any intercourse with the larger world beyond Virginia. His brief voyage to the West Indies with his brother had shown him something of the sea (on which it had been his first ambition to spend his life), but little of men; and those he dwelt among were of the same mold as himself, though few were of so fine a quality.

Therefore the maxims of his first schoolmaster, old Hobby, and those impressed on his mind by James Marge, added to the teaching of his mother and the examples of his brothers remained fresh and powerful in his mind and heart and gave him the proud austerity that, for all his passionate nature, permitted him so serenely to throw down all his ambitions when he believed his country's dignity was affronted. Those who sought to draw him on the subject of war in the Ohio Valley got little for their pains; Mr. Washington turned their questions with perfectly courteous rebukes.

So he lived and worked at Mount Vernon, grave beyond his age and wonderfully silent, and a year went by, things moving slowly in England, despite the energy of Dinwiddie's representations to the government. In the November, however, following the surrender of the British to Coulon de Villiers at Great Meadows, General Braddock, a soldier with some fame in Europe, set sail from England with a thousand men and commands to recruit four hundred more in the colonies.

The spring had come before the British commander held his council of war at Alexandria, which was attended by the governors of most of the colonies. Mr. Washington's eyes flamed when he heard an account of this, but he said nothing, and rode among his slaves working in the tobacco fields and corn fields under trees breaking into blossom.

Then, sudden as a thunderclap out of a cloudless sky, came a letter from General Braddock, requesting the honor of Mr. Washington's presence in Alexandria. The young Virginian put his affairs in order, mounted one of his beautiful horses and, accompanied by a colored servant and Van Brahm, his old fencing master, proceeded thither at once, an action which somewhat surprised his friends, who had believed him obstinately set against the English. On his arrival at Alexandria he at once waited on Governor Dinwiddie, who received him somewhat coldly.

He had already described him to General Braddock as a "dangerous young fellow," and Braddock had replied that he "liked 'em dangerous."

The next day he came before the British general, who was quartered in one of the modest houses of Alexandria which had been furnished with the costly and ponderous equipments Braddock had brought with him from England, expecting America to be a wilderness of barbarism.

Late in the afternoon of a June day the two men came face to face in the front parlor of the general's house; the room was dark and somber with heavy furnishings, but outside the chestnut, the maple, the tamarisk, and jasmine were in bloom, and the little garden beneath the window blazed red and white with roses.

As Mr. Washington entered, the general, who had been seated near the open window, rose, and the Virginian, greatly appreciating this mark of courtesy, bowed very low.

Then, in a pause of silence, they looked at each other. Mr. Washington saw a man of middle age, alert and pleasant looking, yet haughty, attired in the white breeches and waistcoat, scarlet coat, gold braid, and crimson sash of the uniform of the British army. His hair was powdered and arranged in full military side curls, and a snowy cravat of needlework emphasized the brown freshness of his thin face.

He, for his part, saw a young man, not more than twenty-three, over six feet in height, and of a most winning attractiveness of countenance, wearing a clear violet traveling coat, black satins and waistcoat and carrying a hat with a great bunch of white plumes.

It was a figure that would have graced St. James' Court in London.

"You are Mr. George Washington?" asked the Englishman.

"Yes, Sir."

"Be seated," said General Braddock.

Mr. Washington took the deep chair with arms facing the general's seat. As he waited, smiling slightly, the Englishman grew almost confused; he felt at once that he was handling unusual material.

"You commanded the last expedition against the French?" he asked.

"Yes, General Braddock."

"It was your first experience of war, Mr. Washington?"

"Absolutely."

"And not wholly successful, eh?"

"Sir," answered the young Virginian, "my first attempt consisted of much impatience, more boasting, a little victory, and a larger defeat. I knew nothing."

"Enough to fire the shot that made war inevitable, Sir," said General Braddock.

Mr. Washington flushed slightly. "I hope you have heard the truth of that affair, Sir; the French say that Coulon de Jumonville was shot while parleying, but it was not so. And, for my part, I was always sorry for his death."

General Braddock looked at him keenly. "Why did you resign?" he asked.

"Governor Dinwiddie must have told you," answered Mr. Washington.

"I want your version."

"It was because I could not agree to His Majesty's commands that all British officers were to take precedence over the colonials."

"You speak strongly."

"I feel strongly."

"You have a hot temper," remarked General Braddock. "Eh?"

"Perhaps, Sir," smiled Mr. Washington, "but this was scarcely a question of temper."

"Well, you appear to have thrown away a chance most young men would give ten years of their lives for, on a question of mere pique."

Mr. Washington lifted his head. "You do not understand, Sir," he said superbly. "It was not a question of pique — but of the dignity of my country."

"Your country," said the Englishman keenly, "is the same as mine. Your king is my king. His Majesty's commands are binding on you as on me. Your action, Sir, breathes to me of disloyalty."

Mr. Washington was silent, not as one who has nothing to say, but as one who has too much too say. At last he said quietly, "Did you send for me to tell me this, Sir?"

General Braddock suddenly smiled. "No," he answered.

"What, then, Sir?"

"You are, I think, an expert woodsman," remarked the general.

"I have had a long training in that craft, from Indians and woodsmen, also I learned much when surveying the estates of my Lord Fairfax — but I think that there are men better equipped in this particular, notably Christopher Gist."

"Governor Dinwiddie," returned the Englishman, "told me that as a woodsman, a horseman, and a shot you had no equal in Virginia. I am prepared to believe it."

Mr. Washington flushed from chin to brow and bowed, stiffly from the waist, without rising from his chair.

"I have heard other reports of you," continued the general, tapping the fingers of his right hand on the dark surface of the table. "You did as much as any man could last year. Would you not like to gain a little more experience in war?"

"With all my heart," answered the young man, still with the flush on his face, and now with a sparkle in his expressive gray eyes.

General Braddock smiled again. "Of course, this war is of no great importance," he said; "you will understand that."

He spoke with the assurance of one who had played a part of some distinction in the wars on the continent, and who had commanded in Gibraltar. "It will only be a few skirmishes with the savages before we will bring them to their knees. And I do not count the French as much."

"Sir, you underrate both," cried Mr. Washington boldly; "these Indians are no mere savages, but men highly trained and cunning."

"I make no count of a parcel of painted blacks," returned General Braddock.

The Virginian looked at him thoughtfully. "Do you know the country?" he asked.

"I have seen a map."

"Sir, there are places between here and the Ohio Valley that are not on maps and yet are most expedient to know."

"Are you thinking I shall lose my way?" smiled General Braddock.

"How could a man find it," replied Mr. Washington simply, "save he knew the country from his own eyes and judgment? It is, Sir, largely untracked and uninhabited save by a few settlers."

The Englishman looked interested and amused; his sharp eyes dwelt in a kindly fashion on the young colonial who was so modest yet so outspoken.

"As we are speaking plainly, Mr. Washington," he said, "I do not like the look of your men here. A motley crowd of fellows not amenable to orders and slack on parade."

"See them under fire!" flashed Mr. Washington, "the first and last test for a soldier, after all."

General Braddock took a pinch of snuff from a tortoiseshell box. "Not quite," he answered dryly. "You are playing at war here. If you are fond of soldiering, Mr. Washington, you will be interested to see trained troops — the very look of which will frighten these gangs of savages you think so much of."

The Virginian's eyes sparkled with suppressed excitement, but he said nothing.

"Why did they send Fry and you with so few men?" asked the soldier suddenly.

Mr. Washington was afire at once. "Why, Sir, there were no more to be spared. The other colonies were slow in their help, and we could not take from Virginia every man able to carry a rifle and leave our homes at the mercy of the Negroes. Besides, Sir," he added, with a quick flush, "if I had had twice the number the end would have been the same; I wasn't equal to the task."

"You'll make a good soldier," said the general, "if you are not too proud to listen to the older men."

He leaned back in his chair and looked thoughtfully out of the window at the sunlight in the rose garden, then he turned his head slowly and surveyed with a critical eye the ardent young colonial whose beautiful face had lost its stately reserve and showed a very youthful and charming interest and eagerness.

"Mr. Washington," said the general, "my plan of campaign is this: I and the British troops are to march to the Ohio Valley and regain that prestige in the eyes of the Indians which the late defeat forfeited. Three bodies of colonials are to march against Acadia, Crown Point, and Niagara — you will see that I am myself undertaking the most important operation." He paused, with the effort of a stiff formal man to exert himself to active graciousness. "Mr. Washington," he added, after a second, rather red in the face, "I am sorry to have displaced you. If you will volunteer for this campaign I will make you one of my *aides-de-camp*, with the rank of colonel."

It was a good deal from a soldier with a reputation to a youth who had only smelled smoke once; it was more from an arrogant Englishman to one of those colonials whom he openly despised; it was beyond what Mr. Washington had expected.

He read in it some personal liking and the British sense of justice that acknowledged as right his action in resigning; he responded instantly and with his whole heart to the touch of magnanimity and generosity. He rose and bowed.

"I accept," he answered, "with gratitude and pleasure the opportunity of learning from General Braddock something of the art of war."

"Well, we hope to teach the French a lesson," replied the general; he slipped his snuff box into the pocket of his gold-frogged waistcoat and exclaimed with sudden irritation: "but of course I haven't got enough men — when did a British government ever send enough men to open a campaign?"

And his face darkened as he thought of the fourteen hundred that were his sole army; then, having repented that he had said so much, he rose abruptly to intimate that the interview was at an end.

"How old are you?" he asked curiously.

"Twenty-three, Sir."

"Well, you have not done so ill for your age, eh? Get together your equipment and make ready for the campaign, Sir."

Twenty-three and another chance being offered; another opportunity to learn with honor, to serve with pride. The young man rode away under the trees laden with white chestnut blooms, heavy with fragrance; the world was not complete for all this golden glimpse of glory, no, not so complete as it had been a year ago.

Martha Dandridge was Martha Custis now, with a baby on her knee. He ground his teeth that he should have thought of this at such a moment, but the thought had come and would not go.

CHAPTER XI
MONONGAHELA

The campaign which the enthusiasm of Dinwiddie and Shirley had conceived as likely to end the war was from the first unfortunate.

The sloth of Pennsylvania put delays in the way; the assembly would do no more than vote twenty thousand pounds, though this colony was the most defenseless and the most tempting prize. Nor would they show any energy in providing the necessary stores for the troops, nor take any steps to raise men. Their lack of zeal had an ill effect in another way; Braddock could have marched to the Ohio either through Virginia or Pennsylvania; both routes looked the same on the map, and the British general chose the one through the loyal colony, ignorant of the fact that, whereas Pennsylvania was full of good roads with abundant facilities for transport and plentiful supplies of food, Virginia was an untracked wilderness.

His choice was encouraged by the members of the Ohio Company, who hoped their trade would benefit by the military road he would be obliged to make, and so the campaign commenced with insufficient men and money and an initial mistake, and also not before the French had got a thousand men on the Ohio and their Indian allies well advanced and stoutly encamped on British territory.

The plan of campaign itself, though sound in the main, became absurd when working out with such a handful of men. The niggardly policy of the home government and the indifference and carelessness of some of the colonies alike tied Braddock's hands. His own ignorance of the country and obstinacy added to his difficulties; he refused to listen to the advice given him by many of the Virginian gentlemen against the route he had chosen and the equipments he was preparing to take with him into the wilderness, and toward the end of June he left Alexandria for the Ohio, taking with him the thousand British troops, the four hundred Virginians, several heavy guns, and a great quantity of baggage.

They left with drums beating and flags flying, every soldier neat and smart in his scarlet coat and shako, his white belt and straps and his well-polished musket, all with a jaunty air and some laughing in the confidence of an easy victory and a quick return from what promised to be a pleasurable adventure.

Mr. Washington, now a volunteer colonel, watched them depart. He had yet to transact some business in Virginia and was to join the general in Maryland. From his first sight of these well-drilled, well-uniformed stalwart troops, most of them from regiments that had seen hard service in Europe from the days of King William of Orange, he had been enthusiastic in his admiration, and inclined to agree with Braddock that the mere sight of their even ranks, their glittering bayonets, the mere sound of their powerful cannon would serve to dismay and discomfit the Indians and that the French themselves would not long be able to resist such a veteran force.

The two mistakes, the route and the huge quantity of baggage, he thought serious, but not fatal; he had a considerable trust in Braddock, who had given the brilliant young colonel his full friendship and confidence. But when Washington joined the army in Maryland he found matters already in a bad pass; Braddock was floundering through the untracked woods like a blind man in the surf, cursing the route he had taken, the French, the Indians, and the colonists.

The guides had lost their way, and several days had been spent in circling round the same spot. Considerable delay was also involved through the troops having to make their own road, to fell trees and bridge rivers, none of which, Braddock hotly declared, were on the map.

The young Virginian colonel, ardent and full of enthusiasm, longed to get the direction of affairs into his own hands, but curbed himself, and gently suggested to the general that it would be quite impossible to drag the baggage wagons and cumbersome artillery over the mountains that would presently have to be traversed. This was the signal for Braddock to lose his temper; he cursed the whole country and declared that he had never carried less baggage in Europe and had always found roads prepared for him, adding that the colonists were doing their best to hinder him and that such a country as this was not worth fighting for.

The Virginian could not reply to such a line of argument, and the army toiled on, painfully dragging through the virgin forests the heavy tents, the elaborate camp furniture, the silver services, the costly wines of the officers, the ponderous belongings of the men, a huge supply of ammunition, sufficient bombs to shell a town, palisades, engines, sacks of sand to line trenches, fodder for horses, and all the elaboration of the complicated wars of Europe.

The strenuous and able mind of George Washington began to fret terribly. To him, who was used to carrying no more than he could put in his saddle bags, who had forded the streams and climbed the mountains and done his fifty miles a day, this ponderous progress would have been absurd if it had not promised to be tragic.

"They halted," he wrote, "to erect bridges over every brook and to level every molehill."

General Braddock prided himself on the thoroughness of his tactics; he neglected no precaution of continental warfare, with the result that soon his army was doing three miles a day, and sickness had broken out among the troops owing to the exhaustion of the fresh food supply.

Colonel Washington himself fell ill, more from fret of mind than weakness of body, and had to be left behind for several weeks. Persuading the surgeon to allow him to start before he was completely recovered, he traveled in a wagon to the Monongahela, where he rejoined Braddock who had now been forced to abandon some of his baggage through the sheer inability of horses or men to drag it up and down the mountains, but enough had been kept (with almost superhuman difficulty) to sufficiently hamper the army.

Washington, still sick, allowed his passionate temper vent and spoke hotly to the general on the folly of the course he was pursuing. Braddock retorted with equal heat; he, too, had his grievances, genuine enough: the colonists had supplied horses of so poor a quality that half were already ill from the exertions of the march, and his stock of good mounts had been seriously depleted by the horse-stealers who followed in the wake of his army. Add to this the fact that guides and maps were alike unreliable, and there seemed other reasons beside military pedantry and obstinacy for Braddock's delays.

But his refusal to take any advice from the colonists, his unyielding adherence to the most formal detail of all the traditions of European military tactics were, at least to Colonel Washington, inexcusable. A coolness sprang up between the two men who had been on the way to a close friendship; Braddock left some of the heavier baggage behind with General Dunbar, and divided his men into two portions, but he would make no further concession to the advice of Washington, who was the only colonial officer he would even listen to.

The army under command of Braddock, consisting of about twelve hundred troops, was now at the junction of the Monongahela and Youghiougany; the first stream was fordable at a point eight miles from Fort Duquesne, which Braddock rightly regarded as the key to the valley of the Ohio.

His plan (and here Washington was with him) was to carry the fort by assault and from there to conduct his operations on the enemy's side of the frontier.

This fordable point of the river was reached early on the morning of July 10th, and Colonel Washington, who had received information from an Indian that Contrecœur, the Commander of Fort Duquesne, had been informed of the approach of the British as early as July 3rd, sunk his differences with the general and hastened to give him this news.

Braddock treated it as of no importance; Contrecœur might know, but what could he do? Only fortify himself against attack, and probably he had done that in any case.

The young Virginian tingled with impatience; he felt all the needful capacity, energy, and knowledge at his finger tips. He *knew* this country;

Fort Duquesne was built on the site selected for a British fort last year and had been surrendered to an overwhelming force of French while Washington was fortifying Wills Creek and the trading house there.

That had been before the first shot was fired, and now when the war had dragged a year the thought of regaining and renaming this fort, of hauling the lilies down and running the Union flag up, was inspiration and spur to the young Virginian. But how was this to be accomplished if Braddock so persistently refused to adopt the tactics of the country he was invading — tactics in which the French and their savage allies were such adepts?

The young *aide-de-camp* had parted from his general the night before with a hot heart, but a restless vigil in the close dark (he was yet under the effect of fever) showed him that no pride nor temper on his part must be allowed to stand in the way of his final warnings.

Lately, in his opinion, the general had committed several serious errors; he had neglected to encourage or reward the friendly Indians; he had refused the help of a band of settlers, who, painted and dyed like savages, had appeared at his camp mad from the loss of their families by the Indian tomahawk, and now he was proposing to ford the Monongahela as if it had been the Rhine; *i. e.*, to march his men in review order across the stream and up to the fort with all their artillery, scaling-ladders, etc., and the baggage, with the sick and stores. This baggage was a nightmare to Colonel Washington. He had visions of it lumbering through the water and the troops waiting for it on the opposite bank that nearly drove him mad.

What he feared was an Indian ambuscade. He had not lived all his life in the wild without learning the ways of it. He could not believe that the Indians would permit the British to cross the river and gain firing distance of the fort without an attempt to divert them, and that attempt on unprepared troops with a commander like Braddock might spell disaster.

The young Virginian dressed himself with his usual neatness in his blue coat trimmed with scarlet, his white breeches and black boots, mounted his horse (he was still rather stiff in the saddle), and reported himself at the general's headquarters. He found that the troops were already ranged in order of battle and preparing to ford the stream.

General Braddock was in a good humor; he was surrounded by his officers; all had been drinking heavily the night before and some were not yet sober. They were making comments on the French and Indians and disparaging remarks on both; they were all pleased at the prospect of taking Fort Duquesne and at some respite there from the labor of pushing through the wild forest.

Still pale and a little feeble in his saddle, Washington rode up to the general, who greeted him amiably, as if he had forgotten the argument of last night, as indeed he had, having washed away his ill-temper with several bottles of port.

At the sight of the ardent young face of his favorite *aide-de-camp* he unbent from his usual formal haughtiness and asked with the excitement, controlled but ardent, of a man going into battle, if the men did not look well.

The Virginian replaced his hat with the gold lace on his flowing brown hair, which was loosely knotted with a black ribbon in his neck, in great contrast to the powdered and curled locks of the British officers, who were all very flourishing in their dress.

"Sir," he said earnestly, disregarding the general's question, "I have come to beseech you to send skirmishes out to discover if there be not some ambush on the other side of the river."

"I am not afraid of savages," returned the general.

George Washington bit his lower lip. "I greatly dread an ambush," he repeated with great force and an almost piteous intensity in his eyes, which he kept fixed on the general's countenance. "If you would send an advance party of the Indians . . ."

"Sir," said General Braddock coldly, "I have never done such a thing; it is not done in Europe."

"But we are not in Europe!" cried the Virginian desperately.

"There is no need, I assume, Sir, to adopt the tactics of savages because one happens to be in a savage country," replied the general, adjusting his sword-knot. "As for the Indians we have with us, plainly, I would rather fight without them." He glanced at the young man's flushed and downcast face in a not unkindly fashion. "You are overzealous, Colonel Washington," he said. "And you do not know much about war."

An officer near him, who was more than half intoxicated, gave him a friendly slap on the back.

"Too cautious," he said. "That is what is the matter with you."

"I hope, Sir, I may be," replied the Virginian sincerely.

"You aren't afraid, I hope?" asked another with a short laugh.

"I am very afraid of a defeat," smiled the young colonel, at which they all good humoredly laughed together, shaking in their saddles till the powder flew out of their hair and their comely faces were as red as their coats.

General Braddock did not laugh because he always maintained a sober habit, and Colonel Washington did not laugh because he could not rid himself of that sensation of intense anxiety. The crossing of the stream was accomplished without incident and in beautiful order, which the general pointed out to the colonials with no little pride. One of these, Mr.

Benjamin Franklin, ventured to indorse Washington's opinion that it would be well to reconnoiter at the opposite bank.

General Braddock turned on him haughtily and in a manner that admitted of no further argument.

"Sir," he said, "British regulars have no need to fear the tricks of savages."

The army had now re-formed on the opposite bank and in perfect order swept forward across the natural clearing where they had landed, with their flags fluttering, their polished weapons glittering, their drummers beating a tattoo, as if they had been on review in Hyde Park.

The even ranks, the showy uniforms, the mounted officers, the standards, and the drums combined to make it a spectacle as brilliant as it was incongruous with the surroundings of unbroken wild forest-clad hills.

Colonel Washington was impressed; he felt his confidence return. Surely these veterans would face anything, he thought, as, drawn up beside General Braddock and the other members of his staff, he watched them file past. And it seemed as if there was to be no ambush.

Then suddenly from the forest a shot rang out.

CHAPTER XII
DEFEAT

The shot was followed by another and another, mingled with loud, fierce yells; threats of flame and puffs of white smoke broke from the wooded heights.

"Ah!" cried Colonel Washington, "we have marched straight into an ambush."

The front ranks of the British had already fallen, and those behind them, utterly at a loss in circumstances entirely new in the experience of war, were slowly falling back in confusion and bewilderment. On the other hand, the Virginians, who knew exactly what had happened and the deadliness of the peril, instantly divided their ranks and took cover, after the method of the enemy, behind the large trees that edged the open space where the British were gathered. General Braddock sat his horse taut and pale: his bare sword was in his hand and his eyes gleamed like hellfire as he saw his men falling back from the fusillade of their invisible foes. George Washington turned to him in a passion of appeal.

"Sir, they must take shelter. It is the only way, or not a man will be left alive."

"Shelter after the fashion of your colonists?" cried Braddock in a tone of fury, pointing to the Virginians who had slipped behind the trees. "Let me tell you, Sir, that British troops are not used to show cowardice in the presence of the enemy — nor will they begin now."

The young Virginian's eyes blazed, also. "Sir," he answered, "this will mean a massacre."

"Better," retorted the furious general, "to be massacred like Englishmen than saved like savages." So saying, he put spurs to his horse and dashed full into the deadly bullet-swept space where the huddled masses of the bewildered infantry were being rapidly mowed down.

Many of them had followed the example of the colonists and were lurking in the shelter of the trees and the thick July undergrowth of creeper and plant.

"What is he going to do?" exclaimed Washington, instinctively following his commander into the danger of the open.

What Braddock did was the incredible. Riding up to where many of his men were sheltered, he drove them forth with the flat of his sword, and, bidding the standard bearers advance the colors and raise them as rallying points in the full open, he re-formed his troops in close ranks under the steady and murderous fire of the ambuscade, who were taking full advantage of their unbelievable opportunity and keeping up a steady volley of musketry at the lines of red coats that were clear and steady as a target before them.

As if they had been on the moors of Scotland or on the banks of the Rhine River, the British loaded and fired — fired in vain at every puff of smoke that issued from the trees, and as often as not brought down a Virginian.

Colonel Washington could scarcely credit his senses; he saw Braddock's figure on the white horse in the middle of the fast diminishing red square and the officers with drawn, useless swords rallying and encouraging their men, and he saw that it was too late for argument. With a quick and thorough grasp of the situation, he saw that the only possible hope lay in the artillery which had just been brought across the river.

Wild and desperate to save the day, he dashed to where the gunners were laboriously mounting the heavy pieces on the carriages, flung himself from his horse, and in his eagerness and fury helped to serve one of the guns himself and to drag it into action.

The whistle of bullets was continuous and the smoke had blotted out the sky; he heard the thud on the cannon, on the grass, the rip and whistle through his own clothes. One even passed through his hair and grazed his cheek. His bright blue coat with the scarlet facings, his great stature and unusual action in serving the gun himself, made him a mark for the hidden French and Indians, and more than one bullet was destined for his heart or head. He gave no thought at all to this; he got his gun into range and was directing the firing of it when he saw the gunners drop, one after another, until he stood alone by the cannon.

At that he flung himself into the saddle of the first riderless horse and galloped back into the *mêlée*, where General Braddock was still endeavoring to rally his broken ranks around that piteous, proud standard of England that, riddled by a dozen bullets, still fluttered through the smoke.

But the thing was fast becoming impossible; sixty officers had fallen in a few moments; the wine-flushed gentlemen who had laughed so good-humoredly at the young Virginian's fears an hour before had one after another fallen in their attempt to encourage their men. Braddock was surrounded by a carnage and now the ranks began to break. One man had caught sight of a hideous painted face peering from behind the nearest trees. He was fresh from an English village and he threw his musket down. "This is hell," he said and broke from his line.

It was the signal. The ranks wavered, fell into hopeless confusion, and the men began to run; many thought that the forces of Hell were, indeed, let loose on them, for the Indians, no longer to be restrained by the French officers, began to rush into the open with horrid yells, and to men who had never seen a savage before their sudden appearance at such a moment made them appear like devils incarnate.

Those who were mounted galloped away; many cut the traces of the artillery horses and, springing on their backs, fled across the river; in vain the remaining officers tried to rally them. They would not stop nor listen, and soon there were few save General Braddock himself beside the rallying point of the English flag.

Colonel Washington rode up to him through the rain of bullets. General Braddock turned and looked at him; his face was inhuman in its livid tint and horrible expression. "British troops never ran away before," he said.

"They were never handled so before," answered the Virginian. He added, "Are you wounded?"

The general's lace cravat and white waistcoat were stained with blood, and he held his left hand to his heart, while the other hung down against his saddle, gripping his sword.

He shook his head and opened his mouth as if to speak, but the blood rose to his lips and prevented him. Washington seized his bridle and turned his horse's head toward the river. The wounded man's head sank forward on his breast, the sword clattered out off his hand, but his knees still gripped the saddle and his body was erect.

Followed by a fusillade of shots, Washington guided him through the mass of the dead and the stampede of the living. As they neared the river another bullet struck the general between the shoulders. He shuddered into an upright position and flung out his right arm.

"English soldiers," he muttered. "English soldiers!"

Then he fell sideways out of his saddle against Colonel Washington, staining him with his blood; the Virginian flung his arm around him and, holding him so on his saddle, spurred his horse and led that of the general of the carnage to where some officers were endeavoring to turn their fugitive men back to the slaughter.

"This is no use," he cried to them. "This day is lost, and if we do not use our wits every man is lost, too. Bring the remnant across the river, and by hard riding we may get up with General Dunbar before they overtake us."

They listened.

"Who is in command?" one cried.

Washington knew him. "I am, Captain Gates," he answered. He pointed his free hand at the huddled figure he was with difficulty maintaining on his horse. "The general is struck to the death — help me get him across the river."

To his tone of authority, to his presence of mind, to his obvious knowledge of the only remedy possible in this desperate strait, the

Englishmen submitted, though all were older men. They were subdued, too, and horrified by the spectacle of their general wounded to the death.

One took his horse's head upon the other side and helped guide him to the river. Before they reached it, however, they were set upon suddenly by a band of Indians.

Washington, turning fiercely at bay, recognized in the leader of the troop, who was mounted on a powerful white horse and painted and feathered like a savage, the Frenchman De Beaujeu, whom he had seen at Fort le Bœuf. The Frenchman recognized him also, and waved his hand in mocking salute, while he cried to his followers to take aim at the blue coat. A dozen muskets fired and all missed, though the officer next to Washington dropped, shot through the head.

"The fellow bears a charmed life," cried De Beaujeu.

The Virginian laughed with excitement. He lashed at Braddock's frightened horse, and dragged man and animal with him to the ford.

There, clear for a moment of the musketry, he and the Englishmen lifted the general into a wagon, and in this way Braddock, who was now speechless, was conveyed from the battle, while Washington dashed back to gather the remnant of the forces.

The young Virginian's desperate efforts succeeded in gathering the survivors together and in bringing them out of the line of fire. But even his promptitude and courage could not have saved them all from being cut to pieces if the Indians, who had already disobeyed their French leaders by breaking cover too soon, had not again proved capricious and, refusing to join in an organized pursuit, stayed to scalp the dead and dying and plunder the wagons, while the French themselves could not resist the opportunity to capture English flags and English guns. This delay proved the salvation of the English remnant; Washington, assuming sole command, drew them off in a masterly fashion and proceeded at a headlong pace back to the camp, where the heavy baggage and artillery had been left under command of General Dunbar.

On the way Braddock died. He never spoke, but those about him thought that his awful eyes showed that he retained his senses.

By dint of hard riding Washington and the vanguard reached Dunbar and brought him up to the assistance of the fugitives.

The Virginian's counsels were for still pursuing the advance on Fort Duquesne and not at any cost to abandon the campaign, which would make them a laughing stock before the world.

It was clear, he argued, that the French force was small, that they owed their victory entirely to their ambush, that they had never hoped to do more than delay the English, and that to retreat now would give them a very easy triumph.

But Dunbar took another view. He saw the best troops in Europe decimated and thrown into a state of panic; his general, his officers had

Death of General Braddock

gone; he was under conditions entirely new to him. He could not trust his unnerved men, and he decided to fall back on Fort Cumberland, sixty miles away.

Colonel Washington saw that all arguments were useless. He left Dunbar with these words, "Some day *I* shall come back to Fort Duquesne."

And with that he consoled himself; some day he would come back and meet French and Indians on their own terms; the Union flag would yet fly above Fort Duquesne.

Before the army departed for Fort Cumberland there was one duty to be performed. The unfortunate Commander had to be left in the wilderness that he had hated and that had snared him.

"We will not leave Braddock's scalp to the Indians," said Washington. He had a curious tenderness for the dead man; his incredible action seemed to him to have something more in it than the sheer obstinate stupidity it would be named.

There would be no pity for Braddock either in the colonies or in Europe. The young Virginian knew that, but in his heart he felt a thrill of admiration for that very obstinacy that had elected death in the ancient methods of the old country instead of safety in those new tactics that were barbarous in the eyes of a European. Had Braddock lived, Washington might have blamed him; but he was dead from four hideous wounds, and he had been a man who had loved life. He was taken in silence from the wagon and laid on his spread blue cloak beneath the tall pines, walnuts, and maples, among trailing clusters of creepers and jasmine and wood lilies.

George Washington knelt beside him and looked into his hard, proud, and now stiff features. Clotted blood stained the white pomaded curls, the fine lace ruffles, and the brilliant uniform, and his hands were clenched stiffly at his side.

The young Virginian's mind traveled back to his first interview with this dead man in the house in Alexandria. How composed, self-confident, and arrogant he had been — kindly, too, and courteous — how soon he had paid for that arrogance!

He was folded in his cloak, after Washington had wiped his face and covered it with his own lawn handkerchief, and four of the English gunners dug a grave among the fragrant lilies and wild, untouched leaves and blossoms.

The army chaplain was among the slain, but George Washington, standing erect and bare-headed by the grave, read in a solemn voice the burial service from his own prayer book, which he always carried in his pocket.

The soldiers took off their hats as their general was laid in the fresh virgin earth that quickly covered him.

Then Washington closed the prayer book and stepped back from the new grave, which, in order to efface all traces of it from the enemy, the entire army, artillery, and baggage marched across, with dipping colors and muffled drums.

Colonel Washington leaned against the great stem of a fine tree. He was pale from exhaustion brought on by the violent exertion he had undertaken while still ill. His hair hung disheveled and his coat was tattered by bullets and stained with blood, but his eyes were brilliant with the light of an indomitable resolution.

When the last soldier had marched across Braddock's grave, the exact position of which could not now have been found by the men who had themselves dug it, George Washington mounted a white horse and rode away to join General Dunbar's staff. As he mounted he looked back at the track beaten by a thousand feet of men and horses, somewhere beneath which lay the proud, still figure of the Englishman.

"Farewell, General Braddock," he whispered. "I salute you. England was turned back today. But the colonies will go on."

CHAPTER XIII
FORT DUQUESNE

Four years after General Braddock had been buried in the forest, Colonel Washington justified the prophecy with which he had then consoled his eager spirit for the tardiness of General Dunbar.

Though the English were slow in learning their lesson, and another large force had been ambushed and cut to pieces not far from the scene of that disaster under Braddock that had forever destroyed the confidence of the colonists in British generalship and British soldiery, still the dramatic taking of Quebec by Wolfe and the death of Montcalm had lost Canada to the French, and Washington, marching again on Fort Duquesne, found it abandoned and a mass of smoking ruins, the French having fired it before they vacated it. Colonel Washington, as the vanguard of General Forbes' army, raised the English flag on the site of the fort that he rechristened Fort Pitt, in honor of the English minister, and the campaign was over. The victory for Britain was complete, but her triumph had nothing to do with the operations of her generals and soldiers in America. The successes of this backwoods war, continued through four years of massacres, sieges, and all the miseries of a frontier warfare with savages, had been contributed by the colonial troops under their own officers, and Colonel Washington, though he had gathered much technical knowledge from the English during his first campaign, ended it none the less with the firm conviction that the colonial soldiers were unequaled in their native woods and valleys, and that the British would never command the affections of the colonists nor the allegiance of the Indians.

For himself he had largely achieved his ambitions. The young land surveyor, who had been entrusted with the mission to Fort le Bœuf, was now a brilliant soldier of Virginia (where he had been recently elected as one of the burgesses of the Assembly) and the admired of England, where he had been commanded and praised. At twenty-seven he found himself one of the most important men in the colonies, and if the end of the war meant his retirement from active service, it did not mean the end of his public career, for, as one of the law-makers of Virginia, he felt as powerful for her good as he had done as one of the defenders of her frontiers.

Before Forbes joined him, and while he was still encamped around the ruins of Fort Duquesne, a letter was brought to him in a lady's hand. Though the writing was unknown to him, he received it with some agitation of mingled pain and pleasure, for it came from Williamsburg, and Williamsburg was the home of Martha Custis, now two years a widow, and reputed about to marry again. Gossip named her suitor as Mr. Conway, now in the army, and a former admirer.

George Washington dallied in opening the letter. He had neither seen nor heard from the lady since he had parted from her in Mistress Driscoll's house in Williamsburg nearly five years ago.

He found himself picturing her face, wondering about her. As he gazed at the folded and sealed letter, picture after picture of every assize ball, race meeting, or tea party at which he had ever met her rose before his mind.

So absorbed was he by these reflections that he startled and flushed when one of his officers entered.

The young commander put the letter (together with another package he had received from home) into the pocket of his blue coat and looked up, still with that uncontrollable look of expectancy and surprise on his handsome face.

"Sir, there is a woman to see you — she will by no means be denied."

The flush deepened in Colonel Washington's cheek; foolish as it was, he could not help thinking of Martha as he had last seen her, in a white and lilac striped gown, with a cluster of pink hyacinths in her hair, and he imagined this exquisite vision standing now outside his tent in the snow.

"A woman?" he repeated, endeavoring to dispel these wild fancies, "a white woman?"

"Yes, Sir."

The young general straightened himself in his rough chair. "Who can she be?" he asked, and his hand instinctively went to his bosom, where the letter in the lady's writing lay.

"She would not say, Sir. I would not have troubled you save that she was so persistent I thought that if I could get a definite offer from you for her to go it would be the best means of silencing her."

"But what is a woman doing here — and abroad this time of the year? It must be some settler's wife — perchance with important news. I will see her — at once, Dennis."

The officer saluted and retired; Colonel Washington rose and turned up the wick of the hanging lamp that was the sole light the tent afforded. Though the weather was fine for mid-winter, it was, even under the tightly pegged canvas, cold enough, and the young general was wrapped in his heavy white and scarlet cloak.

When he had turned up the light he seated himself behind the table that faced the entrance. Save for another chair, a few portmanteaux, and a camp bed covered with skins, there was no other furniture in the tent.

In a few minutes, the *aide-de-camp* returned, followed by a woman clumsily swathed in a huge bearskin cloak that she grasped at her bosom; her head was covered by a hood of violet velvet that concealed her face.

Colonel Washington rose and bowed. By the whiteness and delicacy of the hand clasping the dark rough fur he knew that a gentlewoman stood before him. Captain Dennis withdrew and the stranger, as if a restraint had been removed, sank down onto the chair between the table and the now closed entrance flap. The color was still in the young commander's face and his heart fluttered in a restless fashion; he could not rid himself of those absurd visions of the lovely Martha Custis.

"Who are you, Madam?" he asked in a moved and gentle voice.

The lady was silent; her head sank on her breast and her shoulders heaved, while her hand crept from her bosom to her face.

"Can I help you?" asked the soldier, earnestly gazing at her shrouded form.

She did not speak, but she raised her head and pushed back the worn velvet hood and looked at him.

No carnation lingered in her face that was blanched as a lily and looked as fragile. Her forehead and her misty, melancholy eyes looked as if they shed perpetual tears. Her neglected hair was fastened in a knot at the back of her neck and the portion of her throat that showed was white as freshly drifted snow.

"You do not know me?" she asked in a fair English, with a pretty, hesitating French accent.

Colonel Washington strove to recall this cold, white, sad beauty. He felt as if he had seen her, but seen her in a dream.

"Alas, Madam . . ." he began.

She stopped his courteous excuses with a pretty, deprecating gesture of her fair head.

"Why should you remember me! You only saw me once and I must have changed. It was at Fort le Bœuf, Monsieur."

George Washington remembered. He recalled the delicate girl who had reminded him of white violets, seated at her clavichord and complaining with a gentle melancholy of her enforced exile.

"Mademoiselle Hortense!" he exclaimed swiftly.

She gave him a wan smile and answered with some dignity, "Madame de Beaujeu these three years, Sir, and wholly at your mercy."

"What should you have to fear from me?" he asked.

He spoke very tenderly; neither professional insensibility nor all the sad spectacles he had seen among the settlers, or weeping women and ruined homes had steeled his heart; he was easily touched by any distress, deeply touched by the sorrow of this gentle lady.

This gentleness in his voice and look seemed to rob her of her little strength; she rose and wrung her hands in great agitation.

"Ah, it is such a little claim I have on you — just that one meeting and you were our enemy then, but you saw what I was and you see me now and perhaps you may have some pity." Suddenly, with the abandon of her race, she flung herself on her knees and the bearskin cloak falling open, showed her poor torn finery of tarnished blue satin and tattered lace. "Oh, you are good and kind, I know," she cried, pressing her pale hands together, then hiding her face in them, "and you will help me."

Colonel Washington, scarlet at seeing her kneeling, stooped hastily and drew her to her feet.

The poor creature shuddered and sobbed. Then, calming herself under the influence of his strong, gentle reassurances, she gave her story, in broken sentences of French and English that he had some difficulty in following and understanding. She had, it seemed, been in Fort Duquesne when it was decided to abandon it, and, her husband being dangerously ill, she had refused to leave him; he was obviously dying and could not be moved. The retreating army had left her behind with him and some other of the sick and an escort of Indians to transfer them from the fort or look after them till they could be moved or until they died.

The fort had been fired and the sick left in some of the outbuildings, but on the approach of the English the Indians had abandoned their charge and fled.

The other sick men had died under her eyes, but her passionate care had preserved her husband, and by some miracle of love she had managed to convey him from the ruins of the fort to a deserted wigwam in the forest where they had been unnoticed by the British. But the severe cold, the lack of food and fire had proved worse enemies than the English soldiers could possibly be, and Hortense de Beaujeu, hearing that Colonel Washington was in command of the vanguard of the British army, and remembering his brief visit to Fort le Bœuf, had resolved to throw herself and her sick husband on his mercy.

She ended her recital with slow and bitter tears and a piteous wringing of her hands.

"Terrible!" cried the young soldier, much moved. "Why did you not come to me before? Surely you could not but believe that a sick man and a woman were safe with us?"

But Madame de Beaujeu was used to the horrors of savage warfare, the cruelties of her own people who often encouraged the Indians in their ferocities and all the lawless miseries of unwatched, unchronicled wars in a wild country.

It was plain that only desperation had driven her to this step, and that she still could not grasp nor believe in the proffered kindness.

"If you will give me a little food, a little wine," she murmured, "I will go back to him and trouble you no more."

"No," answered Colonel Washington, with eager pity. "He must be brought here and tended." She looked at him with timid and pleading eyes as if still doubtful of betraying the piteous hiding place; then she said, as if seeking to further stir his compassion, "My child, too, Monsieur, I have my child, there — I must get back to it."

Then she sank across the chair, being indeed half dead herself from lack of food and harrowing anxiety.

Colonel Washington clapped on his hat and, resolutely putting his arm about the lady, drew her to her feet.

"Come," he said, "we will go to Monsieur de Beaujeu."

She was too weak to make any resistance; he called Captain Dennis and several other officers and, when they had forced the unhappy French lady to drink a little wine, they started out toward the forest, accompanied by a doctor and a servant with provisions.

It was not snowing, though the ground was white with the fall of a few hours ago. The moon was up above the high bare trees, and the air was clear and cold; it was just such a night as that on which George Washington had ridden away from Fort le Bœuf between Van Brahm and Christopher Gist five years ago.

The poor lady, her anxiety conquering her utter weakness and deadly fatigue, plunged into the forest, guiding them through the dry undergrowth and thick press of trees that the moon could not pierce even in midwinter. The Americans needed all the light their lanterns could give to enable them to follow her, but she was sure-aimed and unfaltering as a bird returning to her nest, and seemed to be led by some divine instinct to the spot where all she held dear was concealed.

Presently a dim light began to sparkle fitfully out of the darkness of the forest, and in a few minutes more they found themselves outside an Indian wigwam, before which a feeble lantern burned, well hidden behind a great group of huge pine trees on the slope of the river bank.

Madame de Beaujeu stepped forward and undid the flap of the tent, took the lantern that hung above it in her hand and entered.

Colonel Washington followed her. As he stepped into the dark interior that the pale beams of the lantern held in Madame de Beaujeu's trembling hand only partially lit, he thought of the two occasions on which he had seen Monsieur de Beaujeu before: once at Fort le Bœuf, amid that elegance the fair Hortense had managed to conjure up even in the wilderness, and once on that fatal day at the Monongahela ford, when De Beaujeu, painted and feathered, had led his yelling Redskins against the retreating ranks of the British, and had again and again pointed out the blue coat of the young Virginian as a target for their muskets.

Glancing hastily round the tent, he saw this man whom he had last parted from amid the terror, confusion, and excitement of battle, lying wrapped in a couple of heavy cloaks, with his head supported on a pile of Indian skins and rugs. Even in this ill light Colonel Washington could see that his hollow, unshaven, and sad face bore the livid hue of death, and that his eyes were beginning to be bemused by eternal darkness, for he seemed not to recognize his wife when she flung herself on her knees by his side and drew his head on to her bosom. Colonel Washington caught the lantern from her and held it high; as the flame sank then leaped with the movement, he perceived a small and beautiful child, with hair so pale as to be almost silver, wrapped in the blue and white uniform of a French officer, asleep near the feet of the dying man.

He stepped back to summon the doctor, but Madame de Beaujeu arrested him by suddenly throwing out her hands with a cry. He came quickly to her side and bent low over Monsieur de Beaujeu. The Frenchman opened his eyes, over which the lids had fluttered heavily, and smiled in a distorted fashion, as if he recognized in the man who had come to his succor the man he had so persistently endeavored to kill.

"They are safe," said Colonel Washington, with a gesture toward the woman and child.

Monsieur de Beaujeu moved his head and tried to speak, but it was too late. His lids sank down again with a terrible finality, a long and painful breath heaved his body; his wife flung herself upon him and pressed her lips to his worn cheeck. There was a reverent hush, then Colonel Washington stooped to lift up the woman who was as motionless as the dead heart on which she rested.

As he tenderly and compassionately raised her he felt her weight slack in his hold. At first they thought she had fainted, but the brave spirit had left the frail body, and when her husband had drawn his last breath Hortense had expended hers in that kiss on his cold cheek.

Without a word Colonel Washington gathered the still sleeping child in his arms and bore it from that place of death to his own tent in the English camp.

In the chill glimmer of the sad dawn following this obscure tragedy he read the letter from Williamsburg. The writer was Sarah Mildmay, and the letter contained these words:

> *"When you return from the war, call at Mrs. Martha Custis' house, where I am staying, and celebrate the peace with us over a dish of tea."*

The young soldier glanced down at the little friendless, forlorn child. Then he kissed the letter that might have been touched by Martha Custis.

CHAPTER XIV
HOMECOMING

The snow fell noiselessly against the diamond pane and lay in an ever-increasing heap on the sill; the flames leaped cheerfully from the pile of great logs on the hearth and shed a strong warm glow over the room already beginning to be dimmed by the dusk of a winter afternoon. It was a charming room, showing evidences of taste and wealth. On the fresh white walls hung pictures in gilt frames, above the mantelpiece was a round diminishing glass crowned by two Cupids holding a wreath.

The chairs and little work tables were polished till each portion of them reflected a little red flame from the fire and, as flowers were not to be had, a fine china *beau-pot* of rose leaves and lavender, mingled with orris and iris root, stood on the dark bureau by the window.

In this pleasant chamber Sarah Mildmay waited for Colonel Washington. She was attired in her best gown, a rose-colored brocade with a Dresden apron and a cap of real Flanders lace with lapels fastened under her chin.

She was seated by the fire, before which she had drawn a screen of clear silk that slid up and down a polished wood pole and was worked with a design of bright birds resting on bright flowers.

She was making a pretense at work and a trifle of lace and muslin lay on her lap; but in truth her eyes were ever on the door, and her attention wandered and she made every possible excuse to divert it from her sewing, such as picking the fine white threads off her glistening skirt and tying them into neat bundles, or moving the fire screen from one notch to another, or unfastening and clasping again the diamond with the paste buckle that was round her throat.

At last the door opened; she looked up at the diminishing mirror and saw a tiny clear figure of a gentleman in a gray coat sprigged with pink buds and a pale blue cloak, carrying his hat and looking about him in some embarrassment. She tossed her sewing onto the work table beside her and rose.

"Welcome back to Virginia," she cried, laughing and flushing. "Do you know that you are a great hero, Sir, and that I am proud to be one of your poor acquaintances?"

"Madam," he replied, "I am more at a loss before your raillery than before any French guns."

"Oh la!" she smiled, then suddenly laid her finger on her lip. "I must confess to you Martha is angry with me."

He cast his eyes down, and slightly winced, she thought, at mention of that name.

"She thought," continued Sarah, "that it was overbold of me to ask you here."

He glanced up now flashingly. "She . . . did not know?"

"No!"

He colored painfully. "Then I fear I am in Mistress Custis' home on false pretenses ."

"Would you fly?" she mocked. "If you are afraid of her say that you came to see me."

"Will she not receive me?" he asked.

"Now you are in her house could she refuse? As a loyal Virginian, Colonel Washington, she admires you very much."

He looked at her intently. "Why did you put this trick on me?" he demanded, with a sudden charming smile.

Her blue eyes were bland and innocent as she answered. "I just thought to pay you honor, Sir; you are the toast now — having displaced all the poor belles, and I thought I should like to see you again —" she rang the bell, "and give you a cup of tea and see you drink it!"

"It is very agreeable of you," said the young colonel.

He placed his hat and cloak at the end of the settee and seated himself. Sarah Mildmay surveyed him, clasping her hands behind her back.

"I wish you would give me some good advice," she said.

"Good advice, Madam?" he echoed.

"On the subject of Martha."

He held himself in a contained fashion and kept his gray eyes very resolutely on her face.

Mistress Mildmay smiled mischievously as she viewed his controlled stateliness, the perfect schooling of his handsome face and figure.

"About Martha," she repeated demurely, "and Mr. Conway — or I should say Captain Conway now."

He was still inscrutable, but she glanced at the long ruffles on his breast and saw that they were heaving unevenly.

"It would be such an unsuitable match," she added, gazing into the fire.

"Is it —" asked Colonel Washington, in an unnaturally level voice — "a match?"

"Oh, not arranged," she answered, "but if she is *plagued* much more it will be, for she has no heart to withstand him — no heart for anything, I think; and when it is a case of a great beauty and a swinging fortune it is like the flies and the honey pot — there is no keeping the gallants away from Martha."

"In what way," he answered, "could I be of any use in Mrs. Custis' affairs?"

She flashed her bright face round on him. "Oh, advise me how to save her from Mr. Conway so that she does not, in sheer weariness, fall into his net."

"Maybe she favors him," replied Colonel Washington shortly.

"Sir," said Mistress Mildmay earnestly, "I tell you that she favors *none* of the men at present crowding round her, but she is so dismal and moped that, in despair, she will even take the most persistent."

"Why should one so beautiful and fortunate be in such a case?" he asked.

Sarah looked again into the fire. "It is pride," she answered; "what was her last match but a loveless one through this same pride — and the stupidity of a man who *would* not speak? There is a kind of courage more needful than battle bravery, Colonel Washington, and more rare. Lack of it has broken many hearts. It would be a pity if Martha's were to break through pride on her side and this manner of cowardice."

There was silence at the conclusion of this speech, and she did not dare look round at her motionless listener, but raised her eyes from the fire to the diminishing glass, wherein she saw a beautiful figure lifting the curtain that hung behind Colonel Washington and stepping into the room. Whereat Sarah Mildmay sprang up and, exclaiming, "I must hasten those wretches with the tea service," left the chamber.

At this exit of hers Colonel Washington rose in confusion and, turning, found himself face to face with Martha Custis.

She was a vision that transcended any embodiment of his long dreams of her; she was beyond all his shadowy imaginings — real and glowing and resplendent. All his life long he remembered her in the attitude in which he now beheld her.

With one hand she held back the curtain, that was of the color of lees of wine, and the other lay lightly on her breast. Her gown was a lavender blue silk, and she wore a little fichu of white lawn embroidered with a thousand little roses of manifold hue.

Her soft hair, though firmly confined by a black velvet band, yet escaped in several large curls that rippled down her neck. There was a clear flush on her lovely lace, and her eyes were wide and sparkling. For one moment she stood so, her expression half expectant, half challenging, for one moment only, but sufficient to fix herself upon his mind forever.

Then she dropped the curtain and came forward with a light step.

"I fear Mistress Mildmay was too informal," she said, as she curtsied; "we scarcely knew you well enough to bid you wait on us when all Virginia is waiting to do you honor." She spoke gently, with frank eyes sweetly on his face.

"All Virginia," he answered, suddenly flushing, "could offer me no pleasure equal to this." She gave him her long white hand.

"Did you learn that at the war?" she asked. "You used to not be so ready of tongue."

He kissed her fingers as they lightly lay on his. "Did I use to be a fool, perhaps?" he asked.

Martha laughed below her breath. "I wonder? At any rate you are a great man now." She raised her glorious eyes as she withdrew her hand and fixed them earnestly on his face. "Colonel Washington, I always believed and thought that you would succeed."

His proper complexion paled beneath the darkness of outdoor living. "Thank you, Madam. But I have done nothing." He spoke sincerely; his own exploits seemed to him very small. In his modesty he felt that it was not he who had done anything remarkable, but others who had failed in foresight, in patience, in daring, and in resource.

She seated herself where Sarah had been and clasped her hands in her lap. "You would do more," she said, "if you had the chance."

He answered, half in a tone of regret, "The war is over and I am no more than a gentleman of Virginia."

"Peace may not last forever."

"Canada is British now; the French will never make an attempt to regain it, I think."

"You will return to your plantation?"

"To Mount Vernon, yes, Madam. Since my brother Lawrence died I have his property to manage, and my hands will be full."

"You are glad to return home?" she asked gently.

"For many reasons, yes."

"Your lands will have missed you," she smiled.

Her tone, though sweet and friendly, was not in the least intimate, and the perfect frankness of her glances seemed to be intended to repel the intense eager questioning of the young soldier's gaze which belied the courteous formality of his manner.

He had remained standing, and now he moved to the hearth and stood near to Martha, looking down at her with certain masterfulness.

"Madam," he said, "a sad thing occurred when we were encamped outside Fort Duquesne. A certain lady, whom for one moment I saw years ago when I was at Fort le Bœuf, came to me with a distressful tale. She had her sick husband and her child in hiding, and did most piteously entreat me to go to their succor, though she was loath to betray the secret of their concealment, having seen too much of war to trust white or redskin. At once I accompanied her, and she brought us to the poor wigwam where Monsieur de Beaujeu (such was his name) sheltered, but at our coming he was almost gone, and no sooner had the poor creature knelt beside him to say that help was at hand than he breathed his last, and she, feeble with misery, expired as she endeavored to call him back to her. And, wrapped in her father's uniform, we found Monsieur de Beaujeu's daughter, a maid not above two years, and have brought her with us to Williamsburg."

She looked up with eyes brilliant with tears. "Yet she was happy that she did not survive him!"

"You think so?" he asked quickly; "it was a fine manner of love. I had a reason, Madam, in telling you this. I wish you would take some interest in this sad orphan . . ."

Martha interrupted hastily, "Should you not ask Mrs. Washington?" she said.

"I ask you," he answered; "I wish you would do me this service. As I said, I have so much on my hands; still I intend to be the guardian of this child and to bring her up as a gentlewoman, and you can put me on the way to this end."

"If you wish," said Martha.

"You are very formal with me," he exclaimed suddenly. "You are keeping all of yourself from me; you show me a mask . . ."

At this abrupt rending of the veil of their conventional attitude, she flushed scarlet and rose.

"Look me in the face," added Colonel Washington, "and deny it."

She did not lift her eyes; her whole body trembled piteously. He came a step nearer.

"Is it true," he asked, "that you are going to marry Conway? You and Conway! No, it is not true!"

"And if it were?" she commanded herself to say.

"I should not believe it — I could never believe it. Conway is — no use!"

She lifted her eyes; there was a sudden wildness in them. "Mr. Conway is nothing to me," she said. "Yet — again — if it were true?"

The color swept into her face once more, and she laid her hands on her bosom as if she in one gesture defended and stilled her passionate and rebellious heart.

He never moved nor lessened the strength of his gaze on her.

"Why did you send me away so cruelly — those years ago?" he demanded. "Speak to me sincerely for this one moment. And tell me."

She swayed on her feet. "Please tell *me*," she murmured, "what you mean — what you *can* mean, Colonel Washington."

"You know," he answered, in a masterful tone.

She looked at him bravely. "No," she said, "I never knew — or rather I knew myself too well."

He took a step from her, and the flaming ardor of expectancy died in his eyes.

"You are going to send me away," he said sternly; "I was foolish to return only for this. What use for me to again view your coldness — your indifference?"

"Colonel Washington," she answered, "I was never indifferent; really, I was not. Do you not remember," her voice broke a little, "with what good wishes I blessed you and the troops you led — how ardent I was for the cause of Virginia."

"Yes," he replied stormily, "you were ever a good patriot."

There was a moment of intense silence; Colonel Washington moved to pick up his hat and cloak; she stood before the fire that stained her lavender blue dress golden rosy in the front folds and flushed her lovely pale face with color.

"Bring me the little French girl," she said, at last, without looking round.

He paused, arrested. "I will not bring her to a stranger," he answered.

Martha did not move. "No," her voice fell exquisitely, "bring her to *me*."

He flung down his cloak and turned to her. "Martha!" he cried, as soon as he could catch his breath.

She swung round, flushed with sudden passion. "No — no," she breathed, "say no more — go . . . go . . . you know the truth now, all the truth . . . you have always known it, perhaps . . . ah, love! . . . it is beyond denial now! But leave me."

She shrank back against the wall out of the flutter of the firelight till the shadows veiled her beauty, her tenderness, her sweet confusion.

He put his hands before his eyes like a man who is giddy. "I may come back?" he whispered.

"When you wish," she said, "and forever, if you will."

PART TWO
THE CAUSE OF LIBERTY

"I flatter myself resolution to face what any man dares, as shall be proved when it comes to the issue."
— Washington to Dinwiddie.

Destruction of Tea at Boston, 1773

CHAPTER I
RUMORS OF WAR

An elegant traveling coach and four drew up in front of the entrance to the extensive and beautiful gardens of Mount Vernon; a young man who was riding beside the heavy vehicle dismounted and opened the gate.

A lady descended and thanked him with a smile; one of the postilions took the gentleman's horse and the coach turned away to the stables while the couple proceeded slowly across the fragrant sweep of grass that led to the comfortable farmhouse.

They were in every way a remarkable couple, well matched in beauty, though their expressions betrayed souls utterly dissimilar.

Her curious and unusual beauty largely consisted of her silver fairness; her hair was pale as gold thrice refined, her skin had the glowing palter of a white rose and her eyes were of a blue as delicate as the tint of an early spring sky. Yet, despite this appearance of delicacy, the cast of her countenance was resolute and proud, and she walked with an alert and eager step.

Her pelisse and gown, both of a coral red, were of rich material and fashionable make, and a coquettish straw hat trimmed with sarcenet ribbon shaded her face. Her companion, who was of about the same age, had all the appearance and appointments of a man of fashion, his riding cloak was of silk, his coat of velvet, and his hat displayed a huge cockade of white feathers fastened with a diamond clasp.

His figure was elegant and graceful in the extreme, but his face, though handsome in line and color, wore a disdainful and haughty expression not pleasing.

The lady lightly touched his arm (she seemed a little afraid of him), and invited him to look round the prospect of trees, flowers, and shrubbery, bounded by the gleam of the river, that looked beautiful even beneath the mild fires of a misty June sun.

"Is it not a fair place?" she asked wistfully, and with a little air of deprecation, as if she hoped to forestall some adverse comment from her companion.

"It is well enough," he answered, "for a place in the wilderness."

"A sweet wilderness," she exclaimed. "I spent, Sir, much of my childhood here."

"Then it is, indeed, a sweet spot to me," he replied, and she received the conventional compliment with a flush of genuine pleasure and gratitude.

"They call it Hunting Creek," she said hastily. "The hounds meet here three times a week in the season — Mr. Washington has the finest pack in Virginia."

"Though I do not doubt that it would make a sorry show in England," smiled the young man.

They were now approaching the low modest looking house with the long white stables commanding the wide prospect of gardens, fields, pastures, new roads, barns, and plantations that sloped to the huge and splendid woods that shrouded the horizons with an air of mystery.

The air of peace and plenty, of refined leisure and prodigal abundance of natural beauty and natural riches, the sweep of the tobacco and grain fields, the rows of fruit trees, the well-kept parterres and box hedges, the flower beds and paths, the scent and sight of the first flowers of early summer that bloomed on every side in rich profusion, combined to weave a spell to which even the young Englishman with all his inherent contempt of the colonies and the colonists was not altogether impervious. The quick sense of a business nation made him appreciate what he looked on.

"Much time and money has been given to this," he said.

The girl seemed as pleased with this compliment as she had been with that directly addressed to her.

"You shall see the other side tomorrow," she said, "that toward Lord Fairfax's lands and Blue Ridge." She broke off abruptly and flushed in some agitation.

Save for some Negro slaves working in the distance they had hitherto seen no one, but suddenly the girl caught sight of a tall man in a gray coat coming round a great bush of laurel with a pack of different colored dogs after him.

"It is Mr. Washington," she murmured.

She was obviously confused, and her companion smiled in amazement, though he knew that her embarrassment rose from the fact that she was not at all sure of the welcome he would get from the master of Mount Vernon. Urged by the gallantry in her blood that made her the more daring as she was the more afraid, Hortense de Beaujeu stepped forward and, with a confident mien that belied her beating heart, hastened along the neat gravel path. The gentleman she approached lifted his head and saw her; he took off his black beaver and greeted her with a charming smile.

"Why, Hortense, child — we did not expect you so soon." Then he instantly saw her companion. "Who is this gentleman, Hortense?"

With mingled pride and defiance she made the introduction.

"It is Governor Tryon's son, Sir, who has escorted me and Mistress Dennis from New York to Williamsburg — and then would ride with me here, so I gave him (forgive my boldness) the hospitality of Mount Vernon for a day or so."

Mr. Washington glanced at the young exquisite and his handsome face clouded. His hospitality was lavish, and uncounted guests were always coming and going at Mount Vernon, that was famous for dances, dinners, and hunting parties, and one more or less made no difference in any way to Mr. Washington, but in the face of recent political events he did not and could not feel friendly to the governor of New York; nor was he prepossessed by the cool carriage and slightly contemptuous air of the young man who made it obvious enough that only the fair face of Hortense had lured him into that wilderness he had so often heard spoken contemptuously of, and not any desire to make the acquaintance of one whom, no doubt, he dismissed as a mere farmer.

"Mr. Tryon is welcome, of course, Hortense," he said gravely; "go into the house and find Martha. Patsy Custis is away for a while, and Jack is with his tutor."

She saw that he was displeased with her; she had known that he would be. In the letters she regularly received from Martha Washington and Patsy Custis she had again and again been told that the sympathies of everyone at Mount Vernon were passionately on the side of the colonies in the ever-growing disputes with the mother-country.

Politics was a subject in which she was not interested, but since her stay in New York, where she had been a belle and a toast, she had absorbed the English point of view; it seemed to her that all that was fashionable and dashing and showy was on that side. Not that she in the least wished to annoy the Washingtons, to whom she was under the very greatest obligations, but she hoped that they would be able to extend a warm welcome to the son of the man who held one of the highest positions in the colonies, without remembering the tedious disputes that occupied the assemblies.

She saw by Mr. Washington's manner that they could not, and she went into the house feeling grieved and angry. She was not a child, she argued, to be frowned on for doing wrong — and how outlandish and puritanical Richard Tryon would find this home of her guardians (which she had often boasted of to him) if they received him in this grave, formal fashion, so different from the easy manners of New York!

With tears in her eyes and an angry frown on her brow the capricious young beauty flung herself on a settee in the pleasant withdrawingroom and when Mistress Washington entered, full of love and welcome, she interrupted her crossly.

"I have brought Mr. Richard Tryon with me and Mr. Washington is not pleased."

"Brought him with you?"

"Oh, la, he had business in Virginia," exclaimed the girl impatiently. "And then he rode on here with me and I asked him to stay."

Martha shook her fair head. "It was bold and foolish, dear."

"No one thought anything of it in New York," flashed Hortense, "and . . . and . . . I want you to be — *civil* to him."

"Should we be otherwise — to anyone who has crossed our threshold?" smiled Martha indulgently, "but you know how we feel, Hortense, about the new taxes?"

"I am weary of the new taxes," cried Hortense passionately, "and I do not care what Governor Tryon does or says — I like Dick."

"Dick?"

"Mr. Richard Tryon, then, and I want things to be pleasant and peaceful." She glanced at Martha Washington's beautiful face that was set in rather dangerous lines, and added, "You know I have no home of my own to receive my friends in."

"Sarah Dennis has made her home yours," returned Martha, instantly softening.

"But why should he stay with Mrs. Dennis in Williamsburg when I am here?" demanded the girl ingenuously.

Martha laughed. "Oh, Hortense! Hortense!"

Mademoiselle de Beaujeu flung off her hat and pelisse in a temper; she felt that her visit to Mount Vernon was spoiled through the lack of sympathy shown with regard to the unheralded advent of the Englishman, of whose conquest she was immensely proud, and on which, indeed, she wished to be flattered and complimented.

But at the bottom of all her discontent was the fact that she was sorely missing New York and its gaieties, and that Mount Vernon, that had formerly seemed so delightful, struck her as likely to prove dull after the balls and parties, masques and theaters of New York.

Presently Mr. Washington and Mr. Tryon entered, and she was somewhat relieved to see that the host was conversing courteously with his guest.

Her good temper revived a little; she spread out her skirts, shook back her blonde curls, threw back her pretty head, and said, "I am so monstrous thirsty, could we not have some tea?"

The effect this remark produced was instantaneous and extraordinary. In after years Hortense often recalled the scene.

Mr. Washington had just closed the door and stood before it, a figure in gray, his unpowdered hair fastened with a black ribbon, in the white ruffles at his throat a hard red rose bud with a glossy leaf. Before him was the young Englishman, powdered, perfumed, and glittering with brilliants in the brooch at his cravat, in the buckle of the hat he held, and in the hilt of his light dress sword.

In the center of the sunny room stood Martha Washington, in a gown of embroidered lawn, her soft rich beauty, that was then at its zenith, accentuated by the simple white of her dress and the becoming lace cap fastened under her round chin.

On the settee was the frail figure of the girl in the coral red silk, her wonderful silver blonde hair sparkling in the sunlight that streamed behind her, and her wilful face flushed.

She could not understand what had happened; the Englishman had looked over his shoulder at Mr. Washington, who returned his gaze steadily, and Martha had also glanced at her husband with an expression of alarm and vexation on her face.

The girl shivered; she felt as if she had fallen under the shadow of something mysterious and terrible — yet what had she said?

Though the pause seemed long to her, in reality it was only a second.

"We have no tea in the house, dear," said Martha quietly.

Hortense was vexed that this should occur before the fashionable Mr. Tryon. "No tea?" she exclaimed.

The two men were still looking at each other.

"I believe," said Mr. Tryon slowly, "tea is boycotted in Virginia."

"You have heard correctly, Sir," was the dry answer.

"It was a thing that I never credited," returned the Englishman.

"Why not? Since Lord Dunmore closed the House of Burgesses and dismissed its members as a punishment for their protest against England's treatment of Massachusetts, not an ounce of British merchandise has been used in my house nor in the house of any Virginian gentleman."

"That would sound well in New York," said Mr. Tryon, very pale.

"Sir," returned Mr. Washington haughtily, "you may, if you will, report it there."

Richard Tryon laughed. "It would have a disloyal sound."

"Disloyal? That word is lightly used, Sir, disloyal to what?" and, with a light smile that put the young man utterly at a loss, he crossed over to Hortense and began questioning her as to the festivities in New York and the last news from Williamsburg. Hortense answered absently; she was greatly annoyed by the little passage between her beau and her guardian that had been brought about by her innocent request for tea. She had been too long away from Virginia, was too absorbed in herself and too careless of serious things to remember (or, indeed, to have ever noted) the great strength of the feeling in the South against the new taxes, and the resolution that had been taken there, at the instance of Mr. Washington, to boycott English goods as a protest against the governor's action in dismissing the Assembly.

She thought it very foolish and vexatious, and she was angry with Mr. Washington and with his wife, who had excused herself and left the room sooner than speak to Mr. Tryon. And presently her husband followed her, leaving Hortense alone with the son of the governor of New York.

"What a lot of folly this all is," she exclaimed peevishly; "what does it matter whether or not the tea comes from England as long as we have it?"

Mr. Tryon smiled unpleasantly. "You will have to be careful here in the South," he said; "your Virginian Burgesses will be again ordered to disperse, I think, for the high hand they take about the closing of Boston port."

Hortense looked alarmed. "I doubt Mr. Washington knows that," she said; "oh, la, he will be riding over to Williamsburg and there will be no parties, no dances, no dinners, and I shall be moped to death."

"With my company?"

She heaved a great sigh. "*You* will not be able to stay, Dick, I fear."

"Why?"

"Well, because of Mr. Washington," she answered, tears of mortification in her pretty eyes.

"Mr. Washington," sneered the Englishman, "who is Mr. Washington?"

CHAPTER II
NEWS FROM WILLIAMSBURG

The master of Mount Vernon followed his wife into the garden, where she stood between the close-clipped box hedges cutting the long-stemmed roses from the profusely flowering bushes and placing them in the fat willow-wand basket she held over her arm.

An expression of vexation and anxiety clouded her face, and she looked up in some agitation as her husband approached.

"Why did that child bring this young gallant here of all times?" he exclaimed, in a moved tone. "Governor Tryon is foremost in supporting the home government, and this boy may be no better than a spy, sent to ascertain the dispositions of Virginia."

"I do not think so," answered Martha hastily. "Hortense is fine, she would know if this gentleman were sincere or not — surely she would bring no one here she could not rely on. No, I do not think we need suspect any friend of Hortense — besides," she added, in a troubled way, "is there any need to be anxious?"

Mr. Washington answered briefly, looking away over the lovely shimmering prospect. "There is a dangerous time ahead. If they send troops to Boston and close the port — well, the colonies would have to protest."

"You think they will?"

"They threaten it. The last time I spoke to Lord Dunmore he was cold on the subject."

Martha paused with two white roses in her hand. "But is it likely to be anything — serious?"

"No, I suppose not. But if Dunmore dismisses the Assembly again . . ."

"Is he likely to?" she interrupted, startled.

"So they say in Williamsburg."

"You should have told me this!"

"No, why should I vex you — I did not mean to speak to you, only seeing this young man disturbed me. I have no great fancy to entertain Governor Tryon's son. Hortense is too wilful."

Martha was silent; she knew that Hortense had been nothing but wilful since the day the young Virginian commander had lifted her from her dead parents' side in the Indian wigwam; first her piteous history, and lately her beauty, had excused all her faults, but none the less they were frequently vexing enough to those who had loved and cared for her all her life. She had always been perilously fond of luxury, gaiety, and flattery, and she had had more than enough of each at the home of Mistress

Dennis (one-time Mistress Mildmay), who had recently adopted her entirely, as she was without children of her own.

But as much homage as she had received in Williamsburg, it had been nothing compared to the triumphs she had achieved in New York, which had been such as to really bewilder her vain little head.

Martha saw this and sympathized with it, and condoned the girlish vanity that was flattered by having such a notable beau as Mr. Richard Tryon at her service, but her husband was not so lenient.

"Think you this Englishman came hither for that girl's fair face?" he asked shrewdly. "It was rather, I think, to discover what steps the notable men of Virginia will take if they press the matter of Boston."

Martha absently dropped the two roses into the basket. "They will not press it, surely?" she asked anxiously.

"In Williamsburg," he answered, "they talk of a Continental Congress to settle this and other matters — so far neither King nor Parliament have shown themselves reasonable."

"Lord Fairfax," said Martha, "is hotly on the other side — he calls us all disloyalists."

"I know, but what would you expect? The old man was born and bred in England. How can he feel as we feel? But whatever his opinions are, he is honest and just — it is men like Tryon that make the mischief."

"Do you think that this gallant will report us in New York?" questioned Martha. "Yet, no, you are known to be friendly with the royal officials."

"I am safe enough," smiled Mr. Washington. "It is not for that that I am vexed to see this Richard Tryon here — but speech is such a winged mischief and every rumor sent to New York is as fuel to flame, and we do not want this matter to end stormily."

"God forbid," said Mistress Washington fervently and gravely; "how terrible," she gazed round the rich and beautiful scene, "if this perfect peace should be broken."

He laid his arm lovingly on her white sleeve. "It is not likely. Indeed, I see no chance nor possibility of such a misfortune. Only, these long disputes lead to broils and misunderstandings that last as long. And we are in the right," he added firmly, "and must not cease to maintain it."

"Where is this Mr. Tryon now?" asked Martha.

"I left him with Hortense; Mr. Fairfax will be joining them."

Martha looked down absently at the basket that was now quite full of white roses.

"If Mr. Tryon should be in love with the girl, it would be a good match for her," she said abruptly.

Mr. Washington laughed. "Are you scheming to get rid of Hortense?" he asked tenderly.

Martha smiled back at him. "No — but she is wild and wilful and needs luxury and a firm hand, too, and if this gentleman should make an offer . . ."

"It is not likely."

"No, I know it is not — it was a noticeable thing for him to escort her from Williamsburg, and Sarah would scarcely have permitted it if she had not thought him serious."

As she finished speaking, her smile faded; she noticed that he was looking away from her, beyond her, and that his handsome gray eyes were dark and brooding.

"You are not listening," she said softly.

He responded instantly to the changed and intimate tone of her voice. "Dear heart," he answered, under his breath, "I was thinking of the country. I feel that there is trouble ahead, disorder and confusion; there have been so many signs. The English do not understand us — how can they understand a country so far away — so *different*!"

"Do they *try* to understand?" asked Martha, rather bitterly.

"I do not know. Sometimes I think they do not — I suppose they have their hands full in London. And maybe they will withdraw these new duties, as they withdrew the stamp tax."

"If they do not?" asked Martha steadily.

"Then . . ." he checked himself, halfway through a passionate utterance, it seemed.

"Ah, well, let us think of peaceful things."

Martha was silent. Two emotions struggled in her soul; one was an intense desire to keep undisturbed the perfect happiness of her tranquil home that had for so many years given her the best of life, the other was an almost equally ardent wish, new-born but strong, that the man she had always believed in as great and a force and a power, should distinguish himself again as he had done before, but on a larger field and with a wider scope. She recalled the brilliant young officer who had been the toast of Virginia when she had married him, and the thought came as it had come before, that he was too big for Mount Vernon, that somewhere there must be use for those larger activities she knew he possessed. She had always felt that the day would come when some need would rise and call him, and suddenly it seemed as if that day was very near.

Martha Washington was proud and glad, and sorry and frightened. "If . . . if . . ." she said, with trembling lips, "anything happened — there would be need of — a man."

He broke off a sprig of box from the level hedge and twirled it between his long fingers. "Yes, there would," he answered.

"A man to lead — to command — to plan — to encourage."

"If the moment should come it will bring the man," he said.

She looked at him in unutterable pride. "Yes," she replied, "it would, and I should lose *you*."

He looked at her quickly. "Martha, do you think I am that man you speak of?"

"I know it," she smiled.

A flush like the reflection of a great flame passed over his face, and quickly faded. "You overrate me," he said. "There are many others."

"There is no one like you," she answered quietly, "in all America."

"There is no one, I do think, who has more at heart the welfare of these colonies; there is no one who sees more clearly what this continent might be — but there my merits begin and end."

She looked across the garden to the house that was the center of her paradise. "No," she said, in a low voice, but firmly, "they will call you and you will go; and I shall lose you."

"You could never lose me," he answered; "if I went to the world's end you have a spell to draw me back; but I shall not be needed."

"There is no other," she insisted. "In the last war they had to turn to you . . ."

He looked at her quickly. "War?" he said.

The word, low as it was spoken, seemed to ring round the quiet beauty of the garden and linger in the air like the report and echo of a cannon shot.

Martha looked at her husband steadily. "I have thought," she said, "that it might come to that."

"Who told you?" he asked. "Who told you?"

She smiled bravely. "No one. But I have watched and noticed; lately I have thought that there was only the way of war, looking at our people, knowing you — I could not think of submission."

Again that flush of animation passed over his face; his large expressive eyes flashed, and when he spoke his voice flashed, too. "You know me too well," he said; "I can conceal nothing from you — if the English do not abate, then I think there will be war."

Again the word jarred and shook the heavy sweetness of the summer air, and a sudden coldness came over Martha's heart.

"I knew it," she murmured, "but to hear you say it . . ."

He looked at her face, that was almost as pale as the rich lace that framed it, and the color paled from his own.

"I overleap myself," he said. "I say too much — maybe the Congress will settle everything. I would not have grieved you with this — forget it as mere idle talk."

"No," she answered, in a strong but tender voice, "there are worse things than war. What makes all this peace about us desirable but the honor that planted it here? If it were all planned and laid upon submission and cowardice and oppression, would it yield such fair fruits — should we so enjoy it? Freedom is our heritage and one dearly bought — I often think of that — and how we in this country should be the freest people on earth, for our fathers who came here did so because of wrong and tyranny in the old world, and because they saw peace and liberty in the new. Therefore, it seems to me that it is something sacred, this freedom we have, and that we should guard it" — she paused a little — "at any cost."

"You speak as I would have you speak," he answered, much moved, "and as I feel."

He lifted the fair hand that trembled on the rose bush and kissed it; neither cared to speak.

The tears were on Martha's lashes; she guessed that, from his having said so much, things were nearer a crisis than she had imagined. Though he regularly took his seat among the burgesses of Virginia he seldom or, indeed, never talked of politics, and she knew that the fact that he had been so shaken from his reserve by the chance appearance of the young Englishman showed that he was deeply interested and probably involved in resolutions and schemes for keeping inviolate the independence of the colonies, and his subsequent talk showed her that, even as she had suspected, the prospect of war had already been broached and discussed in Williamsburg. Her mind did not dare to glance at what this opened up; the mere words "rebellion" or "revolution" opened up glimpses of horror untold. Civil war was a fearful thing, worse than the Indian warfare that was the scourge of the colonies, and Martha knew many people who would remain on the King's side throughout everything. Their ancient friends, the Fairfaxes, were among these, and she knew of others, equally dear, equally intimate . . .

She checked herself from dwelling on these things. "Let us go in," she said, with a light air; "I have been gathering these flowers for Hortense's room. Poor child! Do not be stern with her — she has a sad little heart under her gaiety."

"And an empty little head under her curls," he smiled.

"Ah, Sir," laughed Martha, "you have admired curls on a head that was empty for all you could tell yourself — you did not know much about my talents for housewifery and my good common sense when you married me!"

He glanced at her with infinite tenderness. "You have been a success for a blindfold bargain!"

"Do you not think Mr. Tryon might be equally fortunate?"

"Mr. Tryon! I had not seriously thought of him . . ."

"I think Hortense has," smiled Martha demurely.

They had now reached the house, and as they were about to enter, a horseman galloped up.

It was a Negro servant who instantly dismounted and respectfully handed Mr. Washington a letter.

He glanced at the writing which he knew for that of Mr. Patrick Henry, an ardent young member of the Assembly.

"From Williamsburg," he said.

Martha lingered in the doorway as he read, then, as she saw him flush and frown, turned back.

"What news?" she asked anxiously.

He crushed the letter in his hand; there was a peculiar expression on his face, almost the expression of a man who suddenly sights his foe.

"This news," he answered quietly. "The British are sending troops to Boston, and have issued orders that the port be closed."

CHAPTER III
THE SUBMISSION OF THE COQUETTE

Hortense de Beaujeu, after an unhappy night of sleeplessness, lifted the muslin curtains of her bed and looked out, soon after the dawn.

A saddled horse stood waiting before the door. It was Mr. Richard Tryon's horse.

Hortense dropped the curtain and stood motionless a moment, thinking rapidly. He was going away — so soon — before anyone was awake — then what had happened last night after she had come up to bed and left the gentlemen downstairs over their cards? Mr. Washington had been in very good spirits, and his behavior toward Mr Tryon had been courteous enough even to her captious observation, but something must have gone wrong or why was the young Englishman leaving so soon and so secretly? Hortense's spirits were in an unusual confusion; she dressed hastily and ran downstairs.

The house was absolutely quiet; by the newel post she stayed her steps and hesitated. Through the open door she could see the dewy lawns sparkling in exquisite sunshine and the colors of roses, jasmine, clematis, red-bud, and lily hazed in the early shadow. She drew a deep breath and stepped out into the garden.

Mr. Tryon's body servant was coming along the path, leading another horse. Hortense laid her right hand on her heart; she thought that she had never before realized how extraordinarily beautiful this place was, how wonderful were the mingled perfumes, how glorious was the sweeping prospect, how superbly the regal sky glittered above the swell of field and wood.

She sighed and her hand pressed more closely over her heart.

Mr. Tryon came leisurely between the box hedges; he was wearing a fawn-colored cloak and carried his beaver in his hand, and his dark face was raised, as if he, too, were drinking in the marvelous beauty of the early morning.

He saw Hortense before he reached her, and, seeing her, paused. In her blue muslin gown with the white lace fichu flung over her shoulders, her pale hair floating in loosely knotted curls, her delicate face uptilted and crossed by the lovely shade of a softly waving bough of wild roses, she might indeed have been the fairy guardian of the place, and it did not need a young man's fancy to glorify her ethereal loveliness.

To Richard Tryon she was even more alluring now than she had been in the paint and powder of her ballroom attire. He realized suddenly that he was looking at beauty in the abstract; this was not Hortense de

Beaujeu, the coquette and toast, but loveliness incarnate, waiting to greet him in the first pure flush of the morning glory.

"I did not think that you would be up so early," he said, approaching her.

"And you?" She spoke without a trace of coquetry or affectation, but simply and as if from her heart.

"I am leaving."

"Without saying one word to me, Mr. Tryon?"

"I would not have disturbed you for anything so trivial."

"Have you seen Mr. Washington?"

"He is at the mill; I have been to take my leave of him."

"Why are you leaving?"

"I have no excuse to stay," he replied looking at her.

She laughed unhappily. "You never meant yesterday to leave so soon."

The servant had come up with the horse; Mr. Tryon motioned him aside.

"My position was false," he said; "these Virginians are all rebels at heart; I think that they look upon me as a spy. Mr. Washington told me last night that he had had news of the order to close Boston Port, and that he was riding to Williamsburg today to protest. This to my face! I cannot stay under his roof."

Hortense was not interested; the one fact that he was going away dwarfed everything else.

He hesitated; he had been prepared to leave her as a coquette who had a smile for every gallant, but this was no coquette who had come down in this simple attire to see him, and the feelings he had kept under rose to torment him.

"I shall see you in New York," he said.

She raised her large eyes. "No, I do not think that Mistress Dennis is likely to ever go again to New York. Captain Dennis says that it is too expensive." A pause. Then she said, in the same grave tone, "Perhaps you will some day come to Williamsburg?"

"It is not likely. My place will be in New York. If trouble comes, more than ever there."

It seemed as if this casual parting were suddenly assuming tragic proportions.

"This is goodbye forever, then," said Hortense — and each was surprised how the sentence stabbed.

"Not forever . . ." said Mr. Tryon. "We shall meet — some way."

"How?" she challenged.

He tried to regain his usual light ease of manner. "What is to keep us apart?"

The little hand made a sweeping gesture round the domain of Mount Vernon. "This — Mr. Washington — Mistress Dennis and all these Americans with whom I must pass my life."

"But you are one of them."

"No," she answered violently. "No!"

"Are you not happy?" he asked, softly and quickly.

Again she said "No."

Another pause of silence fell between them. Her muslin skirts, her curls were ruffled by the breeze off the river, and his dark locks were lifted on his forehead.

"Why?" he asked.

"I am homesick. I belong to the old world. I am not like these people — but why should I trouble you, Mr. Tryon? Adieu."

He bowed over her hand and turned away toward his horse.

As Hortense looked after him she knew in one unbearable flash that the whole world was only a dim background for his figure, and that nothing mattered at all save that he should not leave her like this. She came after him, pale and trembling, finished coquette as she was.

"Will you sometimes write to me?" she stammered.

He looked sharply over his shoulder at her, then spoke to the servant. "Take the horses away — I shall not leave for another hour."

She stood mute till man and animals were out of sight, looking down at her white sandals and the blowing edge of her blue gown.

Mr. Tryon stood gazing at her, his hands clasping his riding stock behind him, his teeth in his nether lip.

No one seeing them now would have known them for the accomplished belle and beau of New York.

"Are you still playing with me?" he asked, at last.

She did not answer nor raise her eyes; her face was grave and rather sad. He had never seen that expression before on her lovely features.

"You have jilted so many," he said.

"Yes — I have amused myself."

"With me — no more. I cannot endure it."

"I do not ask you to — why do you not go?"

"First, I wish to know what you mean."

She looked up now, and her eyes glistened with tears. "Dick, you know all about it already," she answered.

He still hesitated; he could not believe that he had really won the celebrated beauty who had treated him with no more favor than she had accorded to a dozen other of her admirers.

"Why do you not go?" she repeated.

He flushed with the quick whirl of his thoughts. "Would you come to New York — to the old world — with me?"

She stepped away from him. "I will answer that presently," she said breathlessly. "First, I want you to know about me."

"I do know."

She checked his outburst of passionate words. "Walk with me a little way and let me speak to you."

She moved before him down a walk bordered with box and grown with roses, and he followed her.

When he had gained her side she looked up at him; her face was quite colorless, and she looked older and more serious and more lovely than he had ever noticed her look before.

Her beauty had wonderfully increased with the loss of her childish air of coquetry; her sweetness was no longer tempered with folly, nor her charm with insincerity.

Richard Tryon realized her as a wonderful creature, by some miracle his, and not to be, under any excuse, lost now. Other things must adjust themselves hereafter; now he could only feel the marvel of it that this creature, whose full splendor he had only just grasped, cared for him.

"You know who I am?" she asked. "By birth French."

He nodded — what did these things matter?

"My father, his brother, my mother, her father and her brother all died during the last war," continued Hortense; "there was no one left in France to care for me. A distant cousin came into my father's estates and sent me a generous portion of money that Mr. Washington invested for me."

"What is this to me?" he interrupted impatiently.

"I want you to know. Mr. Washington found me by my dead father's bed and brought me to Virginia. Mrs. Dennis adopted me. They have all been good to me. But I am not grateful."

They had reached a pleasant seat overshaded with maple. Hortense seated herself and motioned to him to do the same.

"I belong to another nation — to the old world," she said, with a force and passion that he had never suspected lay beneath her blithe manners. "I have read of the places my parents came from . . . I think my mother must have been always homesick. A longing for the old world has been her heritage to me — New York pleased me better than any town I have seen. I do not want liberty — I could be very happy at a court. I am not a Puritan — my family was Catholic — all I see round me depresses me; I want luxury and — the *old* things — all the things this country lacks." She paused.

Mr. Tryon understood; he himself thought of the colonies as a wilderness, as a place of exile . . . she should come away.

"Tell me . . . do you care for me?" he asked.

"Yes . . . take me away to a garret in London or Paris . . . but away from Virginia."

But even as she spoke she rose and moved swiftly from him. "Think!" she said; "consider it all — do not take me for pity."

"Pity!" he laughed joyously, and would have taken her in his arms, but she still escaped him and held him off.

"Tell me — could you have gone away and left me here?"

"No — no . . ."

"Yet you were going . . ."

These words brought Richard Tryon back to the other things that had been completely swept from his mind.

"Yes, and I must go," he said, "but I shall come back to fetch you very soon."

She smiled radiantly. "To take me away — really to take me away?"

"To take you away forever. From this barbarous country forever."

She permitted him to overtake her then and kiss her; and neither gave any thought to the ingratitude, almost treachery, Hortense's talk revealed toward those who had cherished her so lovingly and made the alien stranger one of themselves. Only presently Hortense said, "This will please nobody."

"Does that matter?" he demanded imperiously.

"No. But there may be difficulties — with your father and Mr. Washington."

His pride was instantly in arms. "Why should Mr. Washington object?" he added, in a deeper glow of pride and love. "What any of them say is nothing to me. Will you be my wife?"

The color rushed up into her face till it was like a blush-rose under the pale gold of her hair; she came near to him and, leaning her weight against his arm, looked up at him as she answered, "Yes. Do not forget me. Come back and take me away."

CHAPTER IV
OLD CHINA

Mr. Tryon returned to the parlor in a lordly fashion and sent several servants flying for their master.

But Mr. Washington was still in the plantation, and he had to content himself with an interview with the lady of the house since it was no part of his wishes to stay another night under the roof of the Virginian, and he did not wish therefore to delay his departure.

Martha Washington was in an inner room; when he entered her presence he found her standing at a long dark table in a rose-colored cotton dress, and a fine white lawn apron, washing china ornaments. A long row of them stood in the window seat, and others, still dripping wet and glistening in their rich hues, stood on the table with a white towel spread beneath them.

Before Mistress Washington was a great yellow bowl, and her white hands went in and out of the clear water as she delicately dipped piece after piece and stood it in a line with the others to await drying.

The room was simply but charmingly furnished, and the air was heavy with the delicious scents borne in from the garden and the persistent though faint perfume of the sticks of lavender and dried conserve of roses that lay in a white beau pot on the mantelpiece.

The lady lifted her face that was very beautiful in its tranquil sweetness, and greeted the young man pleasantly, though without pausing in her occupation.

"I thought that you had left us," she said.

He bowed with an exaggerated homage that was almost a mockery of her humble mien.

"Madam, I am about to take my departure, but there is first something I wished to say to Mr. Washington."

She paused with a red and white cow in her hand, arrested in the action of dipping it in the water, and her gentle eyes grew grave.

"A message for Mr. Washington?" she repeated.

"It is one I can leave with you," he answered, with a slightly haughty smile that she marked and disliked.

Mistress Washington kept her eyes fixed on his face. "It is about Hortense," she exclaimed quickly.

"Yes."

She plunged the china cow into the bowl and moved her glance to the water as she asked, "Are you going to marry Hortense, Mr. Tryon?"

He replied with an emphasis of his usual grandiloquent manner, "Mademoiselle de Beaujeu has accepted me as her husband, Madam."

Mistress Washington bowed her head gravely. "I hope you will be happy," she said; "do you wish me to give this news to Mr. Washington?"

"Yes, Madam."

He was so obviously unfriendly, so clearly performing a formal duty in a formal manner that Martha hardened against him.

"Neither I, nor Mr. Washington, nor anyone have any claim to control Hortense," she said, rather coldly. "Of course my husband has looked after the child's money affairs since there was none other to do it for her — and on this matter you must see him — for the rest we have nothing to say — can have nothing."

Mr. Tryon smiled, "Begging your favor, Madam, I think no family in America would slight my offer."

A delicate pink mounted to her face. "Ah, Sir," she answered, "there are feelings in America that I fear you have not yet understood — that England has not yet understood. If Hortense were Virginian there might be many objections to her marriage with the son of the governor of New York — with any Englishman just now."

Mr. Tryon flung up his head, "You rate yourselves high in Virginia," he exclaimed.

"We do!" smiled Martha delicately, taking up a richly colored little figure in her dripping hands. "But we were not discussing Virginia, were we, Sir? Hortense is French, which makes a different thing of it."

Mr. Tryon brought his hand lightly down on his elegant sword. "I am sorry to see this spirit in the colonies."

"What spirit?" She was still smiling, but her eyes sparkled.

"That spirit of which I see evidence all around me, Madam, that spirit that is sending Mr. Washington to Williamsburg today to protest against the action of the government, the *British* government, Madam."

Her smiling poise vexed him.

"The burgesses of Virginia have been dismissed once," he reminded her, "it may happen again."

She glanced swiftly at him. "It may happen," she said, "that Virginia will do more than protest this time."

He bowed, very coldly, stately. "I cannot," he replied, "make a good report of the loyalty of Virginia on my return to New York."

"No?" she answered indifferently, and busied herself with the china and the bowl.

He was about to take his leave on that, when the door opened impetuously and Hortense entered.

It had seemed an intolerably long time since her lover had left her to speak to Mistress Washington, and she had been unable to any longer curb her impatience; fully expecting, indeed, half hoping for opposition, she stood inside the door, defiant, alert, challenging, ready to prove her loyalty to Mr. Tryon by counting everything and person as nothing in the scale against him.

At the sight of her frail, lovely figure and flushed, passionate face, Martha left her task and came affectionately and impulsively toward her.

The girl gave a hard laugh. "What has Mr. Tryon been saying to you?" she demanded.

The tone stayed Martha as if a hand had been thrust out to hold her back. "That he is to be your husband, child," she said, in quivering voice.

"And you are not pleased?"

"I am very pleased that you are happy — but I do not know Mr. Tryon — and it will be a very different life for you."

"I know!" the girl's eyes blazed with excitement.

"And we shall miss you in Virginia, dear."

Hortense softened a little; she laughed again unsteadily. "Forgive me — I do not want to be unkind, but I am longing to get away from Virginia."

"Hortense!"

"Ah, yes." She caught her lover's arm. "Dick and I are going away to the old world."

"Has your life been so hateful to you?" asked Martha. She was deeply moved by this news, and by the girl's manner as deeply hurt; she had a peculiarly tender feeling for Hortense, whose existence was mingled with some of the most beautiful things in her own life.

On George Washington's last campaign he had brought the little orphan home to Virginia, and it had been of her that he had spoken that afternoon he had come to the house in Williamsburg at Sarah Mildmay's request; that afternoon from which Martha dated all her happiness.

Hortense answered carelessly, "La, no — but things are different in New York, and I like them better so — I never belonged here."

Martha returned to her bowl and slowly began drying the china on lengths of fine linen. "There is nothing further for me to say," she said.

"Farewell, then, Madam," said Mr. Tryon, and, bowing low, he left the room, followed by Hortense.

Martha sank into the deep, worn, comfortable chair by the table and stared across the great bar of sunlight that fell from the window, into the shadows of the pleasant room beyond. What was happening that life seemed to have suddenly become so different? First, the news last night — all the various disquieting rumors concentrated and confirmed — then the betrothal of Hortense with this strange young Englishman. Yet there was nothing so unlooked for in either of these events. She had long expected that the colonies were on the eve of some serious and prolonged dispute with the home country, and she had longer been aware that so beautiful and admired a coquette as Hortense must marry soon, even as she had known that she would choose some gallant of New York or Philadelphia. But now these two things had happened they seemed to have changed life more than she had thought possible.

She tried to reason with herself; nothing disastrous, nothing unfortunate had occurred; Hortense had made, from many points of view, a brilliant match, and in one way Martha was relieved that the burden of the capricious girl's destiny was moved from hers and Sarah's shoulders. Yet these things were in the nature of consolations, and Martha knew that if she had been perfectly happy, perfectly content, she would not have needed consolations.

The truth was she felt that Hortense was going into the camp of the enemy, and going with an ungrateful gladness and joy. She could not think of the royal officials, of whom Governor Tryon was one of the most prominent, except as enemies; her heart leaped and her spirit rose at the thought of the closure of Boston Port, and the foolish and unnecessary monopoly of tea that had led to this climax; Mr. Richard Tryon had spoken in a very curt, masterful manner; he had hinted that those who protested against the high-handed action of the English were no better than rebels, and there had been something like a threat in the way he had spoken of the report he would have to make in New York of the feeling in Virginia.

Martha was not in the least frightened by this, but she was ruffled and somewhat disturbed. Across the serene and beautiful happiness of her life at Mount Vernon she summoned memories of the war; she recalled what she had endured when her young Virginian had been away fighting on the frontier, the terror and scandal of Braddock's defeat, the four years of suspense, misery, of alternate hopes and fears that had followed; the Indian massacres, the burning dwellings, the smoking fields, the disturbance of all the pleasant homely things, the dread of the French marching on to Pennsylvania — all this had been ended when Washington had run up the English flag on the black ruins of Fort Duquesne, and the peace that had followed had been perhaps too intense to be permanent, had lulled them all perhaps too completely into a sense of security. Yet, to imagine another war as likely was madness, as she hastily assured herself — still, what else would armed resistance to British decrees be? And that there would be armed resistance unless the English Parliament gave in, Martha Washington was in her heart sure.

She rose with a sigh and returned to her employment. Washing the old and valuable china, much of which had been brought by her husband's ancestors from Europe, was usually a pleasure to her, for she had a great love of dainty, fragile things, but now the pleasure had gone from the task; her hands moved mechanically and her mind was busy with other thoughts.

Presently Hortense entered, flushed from her lover's last kisses and triumphant from his parting words. She flung herself in the window seat and sighed tempestuously. It seemed to her cruel and unreasonable that she should be left behind with the long summer days before her while he rode away.

Martha looked at her with grave tenderness. "So you are longing to leave us, Hortense?"

"I suppose you think that I am very ungrateful," replied the girl, half defiantly, "but I have always cared for Richard from the first moment I saw him, and wanted to be with him more than I wanted anything in the world."

Martha could sympathize with that well enough. "I understand," she said.

"But you are not *pleased*," cried Hortense.

Martha flushed. "I suppose I wish it had been a Virginian, dear."

The girl laughed. "Could you conceive me married to a Virginian?"

"Why not? It is where you have been bred."

Hortense opened wide her eyes that were almost cruel in their clear sparkling look of joy.

"I never really belonged here," she answered. "You were always very good to me, but I felt an alien just the same."

"Hortense!"

"Yes, I did. And now there is this question of silly, stupid disputes between the governors and the colonies, whatever it is, I do not feel at all with you — Richard says you are all rebels here; well, I do not feel at all a rebel."

"Rebels!" said Martha, startled. "You must not use that word. There has never been any doubt cast on the loyalty of Virginia."

"Richard," returned Hortense, "said the troops might be sent here as well as to Boston, and so I want to go to New York. If I am to marry the son of the governor of New York, I cannot be mixed up in these affairs."

"You do not understand," said Martha, "there is nothing to be afraid of."

"Oh, yes, I understand," interrupted Hortense wisely. "Mr. Conway told me that there was great danger of war."

"Mr. Conway? Do you know Mr. Conway?"

"Yes, he is a friend of Richard's."

"I used to know him," said Mistress Washington. "I do not like him."

"*He* does not like Mr. Washington," replied the girl mischievously.

Martha flushed swiftly. "How did you learn that?"

"Ah, by many things he said."

Martha made no answer; she had a large biscuit paste bust of the King in her hands and, as she flicked the dust off it, she stared down into the full, rather vacant face of His Majesty; for the first time she noticed it and reflected that this was the man who was to rule them all — to decide their destinies.

The door opened sharply; she turned, half startled; the bust slipped from her fingers and smashed into a thousand pieces against the edge of the basin.

She gave a cry of dismay; it was her husband who had entered; he looked at and recognized the fragments of King George.

"It was the King's likeness," she murmured ruefully

"No, only old china," said Mr. Washington cheerfully.

CHAPTER V
THE MAN AND THE MOMENT

At the meeting held to elect delegates to attend the first Continental Congress at Philadelphia, Mr. Washington, who had hitherto been a watchful but silent member of the Virginia Assembly, made a speech that one who heard it afterward declared was one of the most eloquent ever made.

It consisted of very few words, and was delivered with a modesty only equaled by its force.

"I will myself raise a thousand men," he said, "enlist them at my own expense, and march myself at their head for the relief of Boston."

This speech was like a signal; events began to move with almost alarming rapidity. The world found itself bewildered by the spectacle of a federation of colonies, hitherto scarcely noticed, and certainly never considered in European politics, actually preparing to defy the nation that was now, since the decay of the French power, the foremost in the world.

America was arming, and her arming was no jest; when it became evident that neither King nor Parliament was going to take any heed of the message sent by the first Congress demanding justice for all the colonies, and that England's only answer was to prepare to force on America the taxes she found so hateful and so unjust and to prepare to insist on the East India Company's monopoly of the valuable commodity of tea, then all the states in good earnest prepared to meet force with force, arms with arms.

The spirit ran high, especially in the South; the governors of Virginia, the Carolinas, Pennsylvania, Maryland, and Georgia found it impossible to control the Assemblies; they might be dismissed, but they would not submit.

The Virginian troops began to muster, to practice; one, a company raised by Augustine Washington, asked his brother to take their command.

He accepted; he was at that time in Philadelphia, attending the second Congress, which was convened, not, this time, for the purpose of endeavoring to obtain the recognition of the colonies' rights by peaceful means, but to decide on the most proper means of protecting America, for, although the members of the Congress did not yet breathe the word "war," half the continent was arming, and while statesmen in London and Philadelphia were arguing as to how to keep the peace, British soldiers were landing at Boston and armed Americans were riding up from every plantation and farm.

To an observer so keen and so interested as George Washington, the signs were unmistakable.

The spirit of the people rendered submission impossible, and the only means of resistance (since argument had proved ineffectual) was by force.

A firm stand, a little bloodshed, a show of strength, and England might recognize the justice of the colonies' claims. If she did not — then the horrid prospect of civil war was opened. There was no other way. Mr. Washington did not believe that England would prove obdurate, once America showed a determined front.

Again erected as one of the representatives of Virginia, and now commandant of several independent regiments, he left Mount Vernon in early May of the year 1775, and rode to Philadelphia on his horse Nelson, attended only by his colored servant.

The first news that greeted him as he rode through Pennsylvania was that of the battle of Lexington; he heard, too, that the colonists were up and armed outside Boston.

When he attended the Congress he wore the blue uniform with the red facings that had lain by since he wore it in the last campaign against Canada; in these clothes he had ridden back from Fort Duquesne (Fort Pitt as it now was, and the nucleus of a flourishing little town), and in the eyes of most who saw his handsome figure in these stately trappings they were at once a symbol of past success and an omen of future victories. But the Congress would not yet admit there was war despite the patriotic energy of Patrick Henry, who urged action instead of words.

This pretense, however, could not long be maintained; General Gage (whom Washington had known as an officer under General Braddock) was occupying Boston, town and harbor, with British troops and British ships, and the delegates saw the necessity of immediately electing someone to command the various companies and troops who were gathering against the British. Virginia recommended Washington for this post, but the New Englanders who composed the army round Boston would have preferred their own Massachusetts man, John Hancock, had not John Adams, their delegate, argued that the powerful colony of Virginia should have her wishes respected; this argument had the more weight as no candidate was the equal of George Washington as a soldier, either in exploit or practice.

Accordingly, little more than a month after he had left Mount Vernon and waved farewells to the family gathered to bid him "Godspeed" in front of his modest, beautiful home, he found himself elected commander-in-chief of all the forces in the field, the undisputed head of that new creation that had sprung so quickly into existence, *the American army.*

Modestly asserting that the honor was beyond his powers, and stating that he wished to make no profit of his own and therefore would take no recompense for his services, he accepted the command with the immediate task before him of driving the British from Boston. That night he sat up in his lodging writing.

He wrote a farewell letter to his wife, to his stepson, Jack Custis, giving in charge to him the dear home, and to his brother John and his sister.

He also sent letters to the officers of the independent companies who had put themselves under his orders.

When he had finished this task, it was well on into the warm June night, and as he folded and sealed the last packet he came from his absorption with a sigh to notice that the city was asleep about him and an absolute hush filled the room. He rose and went to the window that stood open to the balmy, delicate air of the June night.

He rested his head against the mullions and stood motionless, staring across the darkness that hid the Quaker city. The stars were out, marvelously clear, and flashing like great crosses in the moonless sky; somewhere in the valleys the jasmine and wild rose were out, for the scent of them came and went on the delicate breezes. All the windows, the whole length of the street, were dark, and only here and there a street lamp feebly glimmered.

The commander-in-chief could see no light save his own that indicated any save himself as being awake. He liked the sensation of tranquillity this gave him; he thought that it might be a long while before he again stood like this, in perfect peace, in perfect silence, with nothing but his own thoughts to claim his attention.

His own thoughts were strong, far-flung, tremendous tonight. He foresaw, perfectly clearly, all the difficulties of the immense task that he had so quietly accepted. No man could have been more aware than he of the labors and hardships the position he had taken up required, and no man could have more keenly realized the tremendous nature of the reward to be gained by perseverance and courage at this juncture.

It was the eve of a keen struggle of a nature altogether new in the history of the world.

People of the same blood, the same traditions, the same qualities, the same laws, but widely different in environment and education and separated by such thousands of miles of land and sea that communication between them was slow and laborious, were to meet together to battle for that principle the older nation had first implanted in the new, and then outraged — the principle of liberty.

In England it might appear that the outbreak of hostilities in America was the sign of rebellion, the signal of civil war, or even the revolt of the slave against the master, the inferior against the superior; but the new commander knew that this was not so.

It was the inevitable breaking away of a new powerful people, strong in all those qualities that had made their ancestors great, qualities that had in many cases been developed and ripened by the dangers and necessities of colonial life and brought out by the essential needs of courage, enterprise, and endurance in a new continent.

George Washington saw that it was no mere handful of revolting colonists that he was to lead against the troops of the mother-country, but a nation, young, vigorous, and daring, that was able to defy injustice and demand its charter of liberty.

A nation as yet unformed, as yet uncertain of itself, as yet, perhaps, unconscious of its own power — still a nation — and one rich in all that goes to make a country happy, prosperous, and great.

George Washington, as he looked across the darkness that hid Philadelphia, wondered in his heart if America could ever again be completely held by England, whatever the issue of the present quarrel.

From the governors, from Braddock and the men under him, the Virginian had learned of the careless interest, the superficial knowledge, the arrogance shown by the English where the colonies were concerned. He had seen the disdain shown by the royal officials toward the inhabitants of the various states; he had noticed the frequent rapacity, the frequent indolence of the governors, who treated America as a place of exile and drew all their ideas, all their standards from England, regardless of the different conditions under which the colonists lived.

He had also observed the troubles and confusions arising from the governing of America by men who knew less of her than even the resident governors, men who knew and cared nothing for her, save as a means of raising money by taxation, and who probably had never glanced at the map of the states, and did not know whether they covered an area of hundreds or thousands of miles.

The behavior of the British cabinet during the last war with France had been an instance of this; in sending only a thousand troops and a general entirely ignorant of the country, they had paved the way for the disgraceful defeat of Monongahela and the four years of bloody warfare that followed. That war had once and for all proved to George Washington that the British regulars were not invincible in woodland fighting, that the native troops were more than their equal and that a general who did not know America would have a very poor chance of subduing it, especially if his head was full of prejudices, as poor Braddock's had been.

Putting these things together it seemed unlikely that England would hold America against her will, and while the commander-in-chief did not contemplate ultimate independence of the mother-country, he felt justified in entertaining the certainty that they would be able to maintain their integral liberty and the recognition of their rights as a separate people.

But there was the reverse side of the medal, and George Washington did not shrink from contemplating it. There were two great difficulties to be immediately faced.

The first and most insistent and most alarming was that of forming one united and trained army from the various volunteers, free troops, and companies that at present were scattered, disunited and different in discipline and equipments; added to this was the question of money, ammunition and food, all of which were to be had, but perhaps not immediately, and the two last would be awkward to transport across the immense distances that would have to be traversed.

And the second difficulty was that of the Negro population, the slaves, who would either have to be liberated and armed against the English (an extreme and dangerous course), or, if left in servitude, would require sufficient able-bodied men to be left behind to keep them in order, particularly in the South, and protect the women and children.

Then it was not to be overlooked that the English were well-disciplined, well-officered and had the advantage of a tremendous prestige, nor that all the governors, their relations, dependents, and many of the wealthy people of the Carolinas and Maryland would be on the side of the King, both from policy and the force of inherited tradition.

All these aspects passed rapidly through the mind of the man who had undertaken to lead America against England.

He looked at the task from every point of view, and asked himself: "Am I equal to it?" and answered himself, "Yes."

Presently he moved from the window and crossed the quiet little room that was only lit by two candles standing either side of the mirror above the mantelpiece.

He leaned against this mantelpiece and gazed at himself in the mirror with an intense scrutiny, as if he would read his own soul, test it and probe its strength.

He was now at the very beginning of the prime of life and of a most magnificent appearance. His great height, which made him appear slender despite his powerful build, was in itself sufficient to make him notable; added to his splendid carriage, his regular features, his flashing expression, the charm and power of his fine eyes, it made him a man calculated to inspire confidence and rouse enthusiasm by his mere presence.

A book lay on the mantelpiece, an essay on engineering that he had brought with him from Mount Vernon; he picked it up, scarcely knowing why, and mechanically turned over the pages.

He had been ambitions, and here was a prospect sufficient to satisfy any man's ambition — he had longed for a scope, and here was one.

Could he succeed in carrying this through?

His hand trembled slightly and the ruffles round his wrist shook over the book; he laid it down with the cover open, and lifted his eyes to the dark square of the window which was beginning to glimmer with the silver dawn.

Inside the book was his coat of arms printed; the three stars and the three bars stippled to denote red and blue.

CHAPTER VI
NEW YORK

The campaign that had opened with the dramatic victory of Bunker Hill had been continued by the capture of Boston without the loss of a man, when General Howe abandoned that town and withdrew his troops on board the British man-of-war in the harbor. Though in one way important, this initial success had not been a fair test of what the war would be; bluff had largely helped the Americans, who had been short of ammunition the whole time, and Washington's principal skill had been shown in keeping this fact secret. The seizure of Dorchester Heights would have been impossible if the English general had shown more capacity, and the commander-in-chief knew that he owed his success more to British carelessness than to the qualities of his troops or the help of Congress, the faults and weaknesses of which he could now more plainly gauge. Especially was he annoyed by the law that made recruits liable for only a few months' service; the result of this was that as soon as the men were in training they were leaving for their homes, and the commander had to continually be drilling and forming new armies under the eyes of his enemies.

Convinced that General Howe would endeavor to redeem the loss of Boston by an attempt to capture another sea port, probably New York, he hastened to that town and took up his position there.

Here, he felt, the real difficulty of the struggle began.

New York was utterly undefended; there were no ships to guard the harbor, no forts, only a scanty supply of ammunition and food, and half the inhabitants were loyalists who did their utmost to distract and hinder the "rebels," as they considered them. Nor were there enough soldiers to defend the entrance to the town, and while the commander was at Philadelphia, advising Congress to declare the colonies independent, the general left in command, Israel Putnam, had to watch the English fleet sailing the bay and landing an army at Staten Island.

Much, however, had been done; batteries had been erected on the river fronts, the streets were barricaded, defenses had been raised at Brooklyn and at Long Island, and to reinforce the stores of ammunition the lead had been stripped from the roofs to make bullets.

On a hot afternoon in early June, soon after the commander's return from Philadelphia with the news that Congress had declared the colonies independent, a little company of ladies and gentlemen sat in the sunny parlor of Mistress Richard Tryon's house, and discussed the affairs of the war with whispered terror and disapproval of the Americans.

One was Mistress Tryon herself, Hortense de Beaujeu that was, only a few months married and at the height of her ambition as ruling beauty of New York.

The other lady was her friend and rival, Mistress Margaret Shippen, daughter of a loyalist but betrothed to Benedict Arnold, one of the American officers. There were two gentlemen, friends of the governor (who had fled on the occupancy of the city by American troops), and General Conway, who, although he wore the Virginian uniform, was eager against the commander and the folly, as he termed it, of the Declaration of Independence.

The truth was that Richard Conway was only an Irish adventurer who served where he saw his profit, and though for the moment he thought that it lay with the Americans, he had never liked Washington, and he thought it politic to keep in with the loyalists and malcontents by abusing him and his exploits whenever an occasion offered itself.

After a while the gentlemen left, and the two ladies remained alone in the frivolous white room with the straw-colored hangings, staring discontentedly at the carpet.

"It is hardly worth while to be alive in such times," said Hortense, at last.

"My dear," answered Margaret Shippen, "it will soon be over now."

"The rebellion, you mean?"

"You heard what General Conway said just now — that the Americans have no chance at all, now the English are on Staten Island and their ships sailing up North River." So saying, Margaret, a brunette of remarkable elegance and beauty, very richly dressed and very finished in manner and bearing, leaned back in her chair with her hands clasped behind her heavy curls and her white-kid shod feet crossed under the frills of her pink petticoats.

"A pity, my dear," said Hortense pettishly, "that you had to fall in love with a rebel."

Margaret smiled haughtily. "I am in love with Benedict Arnold," she replied.

"Mr. Washington thinks a deal of him," said Hortense, who was slightly afraid of her friend.

"You should say 'Commander Washington,' should you not?" asked Mistress Shippen lazily.

Hortense rose impatiently. "No, you try to vex me," she said, with tears in her eyes, "and when you know how hateful the whole thing has been to me — why, if it had not been for the revolution, Richard and I should have been sailing for Europe by now."

"Certainly, it is hard," returned Margaret, still in her lazy attitude, and with what seemed a sarcastic inflection in her tone.

"You do not sympathize?" cried Hortense angrily.

"Sympathize?" repeated Margaret slowly, but passionately. "I need my pity for myself, child; you have your Dick with you, safe within the city — while Benedict Arnold is away with the fighting forces."

"Dick would fight if need be," retorted Hortense captiously. "Oh, la, but it is dull, dull here — still when Lord Howe enters we will have balls and fêtes, Dick says."

"Dull? I was awakened this morning by the throwing up of barricades at the end of my street, and the passage of the cannon going through to Brooklyn, and in the garden I found the rolls of lead from the roof, all lying along the flower beds, and a young Southerner, no more than seventeen, gravely giving his orders, while father was shut in the dining room with a fit of choler — no, I do not think that you can call it dull."

Mistress Tryon pouted. "You speak as if you were a rebel," she said.

"Well, as you reminded me, I am betrothed to one."

Hortense was about to reply, and with some temper, for she was in a very ill humor, and found her friend in a vexatious mood, when the door was opened and a black servant announced: "The commander-in-chief."

Both the ladies sprang to their feet with a little cry of surprise; certainly neither of them had remotely expected to see General Washington.

He entered and seemed at once, with his noble and martial presence, to dwarf and render insignificant the pretty little room.

With a pleasant smile he saluted the two ladies. Hortense indicated the settee and he seated himself.

Margaret was looking at him with interest in her brilliant narrowed brown eyes.

"I wonder you have time, Sir," she said, in her clear strong voice, "to pay visits to ladies. You must have much on your mind."

"There is always time for everything in my belief," he answered. "I do not lighten my responsibilities by neglecting civilities, and I desired to see Mistress Tryon on a matter where she can command my attention."

He flung back his scarlet and white cloak and took from the pocket of his blue uniform a package that he handed to Hortense.

"That," he said, "is my final account of your properties and my care of them, together with the monies arising from the sale of the farm in Virginia I bought for you and you lately instructed me to sell. Everything else was settled at your marriage, I think, and handed to you then."

"Thank you," said Hortense; she was a little touched at this final severance of the tie that bound her to the Virginian gentleman who had been such a faithful guardian of her interests and person.

"I suppose you think I am very ungrateful," she said, half defiantly.

"Ungrateful?"

"Oh, I have never thanked you enough — and, besides, I am on the other side now."

"I am aware that I have ventured into the enemy's camp," smiled the commander. "Mistress Shippen here thinks me a rebel."

"What else, Sir, are you?" she asked seriously.

"Ah, Madam, the reply to that is a long one — come and see the review tomorrow when the Declaration of Independence is read to the troops and judge for yourself."

"I dare not," answered Margaret gravely. "My position, Sir, is a difficult one, between my people and General Arnold."

"Ah, I am *glad* Dick is not a rebel!" cried Hortense.

The commander turned his handsome eyes on her with a quiet smile in them. "You have my good wishes always, whatever you do," he said; "it would not be natural that you should feel about this as an American does and must."

"American!" exclaimed Mistress Tryon, "a hateful word! Are you not a colonist, Mr. Washington?"

"Neither a colonist nor Mr. Washington," said Margaret, with a mockery that disguised some deeper feeling of pride or alarm, "but the American commander — why, Sir, this you have undertaken is no less than the making of a new nation."

"Well, Madam," he answered, "is there not room for another nation in the world?"

Their eyes met.

"It is a big task," she said.

"It is one," he replied, "in which Benedict Arnold will have a fine share."

She flushed deeply; then, with a laugh, threw out her hands. "You have defeated me," she said; "I am silent."

"It is the misfortune of loving a rebel," said Hortense, shaking her blonde head. "Now, if you will forgive me, *Commander* Washington, I will go write a receipt for these monies."

She went lightly from the room, and George Washington resumed his seat on the gilt settee.

Now that her hostess had gone, Margaret's manner instantly changed. She dropped her air of mockery, her light manner, and, leaning forward in her chair, she said, in a very earnest tone, "I am glad to have this opportunity of speaking to you, Sir."

He responded at once to her serious tone. "The betrothed of Benedict Arnold may command me," he answered, gravely and courteously.

She drew a deep breath. "I want to know what is really going to happen, if this is serious?"

"Cannot you see that it is — serious?"

"No — I cannot tell. I hear so many different things; people say this and that. Hortense is counting on everything being over in a few weeks — and General Conway seems to think so, too."

"Do not listen too much to what General Conway says."

"He is a friend of Benedict."

"I know. I am sorry for it."

She glanced at him sharply. "Do you then count on this war continuing?"

General Washington remained silent; there was a peculiar expression on his face.

"Oh, you may speak frankly to me," said Margaret; "I have discretion and sense; I can be silent and I can understand. Please speak to me sincerely, General Washington; you are the only man who can really know."

"It will be a fight to a finish," he said quietly.

"You think so?"

"I know it."

"There is no chance that you would lay down your arms under promise of a pardon from the king?"

"None."

"Ah!"

She clasped her hands tightly in her silk lap. "Then it might continue — years?" she added.

"Yes."

"It will be very terrible."

"I think," he answered gravely, "it may be — but the alternative would be more terrible."

She rose in some agitation. "Do you think that you have any chance against England?"

He smiled. "I suppose one has hopes."

"To even hold your own will be difficult." said Margaret.

"But possible."

"And to be victorious . . ."

"That, too, is possible."

She looked at him with wondering eyes as she answered. "How are you going to do it, General Washington?"

He rose and gave her his frank, winning smile. "I do not know, Mistress Shippen, but done it must be."

She rose, too, with a rustle of her fine silk skirts. "Is the stake worth it, Sir?" she asked earnestly.

"The stake is the liberty of a people, Madam," he replied.

Her glance dropped before his smiling earnestness, before the adamantine purpose she read in his handsome face.

"I must give Benedict up to this — indefinitely!"

"A woman could ask no better fate for the man she loved," said the commander; "there is no man whom I trust and believe in more than in General Arnold. If he chooses he may be great."

"But I . . ." she said, in a tone of anguish, "I am a loyalist's daughter."

With a charming air of tenderness he laid his hand delicately on her rose-colored sleeve. "You must obey your heart. Do not wait until the war is over. Marry him, trust him, stand by him, be one of us in this new nation."

"If I dare!" she breathed.

"You will dare. Look out tonight toward Brooklyn Heights and see the watch fires of our batteries there and think for what they stand. There are only a few of us, but we are very staunch and our number will grow. Only a few of us — but when did you see a fine thing attempted by a great number? Madam, it is on the endeavor and the suffering of the few that the greatness of the world is built. It will be on our efforts now that the prosperity and happiness of the youngest nation will stand."

He checked himself with a sudden flush. "Forgive me — but I should like Arnold's wife to be a rebel — too!" he smiled.

CHAPTER VII
THE EVE OF FAILURE

As everyone had predicted, Washington could not hold New York. The landing of the British forces at Gravesend Bay was a prelude to the first American defeat, and though the commander had shown brilliant generalship in bringing off the scattered army from Brooklyn Heights by means of the sailing craft and row boats of the Marblehead and Gloucester fishermen, and had landed the entire force at Spuyten Duyvil without the loss of a man or a gun, still it had been clear to everyone that this masterly retreat was not a victory and could not have the effects of one. The commander, however, refused to admit himself beaten, and for a while the English hung back, hoping for submission.

Their first attempt to induce the colonists to lay down their arms had been unsuccessful; Howe's letter addressed to "Mr. Washington" had been returned unread.

The three men appointed by Congress to talk terms of peace with Lord Howe on Staten Island returned with nothing accomplished; the English would not discuss terms until the Americans submitted again to the rule of King George, and it was too late for that.

It was easy to talk resistance, but to make this resistance effective required genius.

Washington withdrew first to Harlem Heights, leaving Putnam with five thousand to guard the town; these men, however, gave way before Howe's cannonade, and were with difficulty brought off to the shelter of Harlem Heights.

Baffled in an attempt to break through the American lines, Howe fell back on the ships and endeavored to circle the left wing of the Americans by sailing up the Sound.

Washington detected the manoeuver and flung himself across the enemy's path at Chatterton's Hill.

A trial of strength, the battle of White Plains, followed, and Howe hesitated before a second attack, remembering Bunker Hill.

Meanwhile Washington dropped back to North Castle and strongly entrenched himself there.

Howe's counter move was to fall down to Dobb's Ferry on the Hudson, and so to cut off Washington's right wing near Spuyten Duyvil. Fort Washington, which stood at this point, was occupied by General Greene, who, weakened by treachery within and surprised by the sudden move of the British, was captured with his garrison of three thousand men under the very eyes of Washington, who watched from the Palisades on the other side of the river while the British flag was run up over the fort that bore his name. It was a great disaster.

Apart from the loss of a good general and a large number of men, some of the finest arms and cannon the states possessed had fallen into the hands of the British, and the moral effect of the reverse was enormous, and seemed one that nothing could retrieve.

Washington lost no time. Sending a message to General Lee, who occupied the sister fort to that lost on the Hudson, telling him to cross the river and join him in New Jersey, he at once began a retreat with the center of the army that was under his immediate command.

General Lee scarcely received his orders before Lord Cornwallis attacked his fort, and in their haste the rear guard abandoned baggage and ammunition. When they reached the rest of the army Cornwallis was close on their heels. The revolution seemed indeed over almost as soon as it had begun.

All over the country people hastened to profess their loyalty to the British government; Congress fled to Baltimore and the governors began to return to their various towns of residence.

Meanwhile Washington staggered on across the bare, flat plains of New Jersey. It was mid-winter; the troops were ill clad, ill nourished; desertion and death soon thinned their ranks to about three thousand. And every day brought Cornwallis closer behind them.

The little army, as indeed the whole country, was discouraged by the disaster on the Hudson, and there seemed little hope that even the remnant left to him would continue to follow Washington. But Washington pushed on, across the Hackensack, the Passaic, the Raritan, eluding his pursuers this way and that, turning and twisting in his course to deceive them.

So hopeless seemed his case that General Lee would not come to his aid despite his desperate message, fearing to be involved in a general ruin.

Meanwhile the cold increased, and the sufferings of the army were terrible. Many went back to their homes, many dropped dead of want and cold, but still Washington pushed on, in the face of the icy sleet, the bleak winds, the blasts of the first bitter snow. Crossing the Milestone, he made for the Delaware.

There it seemed that all was lost, for while the banks of the river were being sounded for boats the British came in sight, and before the Americans had gained the Pennsylvania shore Cornwallis' advance guard had reached the river's edge.

But the British had no means of crossing the river; the Americans had sunk those boats they could not use, and Cornwallis was baffled. But the Delaware was rapidly freezing, there seemed every prospect of the winter being exceptionally cold, and the English general decided to wait and cross on the ice; leaving Colonel Rall, a Prussian officer, in command of the British with orders to follow and destroy the cornered Americans as soon as the ice would hold, Cornwallis returned to New York preparatory to sailing for England and reporting to His Majesty that the revolting colonies had been forever crushed.

So hopeless did the American cause appear that it was not considered necessary to leave many men on the banks of the Delaware, and General Howe and the bulk of the British troops retired to comfortable winter quarters in New York.

All over the country men laid down their arms and went back to their homes believing that resistance was useless.

The only force remaining under arms was the little hungry, half frozen band who still kept up the semblance of an army on the other side of the Delaware. Lee was moving to their aid, certainly, but with no intention of being involved in a lost cause, and his capture or surrender was only a question of time.

Meanwhile the Delaware was freezing rapidly and would soon offer a safe road for the English on which to cross and annihilate their hunted foes.

Such was the situation toward Christmas when there was a great ball given in New York in honor of the victorious Lord Cornwallis before his departure for London. It was very bright and splendid, for those who would not rejoice kept away, and those who feigned to rejoice had some good reason for so doing and therefore acted their part well.

A thousand lights blazed in the assembly rooms, and the scarlet uniforms of the British officers mingled handsomely with the gold and silver shot brocades of the ladies' dresses.

All that was brilliant, beautiful or charming in New York had gathered together, and the memory of past anxieties, past bloodshed and past differences lent a kind of intoxication of gladness to the pleasure of the hour.

There were, maybe, many there who hid aching hearts, or wounded pride, or affronted dignity; there were likely many who hated the British and would have sooner seen Washington opening the ball than Lord Cornwallis, but these had to mask their feelings and act the enthusiasm they did not feel; for the English flag flew over Forts Lee and Washington, and the new American army had dwindled to a handful of ragged men from whom there had been no news for many weeks.

There was one there whose heart was not in the festivities, whose thoughts were on the banks of the Delaware, and who found the music and the light and the perfume hideous.

This was the fairest lady there, Mistress Margaret Shippen, the ruling toast now that Hortense de Beaujeu was Richard Tryon's wife. Toward the middle of the ball she escaped from the British officer she had been dancing with and fled to the cardroom that chanced to be empty. If anyone could have seen the laughing belle at that moment they would have been startled indeed.

With a groan she flung herself before one of the little walnut wood tables and clasped her hands on her breast; then, snatching a paper and pencil from her bosom, she began to write, with wild eyes, a trembling hand and the color coming and going in her cheeks.

"My beloved," the silver pencil traced, "I must write to you to ease the awful pain at my heart — yet how can I ever send this letter? Dear, I am at a ball; everything is warm and rosy and soft and scented, and all are making me flattering speeches, but I do not think that you, in the bitter wilderness, can be enduring the torments I am.

"What have we done to be so unfortunate? I was on my knees last night praying God to give you back to me. Yet, perhaps you are dead as I write this — such things have happened. If I knew that, Benedict, I would hang myself tonight in that gold scarf of mine you liked and that I wore when last you kissed me. I am a coward to be here, but I have no soul to support me, and Mother loves me and weeps, and so I go about to please her. After all, it makes no difference; I am yours, wholly, forever, whether you ever come back to claim me or not.

"I think I am a rebel at heart, too — I wish I were with you now; I should not mind the cold, the hunger, the sight of blood. This is incoherent; if you ever get it you will not be able to read it — yet I think that you will; I said to my father last night, 'When Benedict Arnold comes home, I shall marry him,' and he answered me, 'If Benedict Arnold ever comes home, alive and free, you shall.'

"I know what he meant, that there is no hope at all. But I feel that he is wrong; I am saying to myself all day that he is wrong — oh, you are coming back, are you not? I wonder what you think about, of me sometimes, I dare to hope.

"This is how I am now — I am sitting in an empty cardroom; the air is full of music and laughter. I wear a pink dress and my hair is powdered and I have your last letter above my heart. If I were to glide across the freezing Delaware and enter your tent would you be comforted . . ."

"Margaret!"

Mistress Shippen crushed together the interrupted letter and thrust it into the bosom of her brocade gown.

It was Hortense, flushed and radiant, who had crept up behind her.

"Margaret, what are you doing here? You have the next minuet with Lord Cornwallis."

"I know. I am coming."

Hortense looked at her sharply. "What is the matter? Are you grieving over anything?"

Margaret rose and flung up her beautiful head. "I was thinking of what a cold night it is."

Hortense stared.

". . . and of those men on the banks of the Delaware!"

"My dear, your heart is with Benedict Arnold!"

For answer the proud young belle hid her face in her hands, flung herself across the chair she had just risen from, and burst into violent weeping. "I cannot go on," she sobbed; "I cannot act anymore! I do not care what they say; I am his promised wife!"

Hortense cast her bouquet of silk flowers on the table and, regardless of her elaborate dress that was of that fashionable shade known in Paris as "dying monkey" and the lofty structure of her pomaded hair, she seized Margaret and pressed her to her bosom with real tenderness.

"I know what I should feel if it were Richard," she said; "but, sweet, you must not love a rebel!"

"How do I know that I do not love a dead man?" sobbed Margaret wildly.

"Oh, la, he isn't *dead*," replied Hortense. She always vaguely felt that disasters happened to "other people," and that some providence watched over those she knew. "But what will his position be when he comes back?" she added, with that practical manner that accorded so strangely with her pale spiritual loveliness.

"If he returns at all it will be sufficient for me," returned Mistress Shippen.

At this moment an officer in the scarlet and gold lace of the British appeared in the narrow doorway that led into the ballroom.

He stood for a moment regarding the two charming figures with the full panniers of pale pink and green pressed together and their laces, frills, curls and ribbons mingling as Hortense bent over Margaret and Margaret leaned toward Hortense. Then Mistress Tryon turned and saw him.

"My dear," she whispered, "here is Lord Cornwallis."

Margaret rose and cast a glance of mingled fright and defiance on the elegant Englishman.

"I had a touch of the vapors," she said, with her handkerchief to her lips. "I pray you, my lord, excuse me this dance."

So saying, and without giving him time for a reply, she turned away, her looped skirt swinging like a flowered bell, and disappeared into one of the curtained alcoves.

Lord Cornwallis looked after her. "She is betrothed to one of the revolutionaries on the Delaware, is she not?" he asked.

"Yes." Hortense paused, then added, "They have no chance at all?"

He smiled superbly. "If they had any chance should I have left them — even," he bowed, "for the delights of New York, Mistress Tryon?"

Hortense smiled, too, and he led her back into the ballroom.

CHAPTER VIII
CHRISTMAS EVE

It was Christmas Eve and of an extraordinary bitter cold. The Delaware was freezing, and in a few days would be able to bear men, horses, and even cannons.

The British and Hessians, under Colonel Rall, were posted at Trenton, waiting for the ice to hold.

General Lee had been captured by the British, but General Sullivan had brought off most of his troops and taken them successfully into Washington's camp.

Even with this reinforcement, however, the Americans were a much feebler army than the squad of British left to watch them, and were in a lamentable condition from cold, exposure and illness through want of proper food and covering.

If those in Boston, New York, and Philadelphia who spoke of the revolution as ended could have seen the little band that still held together on the Delaware, they would have been more than ever convinced that all further resistance was useless when the newly-declared independence of the colonies had such few and miserable defenders as these.

And now, as the cold increased, it seemed that the end must be very near, indeed it seemed likely that before Lord Cornwallis sailed for England with the news that the rebellion was over Colonel Rall would be able to send him a message to the effect that "Mr. Washington" and the entire force under his command had been captured or had surrendered, thereby permitting his lordship to tell King George that the last spark of revolt had been forever stamped out. Late on the day before Christmas George Washington had heard that the Delaware was filmed with ice and beginning to run sluggishly between its banks. He was now face to face, early in his career as a soldier, in the middle of his first campaign, with utter disaster; his masterly retreat across the plains of New Jersey seemed to have led only to this complete checkmate.

He was in about as hopeless a position as a general could be. The only retreat possible was the mountains, and that would mean practically disbanding the men and risking the chance that it might be impossible to get them together again; and the mountains, as Washington well knew from Braddock's campaign, were hopelessly difficult for the transport of baggage and cannon, all of which would have to be abandoned to the enemy.

Yet the only other alternative was to wait till the river rose and face the English with odds that made victory impossible.

The commander sat alone in his rude tent, in the bitter cold that no skin nor canvas could keep out, and faced these things.

He wore his dark blue uniform, heavy riding boots, and a fur cloak fastened across his shoulders. His hair was unpowdered and tied at the nape of his neck with a black ribbon, his face, tanned from exposure, was, in its proper complexion, pale, and his dark eyes were shadowed beneath.

On the plain table before which he sat was the neat pile of his daily letters; letters to Congress, letters home, letters to Sir William Howe with regard to the exchange of prisoners. The camp furniture was of the plainest; across a chair lay his black cocked hat with the white feather, his gloves and whip — his sword he wore buckled to his side.

An oil lamp stood on the table, and by the light of it he was gazing at a rough map of the opposite banks of the Delaware on which he had marked with a pencil the relative positions of the British regiments as he had learned them from his spies who, disguised as countrymen selling tobacco and vegetables, had passed easily in and out of the enemies' encampments. In the arrangement of these forces lay his one chance, a chance so desperate that once it was reduced from the regions of imagination to sober proportions, once it was couched and expressed in official terms of command, the man who had conceived it feared that it would inspire terror as a piece of folly, dangerous and useless.

Before he summoned his little staff to expound this scheme to them he leaned forward in his chair, with his elbows on the table and, taking his chin in his hand, reviewed his position. Only a few months ago he had been in New York, his chances yet untried all before him, Congress confident and applauding him, even those who did not in their hearts wish him success tolerating him, and the vast majority of the Americans warmly in the cause of liberty that he had espoused.

But ever since Putnam had fallen back before Lord Howe in the streets of New York and Cornwallis had carried Forts Lee and Washington by storm, the tide had turned.

The affairs of the Americans had gone from bad to worse, till there was, literally, of all the enthusiasm, hope, confidence, strength, and resolve of the opening of the war, nothing left but remnants of the Congress fled to Baltimore and the remnants of the army wasting on the banks of the Delaware.

The idea of surrender never once entered the mind of the commander of this little army.

The most desperate expedient he resolved was that of taking to the mountains. This was preferable either to being cut to pieces in a last hopeless stand or to surrender. But he knew well enough that it would be the end of the revolution. The flame might possibly be rekindled, the army might be again got together, the patriotism of the Americans might be again roused and the country again called to arms, but for the moment it would be the end. And an end that would leave the colonists dispirited, the English more confident and high-handed than ever.

The commander felt that it would have been far better never to have taken up arms than to lay them down in this fashion. And he did not intend to lay them down.

This moment of difficulty, of loneliness, almost of despair, was the true test of his character.

With no one to encourage, abandoned, unapplauded, unnoticed, with no glamour nor glory about him but the horrors of cold, hunger, and death, champion of a cause deemed lost and hopeless, he yet faced the odds with as much calm and daring as he had shown before Boston or in the trenches of Harlem Heights.

"Why should I expect to be successful at first?" he asked himself. "Why should I hope to be fortunate? There is," and he set his teeth, "a great deal of this to be gone through before the end, I doubt not."

He rose abruptly and, opening the door of his tent, gave the orders for his servant outside to fetch the officers who were to attend him that evening.

This council of war had been arranged with the greatest secrecy; Washington's plan was not one that he could lightly trust to anyone; the officers who presently entered his tent were few and tried, though some of them were young enough and in their first campaign.

As soon as they had all entered and taken their places, the doors were, by Washington's orders, closed, and guarded from without, to prevent any eavesdropping or interruption. The commander lit a couple of candles from a taper in a silver holder and glanced in a flaming, searching way at the little band of men who waited for him to speak.

There were General Sullivan, who had skillfully brought up Lee's forces after the capture of that officer, Benedict Arnold, whom Washington regarded as one of his most brilliant men, Alexander Hamilton, a youth who had attracted attention by his able direction of the guns on Harlem Heights, Greene, whose rearguard had so cleverly covered the last retreat, Lord Stirling, John Stark, the old woodsman and Indian fighter, William Washington, the commander's cousin, and James Munroe, another brilliant youth.

The general seated himself behind the table and kept his eyes on these men, who remained standing. "Gentlemen," he said, in a steady and ardent voice, "the course I am about to propose may seem desperate or even foolish, but it is not until after a keen realization of our present position and the tremendous importance attaching to our next move that I suggest it.

"It must be plain to all of you that the fate of our newly declared Independence rests on the success or failure of our next effort." He paused a moment, and his eyes sparkled from face to face. "I believe, gentlemen," he added, "that there is not one of you who would not prefer to risk death in an attempt to retrieve our late misfortunes than to seek safety at the price of ultimate submission."

"Not one," answered Benedict Arnold. He stood a little before the others and the yellow candlelight was strong on his romantic face with the heavy gray eyes and waving chestnut hair.

"I need not ask, I do not ask," smiled the general. "I only spoke so because the expedient I suggest may appear wild. But wild actions are needed, tame methods never redeemed fortunes such as ours are now. The English are rejoicing in New York and dancing in Boston and Philadelphia; Lord Cornwallis is preparing to sail for England with the news that the rebellion is over — and we must prove that it is *not*."

Old John Stark spoke now. "We are ready, Sir, officers and men, for anything."

"Defeat in open field," said General Greene, "would be preferable to freezing and starving here."

"This," said Washington, "is not going to be defeat."

He spread out the map beneath his strong white hand, and with the end of the silver taper holder pointed to the pencil marks he had made along the banks of the Delaware.

The officers crowded round the table.

"Those are the positions of the British," said Washington; "their headquarters are at Trenton, where Colonel Rall is with the Hessians. It is my intention to cross the river and surprise them."

A profound silence followed; each man's spirit leaped to the daring magnificence of the scheme, and each man in his heart began to count the chances for and against an enterprise so difficult and so dangerous.

"I have good reason to believe," continued the general quietly, "that the British are utterly unprepared. They are thrown out in various loose bodies with no connection with each other, and tomorrow especially, being Christmas day, they will be relaxed and probably drunk.

"It is therefore my design to cross the river tomorrow afternoon and, dividing the army in three portions, to fall on the three divisions of the British tomorrow evening."

At the end of this speech, that he made with great modesty and cheerfulness, he again looked at his officers and quietly asked their opinion of his project.

Greene, Benedict Arnold, and the younger men were transported with delight at the prospect of a plan so bold and promising such strenuous action.

One or two of the others remarked on the difficulties. The crossing of the half frozen, sluggish river, the forced march through the pitiless weather, the poor, starved condition of the troops, the chances that they might well be delayed until the British discovered the surprise.

The general listened calmly and answered courteously. "I know all these difficulties," he said. "But the alternative, gentlemen, is worse, and I intend to try this expedient."

Then, without more ado, he fixed two o'clock of the next afternoon, Christmas day, for the starting of this expedition.

The little army was to be divided into three divisions that were to cross the Delaware at the same time exactly; Washington was to fall on Colonel Rall and the Hessians at Trenton; each man was to carry a rifle, a blanket, forty rounds of ammunition and food for three days.

"And, gentlemen," added the general, "put bits of white paper in your hats so that in the ill light your men may know you."

He paused a second, and then added, "I think it best not to tell the men of the nature of this expedition until it is absolutely necessary; you will start without any explanation."

He rose and came to the other side of the table, a tall figure blotting out the light, and smiled as he held out his hand to each in turn.

"The password, gentlemen, will be 'Death or Victory' — until tomorrow — farewell."

As the door was opened for the officers to take their leave the wind blew in, cold as death and sharp as a knife; a bitter sleet was falling from the starless sky.

The men shuddered and bent themselves together as one by one they passed out of the circle of candle and lamplight into the dark. The last to take his leave was Benedict Arnold.

The general clasped his hand warmly and detained it. Glancing toward the open door to see that all were out of earshot, he said, in a warm manner: "Do you correspond with General Conway?"

Arnold flushed. "It is a week," he said, "since any letters got in, and those had been delayed on the road."

"But you heard from Conway?"

"Yes. It is strange you should know it."

"I only surmised it — for I knew that you had been close friends. I was always sorry for it. I do not like Conway, nor trust him. He has laid down his command, I hear, and is endeavoring to ingratiate himself with the English."

"They say hard things of him," returned Arnold hotly, "as they say them of me because I am betrothed to a loyalist's daughter."

"I never brought that against you, General Arnold. I trust you — absolutely."

"Others do not. I have been ill spoken of in Congress." He controlled himself like someone on the edge of disclosing a bitter grievance.

The general, still holding his hand so closely that their muslin ruffles mingled, answered generously and sincerely. "I am more sorry about that than I can say. You must not brood over it. Remember that I consider you one of my chief supports."

"I am grateful," said Arnold, in a moved voice. "I hope that I shall justify your good opinion, General Washington."

"And Mistress Shippen?" asked the general kindly.

"She is waiting for me — God bless her!"

"I hope that she will not have to wait long. Tomorrow should turn our fortunes. Good night."

The two men parted; as the commander stood in the door watching Benedict Arnold's graceful figure disappear in among the camp lights, a pale streak in the wet heavens showed the dawn of Christmas day.

CHAPTER IX
TRENTON

The cold increased; by the time General Washington and his regiments arrived at Eight Mile Ferry, where the Marblehead fishermen had assembled their boats, it was freezing. A thick coating of ice, not sufficient to bear a man, but more than enough to impede a boat, covered the river. The wind, too, was blowing fiercely from the Jersey shore, and the current was against them; added to this, the black, threatening sky presaged a violent storm at any minute.

Mounted on his chestnut Nelson, Washington kept his station on the Jersey bank through the long, cold hours of waiting, as boat after boat was filled with men, horses, and guns, pushed from the shore and forced through the rapidly forming ice. With wind and tide against them, with the ice to break and the overloaded boats to row, the fishermen's task was almost too much for them. But they remained at their oars and not a single boat was upset in the perilous passage, though the short winter day came to a close without seeing more than a quarter of the army landed on the Jersey shore. And Washington had planned the attack to take place at dawn.

As he sat motionless in his scarlet cloak, watching his silent army file past, clamber into the boats and disappear across the Delaware among the floating ice, wild impatience clutched at his heart, though his countenance was serene and cheerful. Supposing they should be too late? Supposing the English should be warned? Supposing the weather should become impossible and the men only cross to drop dead of cold and fatigue on the frozen banks opposite?

These doubts were as whips to his soul; he caught passionately at the reins as he marched his horse up and down to keep it warm, and prayed to God to help him. For the stakes were heavy; he must either gain now or lose forever; and if he lost, the new nation that had just sprung into being would be lost, too, slain at birth. It was a tremendous chance, a tremendous risk, and the suspense was well-nigh unendurable.

When the daylight failed the embarkation was carried out by the light of lanterns and torches. The flare of these leaped up and died away as the men tramped past their commander, cast a red light over the tall figure in the scarlet cloak on the chestnut horse, then passed on to throw a red reflection over the disturbed black waters and broken ice of the Delaware where the boats struggled against wind and tide.

Hour after hour Washington watched this, the up flare of the lights from the darkness, the following blackness, another light, darkness again and then again torches or lanterns. Hour after hour he heard the same sounds. The steady tramp of the men splashing through the mud, the jolting rattle of the cannon, the voices of the drivers encouraging the horses, an occasional command from an officer, the dip of the oars, the grind of the keels as the boats touched the shore.

The men were silent. In the long red flashes of light that fell for a second over the rows of soldiers, their general saw their faces. All resolute faces, composed, strong faces above the worn uniforms and beneath the ragged hats. The flashing eyes of the general did not discover in one the least sign of discontent, of alarm, of hesitancy; weariness was there, in some sickness, but in none any malady of the spirit.

"If I can succeed with anything I can succeed with these," thought the general.

Near midnight the dreaded storm broke; a wild descent of hail fell beating in the faces of the half frozen fishermen at their oars, extinguishing the torches, and in a few moments soaking the men with chill wet. And only half the troops were as yet across.

Dawn had been the time arranged for the concerted movement against the enemy, but Washington began to abandon all hope of a night surprise, so fierce and persistent was the storm and so tedious the passage of the river. He himself had to keep his horse moving to and fro up and down the muddy bank that was fast becoming frozen, for his cloak hung wet upon him, the sleet was dashed into his face, his hair was drenched, his hat laden with ice. He did not speak to his staff that was gathered behind him, nor, indeed, utter any sound save to sometimes call a word of encouragement as the men stumbled past him, gripping their muskets in numb hands and bending before the force of the bitter drenching sleet and hail.

At last the final boatload embarked and pushed off into the blackness and Washington galloped down to the trampled landing place and, bidding Benedict Arnold hold up his lantern, he lifted his soaked, clinging cloak and drew out of his pocket his watch that flashed gold through the glancing lances of the sleet.

It was nearly four o'clock. The general glanced from the dial of his watch to the shadowy figures of his officers. "Eight miles to Trenton," he said, "with a halt for food we should be there by seven."

They saw his handsome face above the folds of the wet scarlet cloak, shaded by the drooping wet feather, and it was an inspiration to all of them.

No further word was spoken; a fishing skid struggled to the shore; the general and his officers dismounted and stepped on board, leading their horses, and in silence the fishers of Marblehead strained at their oars close to the unseen water, and the boat ground and pushed through the floating ice. Sleet and wind were in their faces and the tide still ran strong against them, but the lights that showed the waiting army were at last gained, and Washington stepped on land on the Jersey shore the moment the boat was beached.

He at once mounted and sent off messengers to ascertain if the other two expeditions were safely across, and prepared to start in conjunction with his.

It was now well past four; the crossing of the Delaware having taken nine hours and all the troops having during that time been exposed to pitiless cold, and since then to an increasing storm of sleet and hail. But neither horse nor man nor gun had been lost, and Washington's eyes gleamed as he thought of the Hessians at Trenton, only eight miles away. As he rode in and out of the troops, reviewing as best he could by the spluttering torches and swinging lanterns, their condition and spirit, his messengers returned. Not a man of either of the other expeditions had succeeded in crossing the river; there was no trace nor sign of them, and it was evident that the ice and the foul weather had completely checkmated them.

The general took the news in silence, but his eyes narrowed and his nostrils distended. He was now with only a third of his army at his command, and it was hopelessly late for a night attack or surprise. But to give up was impossible; to the far-seeing mind of the general even hesitation spelled disaster; in a few moments he had rearranged his plans, and decided on them unalterably. He would himself fall on the Hessians at Trenton and make a retreat back into camp before the other divisions of the British were roused. He at once gave orders to march, and the men, exhausted as they were, responded immediately.

Wrapping their muskets round with their blankets to protect them from the wet, pulling their hats down and turning their collars up, the troops plunged forward through the deep mud, in the face of the bitter storm following the bits of white paper that showed in the hats of their officers. They were divided into two columns, one following the river, the other the upper road that ran above.

About six o'clock, when no more than four miles had been covered, Washington ordered a halt for breakfast. It was still completely dark, and the storm had in no way abated; the general did not dismount during this interval, nor consult with his officers; the two hours' ride through the dark and the wet had not in any way brought reflections that altered his plan. Nor did he show any signs of disappointment or vexation, though, as he rode in and out of the lines, he saw man after man, too exhausted to get the food from his knapsack, lying on the frozen ground, unconscious with fatigue, and horse after horse that had stumbled in the traces of the gun carriages and could not rise again.

It seemed as if the utmost had been got out of all of them; yet somehow, when the order came, the little army staggered to its feet; the sleeping men were roused and dragged up by their comrades; the horses were encouraged to the last effort, the officers went round covering up the ammunition from the wet, the men shouldered their blanket-wrapped rifles, and again they stumbled forward toward Trenton, the frozen ground breaking beneath their feet and the mingled hail and snow in their faces.

Their progress was slow, but their plodding steps were steady, and when the miserable dawn began to stain the black heavens they were within sight of Trenton town, and by eight o'clock in the morning upon the British outposts.

The Hessians were all sleeping soundly in their quarters after Christmas festivities that had lasted well into the night. Colonel Rall, their commander, had been drinking and gambling with his officers until four in the morning and now lay asleep across the settee in the dining room of the house in the main street of Trenton that he had made his headquarters. The shutters were closed, the curtains drawn, and a huge fire blazed on the hearth and sent a red light up the dark paneling of the room and across the figure of the officer in his bright uniform and wine-stained ruffles, who slept with his head turned toward the wall and his pomaded hair hanging disheveled over the edge of the couch.

The air was heavy with the fumes of wine and the smell of smoke; on the large, round, dark table were scattered cards, wine glasses, empty bottles and two broken clay pipes, while on the floor were dropped dice and nutshells.

Two candles on the mantelpiece had guttered out into a long trail of wax, and four on the table had burned to the socket. A brass birdcage clock with a long pendulum hanging above Colonel Rall's head struck eight.

Though the metallic eight strokes were clear and imperative as a summons, the soldier, motionless in his intoxicated slumber, as the dead, did not stir. There was a sound of hurrying feet, shouted sentences, opening and closing doors, but still Colonel Rall did not move; nor did he even rouse when his own door was violently opened and a young officer, struggling into his coat, with his cravat and hair flying wild, entered, shouting: "Colonel Rall! Colonel Rall! In the name of the King, wake up, Colonel Rall!"

Receiving no response from his commander, the young Hessian dashed to the window, unlatched the shutters and opened the casements, letting in a blast of the bitter morning air. Then, returning to the still figure on the settee, he shook him by the shoulders until the powder flew from both their hair.

"What is this?" muttered the colonel; he opened his blue eyes stupidly, and would have fallen back if the other had not yelled in his ear, "The Americans are upon us!"

The commander straightened. "Oh?" he said, and staggered to his feet.

"The outposts," gasped the young man, hastily buttoning his coat, "were surprised and are flying into the town pursued by Washington's men."

"It is not possible," stammered Colonel Rall. "Washington is on the other side of the Delaware."

"No, colonel, he is in the streets of Trenton!"

The other put his hand to his head and gazed round him in a dazed way.

"That letter," he murmured; he looked at the young man.

Last night a frantic loyalist living near the Delaware had ridden to Trenton and entreated to see the commander; upon meeting with a refusal, he had written a note that he had said contained a warning and sent it in; that note lay unopened in Colonel Rall's pocket now.

For a moment fear shook him; then his natural bold confidence returned; he reached out for his sword, buckled it on and dismissed the young officer with orders to send a company to drive back the Americans while he prepared to arrange the rest of the army in order of battle.

But he had scarcely given this order, and was still fumbling in his pocket for the letter of last night, when another officer entered with the news that the greater part of Trenton had already been seized by the vanguard of the American army; and even as he spoke the boom of Hamilton's guns could be heard thundering without. Colonel Rall took his fingers from the pocket, where they were stupidly fumbling for the letter.

"Washington has got the town?" he cried.

"Sir, the Americans are firing from the houses, and our men flying this way and that!"

Colonel Rall tugged his sword from the scabbard and, whirling it in his hand, ran out into the gray wet streets of Trenton.

The air was already full of the smoke of Knox and Hamilton's hastily uncovered guns that had been swiftly dragged into a position that commanded the whole town; the houses had been seized and entered by the Americans, who were picking off from windows and doors all who appeared in the streets where the Hessian officers were endeavoring to form their startled men into line of battle. Cursing and shouting for his horse, Colonel Rall ran up the main street, followed by some of his officers, only to find himself in a net and completely surrounded by the enemy who were advancing down every ingress to the town.

Taken by utter surprise as they were, however, the Hessians, half dressed, half asleep and wholly bewildered, made at first a stand.

Colonel Rall rushed to the head of his own regiment and, with his coat unbuttoned and his hair streaming, led them against the encircling advance of the Americans.

Two wild volleys were fired by the Hessians, but in vain; their own ranks were thinned every second by the incessant fire of ride and cannon and presently broke and fled in a desperate uproar of confusion and terror.

One company succeeded in escaping across Assanpink Creek bridge; Washington, perceiving this, flung his troops right round the town, and when the next body of Hessians rushed forward they found their way blocked and themselves faced by a hideous fire.

At this moment Colonel Rall, running frantically before his huddled troops, fell, shot through the head, at the feet of General Washington, as he rode up on his chestnut horse.

And with that, Trenton fight was over.

The men cast their guns down, and the officers raised their hats aloft on their swords. So a thousand of them were taken prisoner and many guns and horses.

Leaving a garrison in Trenton, General Washington swept back across the Delaware before the other British regiments were aware of the disaster that had overtaken them.

CHAPTER X
THE TURNING TIDE

"Goodbye, my lord, goodbye."

"And I hope when next we meet it will be in England, Madam."

Hortense Tryon, still in her brilliant ball dress, smiled as she answered, "I hope so, indeed, Lord Cornwallis — now all the troubles are over here, we hope very soon to sail for Europe."

He bowed again over her ringed hand, then turned to Margaret Shippen. "And you," he said, "when shall I see you again?"

"I do not know, Lord Cornwallis," she answered slowly, and turned away down the empty ballroom, where the candles were guttering in the sconces, and the long waxed floor glittered with the bugles and sequins that had fallen from the ladies' dresses during the long night of revelry.

Governor Tryon threw a cloak over his gray satins and accompanied Lord Cornwallis down the steps.

The young soldier was riding at once to the quay where he was to embark for England.

As he descended the steps he looked back, flushed and smiling at the ladies who crowded round the door and wished him, in sweet laughing voices, a prosperous voyage and a triumphal reception.

When he had at last mounted his horse and ridden away through the dark streets of New York (for the winter sun had not yet risen) the ladies, suddenly admitting weariness, called their coaches and sedans and dispersed like flowers blown before a gust of wind.

Mistress Shippen and Madame Tryon were staying in the governor's house; Hortense, finding that her friend had already retired, and moved partly by an impulse of pity for the lonely misery of her friend, and partly because she was too excited to sleep, went to her room and entered without ceremony.

A single lamp on the handsome toilet table cast a pearl-colored light over the small and elegant apartment, the rose-colored and muslin covering of the furniture and the beautiful figure cast in an attitude of abandon on the bed with the embroidered curtains looped back from the frilled pillow. Margaret still wore her pale yellow ball gown, and the voluminous folds of the satin spread all over the coverlet.

One foot hung over the edge of the bed, and the gold shoe had dropped from it and sparkled on the gray carpet. Her hair was loose and tumbled under her head; her hands were pressed to her heart and the fingers entwined in the double braid of pearls that she wore round her neck.

On the gilt chair beside her lay her wreath, her fan, her gloves and scarf. Hortense gave her one glance then went straight to the mirror that hung near the window.

"Was it not agreeable?" she asked, surveying her own pretty person in the white and gold dress as it was reflected before her.

Margaret fixed her dark eyes on the speaker, but made no reply and no movement.

"I shall have such a good time in London," sparkled Hortense; "my lord has already promised me that I shall be a toast!" She looked over her white shoulder and added, "La! Meg, have you not moped enough for Benedict Arnold?"

Mistress Shippen was silent.

Hortense pouted. "I believe you are a rebel yourself — are you not glad that the war is over?"

"I am glad — of course," said Margaret, in a lifeless tone.

"Well, then, do be *sensible*; you can never marry Mr. Arnold now."

"Why not?" demanded Margaret. "My engagement with General Arnold stands."

"It is no use, my dear, I will not use these absurd titles; my lord told me that *none* of the rebels had a right to them."

"Rebel or not," said Margaret sullenly, "my engagement stands."

Hortense lifted her shoulder. "Well, it will never be allowed. But what is the use of talking to anyone in love? Anyhow, I do not see why you are so dismal about it."

"You do not see? Why he may not come back at all, and if he does . . ." her voice broke and she lay still.

"They will all be pardoned," answered Hortense; "my lord told me so, the moment they lay down their arms they will be pardoned."

"I do not think *he* ever will lay down his arms, nor Mr. Washington."

"My dear," said Mistress Tryon, "they will *have* to."

Margaret sat up suddenly, and impatiently pushed back the hair from her brow.

"You know Mr. Washington," she said stormily, "better than I. Do you think that he is likely to give up?"

"Meg, do not be unreasonable, he will *have* to!"

"They might all die at their posts. Dear God! I think they will!"

She shuddered from head to foot and put her hands before her eyes.

Hortense answered with some sharpness. "It is not for you to talk so — when your family has been complimented by Lord Howe for their loyalty."

Margaret looked up. "Oh, I know that they are wrong — but it makes no difference. In my heart I feel they are fine and true — and I wonder you can take it so lightly seeing how close you were once with the Washingtons."

"They were good to me," answered Hortense calmly, "and I thanked them. But I never liked Virginia and I was never happy till I met Richard."

"It is Mr. Tryon who has set you against Mr. Washington," replied Margaret.

"Well, what would you have? Is not Dick the governor's son and sworn to King George?"

"Oh, I do not know the rights or wrongs of it," exclaimed Mistress Shippen wearily. "I only know that my heart is breaking — and that if we do not get news from the Delaware soon I shall go mad!"

"There is plenty of news. Mr. Washington sends to Congress almost every week."

"But nothing *happens*."

Hortense yawned. "Well, as you are so dull I shall go to bed — why, it is near seven; the sun will soon be up!"

She bent and kissed the unresponsive Margaret and was leaving with some raillery on her lips, when she was arrested by a sudden shout from the street, followed by the clatter of hoofs. "What is that?" she asked.

Margaret sprang from the bed. "News, perhaps!" She sprang to the window and unlatched the shutters.

The first uncertain light of dawn fell on the figures of the two beautiful women as they looked from the window with eager eyes.

A bell began to ring.

The streets were full of people hurrying this way and that; a detachment of British soldiers in their scarlet and white swung by; a horseman galloped past; another stopped before the government house.

"He is coming here!" cried Hortense, her eyes sparkling; she thought that the messenger was coming to say that the Hessians had crossed the Delaware and forced the Americans to surrender, and that this was the end of the war indeed.

She wanted the end of the war so much; she longed to be free to go to London with Dick; the success of the English pleased her immensely; if only that last band of rebels on the Delaware was captured and there was nothing more to disturb the joyous days she saw ahead for herself and Richard! Here her pleasant selfish thoughts were disturbed by a glance she took of Margaret's ashy face that looked ghastly in the gray light.

"My dear!" she cried.

Margaret wrung her hands; she felt that the long-dreaded moment had at length arrived, but all her agonized anticipation had not softened the actual thing itself now it was upon her. It came with the bitter shock of an unlooked for horror.

"They have been cut to pieces," she moaned through dry lips, "and *he* is dead, of course . . ."

Hortense snatched up the lavender blue shawl from the chair near the window and, flinging it over her shoulders, ran out into the passage. Lights were flashing to and fro, half dressed servants hurrying up the stairs; from below came shouted orders.

Hortense leaned over the baluster to see what was taking place in the hall. She was just turning away to look for her husband, when Margaret came out of her bedroom in her trailing disheveled silk with her face as colorless as the pearls round her throat and her feet thrust into low pink quilted slippers.

"Lord Cornwallis has just come back," she said. Her eyes were shining strangely, and her lips quivered.

"Lord Cornwallis!" echoed Hortense, in an incredulous tone.

"I saw him ride up just now, his horse covered with foam."

The two women stared at each other.

"What has happened?" cried Hortense; then, seizing Margaret by the arm, she half dragged her, almost fainting, down the wide, stately stairs.

In the hall was the governor, breathing hard, cloaked and spurred, Richard Tryon in his dressing gown, several officers, and a motley crowd of colored servants with lights.

And there was Lord Cornwallis.

The young officer, who had so joyously and triumphantly given and taken farewells an hour or so before, was now leaning against the wall, exhausted with hard riding, catching great breaths and struggling to speak, a letter clutched fiercely in his hand, his face bitter and hard.

The two women instinctively divined that something portentous had happened, and not daring to intrude on the group of men, stayed, huddled together by the newel post.

Presently Richard Tryon glanced round and saw them.

His wife gave a thin little shriek at sight of his changed, furious face. "Oh, what has happened?" she whispered desperately.

He came toward her, and she stumbled forward into his arms.

"Dick, you frighten me — what is the matter? Why has Lord Cornwallis come back!"

He answered, stammering with rage. "The cursed rebels have played a surprise on Rall. He is cut to pieces — a thousand prisoners — all the guns and ammunition, and the old fox to earth again across the Delaware!"

"Oh," wailed Hortense, "and so the war is not over?"

"No, my lord has returned — the news reached him just as he was about to set foot on the ship — he is to lead the army against the rebels."

Margaret Shippen, still supporting herself against the newel post, spoke. "Are any of the — rebels — slain?"

"No," he answered grimly, "the news is that they lost neither man nor gun — but Rall is slain."

Margaret gave a great sigh and her eyes gleamed.

"Is this serious?" demanded Hortense.

"It seems so. The news is spreading like wild fire and all the rebels are heartened again and arming all over the country — there is an express from Baltimore to say that the Congress has given unlimited powers to this Washington."

With that he turned abruptly away from his wife and joined his father and Lord Cornwallis.

Hortense, in her rage and disappointment, turned on Margaret. "I believe you are glad, you wretch!" she cried, "that the war is to continue; you are no better than a rebel as I always said."

"I am sorry," answered Margaret, in a trembling voice, "that England has had a blow — but it seems to me to have been a fine thing on the part of the colonists."

With that she turned away; her eyes heavy with unshed tears of thankfulness, and began slowly mounting the stairs. Her politics were a woman's politics and those of a woman in love. What did her country's reverse matter, if Benedict Arnold was safe and had demeaned himself well in a glorious action?

As she turned the curve of the stairs she heard the English lord say angrily and arrogantly, "This time I will sweep them off the continent!"

"No," cried Margaret Shippen, in her heart, "you will not, my lord, while they are led by Mr. Washington!"

PART THREE
THE CAUSE WON

"I shall constantly bear in mind that as the sword was the last resort for the preservation of our liberties, so it ought to be the first thing laid aside when those liberties are firmly established."

George Washington.

English attacked at Germantown, 1777

CHAPTER I
THE INNER FLAW

Despite the brilliant campaign of Trenton, by next year Washington had been defeated at Brandywine and Germantown, and the British had captured Philadelphia. But, against this, France had recognized the independence of the American States. Burgoyne had been captured by Schuyler and Gates; Arnold and Washington, at Valley Forge, had kept together, in face of all difficulties, a large and devoted army, which had gained in prestige by the volunteered services of European officers such as the Marquis de Lafayette and the Baron Steuben.

The commander-in-chief was indeed hopeful of a favorable final issue to the struggle, though his difficulties had lately taken on a new and alarming form.

There was dissatisfaction in Congress; in fact, General Washington was very painfully aware, and had been aware for some time, of a conspiracy, chiefly fomented by Richard Tryon, Generals Lee, Conway, and Gates, to remove him from his command and put in his place the feeble, vain Gates, who had been one of Braddock's officers, and who had been brought into prominence by the victory over Burgoyne (though the credit of it in truth belonged to Arnold and Schuyler).

Several times Washington could have revealed to Congress that Gates and Conway were plotting together with disaffected colonists and loyalists such as Tryon, while he had sure proof that Lee had told falsehoods to discredit him.

But, like all great men faced with the accomplishment of a supreme task, he was too utterly occupied in getting the best out of the materials at his hand, to quarrel with their faults. As long as they would serve him he would overlook again and again insults, slights, ingratitude, and even treachery, in a manner that seemed surprising to those who knew his proud and passionate temper and did not hold the key to his conduct. He believed that not one of the disaffected officers would ever carry his jealousy of him so far as to traffic with the enemy, and as long as they did not do that he cared nothing for their personal affronts to himself.

Naturally the sense of ill-will and opposition was an unpleasant thing to work with, but it came mainly from men whom he had never much cared for, and it was balanced by a vast amount of affection and devotion on the part of the bulk of his soldiers.

Not one native born American had deserted the ranks even when privation and sickness, defeat and death stared them in the face, and when comfort and reward awaited them in the English ranks. Washington would not, for anything, have revealed to these soldiers the bad example some of their officers were setting them; a quarrel among the generals, he considered, would do more damage to the country than another Brandywine or Germantown.

So not one of the men concerned in this sordid intrigue kept the secret of it more closely than the man against whom it was directed, and who was supposed to be absolutely ignorant of any hint of it.

Meanwhile many attempts were made to goad Washington into resigning; several times Congress complained because the troops at Valley Forge were not marched against Sir William Howe, who held Philadelphia for England.

General Washington waited, refusing to risk his troops in an attack on the British, and nursing them with diligent care through the horrible sufferings of the winter of 1778.

By the time Howe, after the famous carnival which was the most gorgeous spectacle the New World had ever seen, had sailed for England, the Americans who had lately been drawing nearer and nearer were in a position to attack the British outposts. Washington, who had managed by incredible labors to feed and clothe the troops and get them in something like condition, also to increase their number to fifteen thousand, now indeed felt himself strong enough to surround Philadelphia and take the town by storm.

As he was making the preparations to move from Valley Forge, he received a letter from New York that moved him deeply. It was the late afternoon of a hot summer day when this letter was brought to him, and he was walking in the garden of the modest house that served for his headquarters at Valley Forge.

On the level sweep of lawn two little trees grew and cast their shade over the fresh grass; against the neat brick grew flowers and bushes; from the lower window, that was only divided by a great shrub from the unporticoed front door, came the sound of women's voices.

Mistress Washington, Mistress Knox, Lady Stirling, and several other ladies were visiting the camp, and their dinner and sewing parties softened the ugly hardships of war.

Washington walked up and down the path that ran round the house, studying the letter that he held still open in his hand. Then, as if on a sudden impulse, he went round to the shed at the side of the house, where Billy, his colored servant, was polishing swords and muskets, and bade him leave his task and go at once to General Arnold's quarters and request his immediate attendance.

After Billy had started, the general turned into the house and entered the small, ill-furnished parlor where Martha Washington and Mistress Greene were mending uniforms and darning colors.

They were both pale and simply dressed, but cheerful in speech and manner.

Martha looked up quickly when her husband entered. "Something is the matter!" she exclaimed, laying down her sewing.

The commander-in-chief folded away the letter he held. "Nothing, indeed," he answered, with a little smile.

But Martha knew him too well to be deceived by his quiet answer; presently, when he left the room to cross to that on the other side of the passage that he used as a work cabinet, she laid down her sewing and followed him.

She found him seated before the plain table he used as a desk, his hand supporting his head and his eyes fixed on the lovely prospect of trees and garden.

"Will you not tell me?" she asked gently, coming up behind his chair.

He looked over his shoulder at her. "Was I so plain to read?" he asked, smiling.

She answered with a tone of unutterable affection. "To me — yes."

"Well, I have had disagreeable news from New York."

"What?" she breathed.

"Oh, a rumor — Heaven grant that it be no more — that someone whom I trust is intriguing against me with the Congress."

"How many more?" exclaimed Martha, with a great flush of anger. "Oh, it is hard to bear indeed that while you are toiling here there should be those who try to blacken you."

"Hush!" he said, rising and putting his hands gently and tenderly on her shoulders; "we must bear this; remember I have trusted you, and you only, with the fact that I *know* I am plotted against."

"Even to me you have not mentioned names," she interrupted; "who is this last one?"

He smiled and shook his head. "Dearest — I cannot breathe it — I hope to disprove the charge this letter brings. I have just sent for Benedict Arnold."

"Is this officer under General Arnold?"

"Yes."

"Well, then, I do not fear him, for Arnold is *almost* like you!"

"Almost?" he laughed; "he is a better soldier than I shall ever be — as you say anyone under him is scarcely to be feared; that is why I wish to speak to him, to enlist his vigilance and wisdom."

As she looked up at him the tears filled her eyes. "It is too great a burden you have taken up," she murmured.

He took his hands from her shoulders and moved to the window with a little sigh.

"No," he said absently, "but this discontent is a great danger to the American cause."

Martha turned to see Benedict Arnold in the doorway. With a little curtsey she left the two generals alone. As the door closed on her Arnold walked to the table, his cocked hat in his hand.

"You wished to see me, Sir?" he asked.

The commander-in-chief stood in the niche of the window, one hand resting on the latch of the fastening. Before him was the modest table covered with papers and maps, and behind him the fair summer blue and green showing through the diamond panes.

His powerful clear eyes were fixed intently on the man facing him; there was a marked pause before he said, "Yes, I wished to speak to you, Arnold."

"On important matters?" Arnold seemed to find it an effort to keep his own gaze steady under the insistent scrutiny of his superior.

"The most important."

Now General Arnold dropped his eyes, and his hand came out and closed on the back of the chair in front of him; he was still weak from a wound. He said nothing.

"I have," continued the commander-in-chief, still observing him keenly, "had evil news today from New York."

"Of what nature, Sir?"

General Washington did not answer this question.

He came round the table and stood directly in front of, and a few paces from, Benedict Arnold, who now raised his eyes.

Both were of the same splendid height and their eyes were on a level as they looked at each other.

"Tell me," said the commander-in-chief, "two things — first — do you know that there has lately been a movement, both among the officers and in Congress, to put General Gates in my place?"

Arnold answered with an obvious effort at coolness. "Yes, I know, Sir."

"My second question is — do you believe that I completely trust you, and believe you?"

"Why do you ask me that?" demanded Arnold sharply.

"Answer me. Have you ever had reason to doubt my friendship?"

"No — no, but, Sir, your meaning?"

"Oh, Arnold, you are my friend; I admire you, and I trust you; you more than any other man have helped and stood by me. I speak to you now as my friend, not as my officer. I have today received a letter from New York, accusing *you* of being one of those leagued in a conspiracy against me."

"Incredible!" muttered Arnold, and fell back a step.

"And worse than that — accusing you of tampering with the British — you and Lee."

Arnold put his hand to his heart; his face was bereft of color and his lips quivered and fell apart. "You — who brings this charge?" he stammered.

"One who claims to be a disaffected secretary of Mr. Richard Tryon and who offers to expose the whole plot to me."

Arnold cried out suddenly as if he had been struck. "The enemies I have! This is beyond bearing! Who has done more than I, and who has been more shamefully reviled! It is because I have married a loyalist's daughter — all have been bitter against me since then! I am overwhelmed, indeed — against these continued charges I have no longer a defense."

"I have always trusted you," said Washington gravely and sweetly, "as I have trusted Lee. Who else should have my confidence if not you?"

"But this — this slander? This continual persecution — ever since my wound rendered me unfit for active service I have been the target for perpetual malice."

"I tell you that you may know what is going on, for I make no doubt that this is some trick of Conway's to put discord between me and my best friends. You do not think that I am asking you to *deny* this?"

Arnold drew out his handkerchief and pressed it to his lips. "If Conway would stoop to that . . ." he murmured, breathing hard.

"Ah," said the commander-in-chief, "you have not watched these gentlemen as I have."

"How long have you been aware of these intrigues, Sir?"

"About a year," was the calm answer.

"And you have been silent?"

"To what purpose should I have spoken? My constant aim has been to preserve at least the appearance of concord." As he spoke he drew from his pocket the letter and, tearing it in several pieces, handed it to Arnold. "When next you light your pipe burn that," he said, with a smile.

A swift red flooded Arnold's face; he took the fragments and stared at them stupidly.

"We need never speak of this matter again," added Washington affectionately.

Arnold drew a deep breath. "I am, I confess," he said, "somewhat shaken at such a charge."

"Arnold, my friend, do not give it another thought."

But the other moved abruptly away with a short and bitter laugh.

"I knew that I had enemies," he exclaimed, in an excited tone. "I did not know that they would dare as much as this!"

Washington picked up a plan of Philadelphia from the table. "I think to march on the town within a day or two," he said quietly; "and I make no doubt that Sir Henry Clinton will retire at my approach. I am certain that he is not strong enough to hold it." Arnold glanced at him in a bewildered fashion.

"When we have entered Philadelphia," continued Washington, "I shall pursue Clinton to New York." He raised his gray eyes, "and while I go north you will be in charge of Philadelphia. You are still not strong enough for active service."

Arnold turned ghastly pale. "I?"

"Yes," smiled the commander-in-chief, "it will be my answer to that letter." And he pointed to the fragments still clutched in Benedict Arnold's hand.

CHAPTER II
BENEDICT ARNOLD'S WIFE

"Oh, you have a heart divided," exclaimed Mistress Tryon angrily, "you cannot sympathize at all."

Margaret Arnold lifted her pale face. "Do not talk so foolishly, Hortense," she answered, in an agitated voice; "you know that I am, and always have been, a loyalist — could you have seen me in New York leading the Carnival with Major André, you would not have doubted it."

"Yet you are the wife of Benedict Arnold," retorted Hortense, "the close friend of Mr. Washington."

Mistress Arnold was silent; in her heart she hoped that her influence would eventually bring her husband back to his allegiance to King George, but she scarcely deemed it politic to say so yet even to Governor Tryon's daughter-in-law.

The two ladies were in Mistress Arnold's little sitting-room in the house the commander of Philadelphia had chosen as his headquarters; Mistress Tryon was soon departing, with many passports and attendants, to join her husband in New York, where he had gone before Clinton vacated Philadelphia, and she had come to say goodbye to her friend, the rebel general's wife.

Beating an idle tattoo on the velvet arm of her chair, she gave a great sigh of discontent.

The winter of the British occupancy of the town had been without precedent blithe, and Hortense Tryon found it too utterly provoking that the unheard of successes of the rebels should have brought it all so suddenly to an end.

She had other and more serious troubles, too, that served to set a frown on her face and fill her manner with impatience.

"I have never had a moment's peace," she declared, "since that villain, Dick's secretary, went over to the rebels."

"Mr. Washington took no notice of his statements," said Margaret. "He has been very considerate in leaving Benedict here — because of his ill health."

Hortense glanced at herself in the mirror that hung on the wall near her elbow, and discontentedly rearranged the comb that held the loops of her wonderful blonde hair in place.

"He may have believed those statements, though," she remarked shrewdly.

Margaret gave a little start. "I think not!" she exclaimed hastily. "They were such — lies."

Hortense made a little grimace. "Well, of course, Dick never talks business with me, but I should say that it is likely enough he is conniving with some of the rebels to crush Mr. Washington. I am sure I hope so."

"The statements about Benedict were false," said Margaret coldly, "and Mr. Washington showed that he thought so by giving him this command."

Hortense glanced at her. "If you are as keenly loyalist as you say," she remarked, "you should be pleased if those statements be true."

Mistress Arnold answered in great agitation. "I may desire to see my husband return to his duty. I think his action mistaken and bitterly regret it — but do you think that I want him to betray his friend and his trust?"

"You ought to," said Hortense, "if you are loyal to the King."

Margaret covered her beautiful face with her long fair hands. "I am in a horrible position," she murmured, "but I could never urge him to be a traitor."

"Do you not think," asked Hortense, lightly and sharply, "that he is perhaps one already?"

Margaret looked up swiftly. "I know that he is not!" she declared vehemently.

"Ah," Hortense screwed up her mouth and leaned confidently over the arm of her chair; "well, I only tell you this my dear — Conway, Gates, and Lee are all in this plot."

"How do you know?" Margaret was staring at her, tense and startled.

"Oh, I have noticed things; I have heard Dick talk — believe me, I am right."

"I trust not," exclaimed Margaret involuntarily.

"Why? There again you ought to be pleased. It is to the advantage of the English."

"It seems — horrible."

Hortense calmly fingered the exquisite long curl that rested on her fine muslin fichu. "It would end the war," she said vindictively. "Everyone says that — if Mr. Washington were displaced the revolution would collapse in a day. For my part, I wish he could be."

Margaret made no answer to this speech.

"What does this plot consist of?" she asked in an agitated tone.

Hortense lifted her shoulders. "I do not know. As I say, Dick does not talk of these things to me — but he did tell me that Mr. Gates would soon be in Mr. Washington's place, and that once Mr. Washington was got rid of, everything would end — and I know Mr. Conway and Mr. Lee are his friends."

"This is an intrigue against Mr. Washington personally?" asked Margaret. "It is not, I mean, any attempt to deliver the rebels to the English?"

"Ah, I don't know," answered Hortense wearily, "but I do wish that the war would end, one way or another."

Margaret was silent; Hortense's attitude of supreme indifference and irritation toward the man who had guarded her youth with such care and tenderness jarred on her, and this supposed plot among the American officers against their heroic commander-in-chief seemed to her most ugly.

Gates, the Englishman who had joined the rebels, was vain and feeble; Conway was an Irish adventurer who had always hated Mr. Washington; Lee was hesitant and impatient. If these men were the leaders of the intrigue, Margaret felt that she despised them and their motives. She hoped fervently that her husband was not involved with them.

She did not think so — was there not the closest personal trust and affection between him and Mr. Washington, and after such a signal mark of confidence as the command of Philadelphia she could not hold it possible that her husband should intrigue against the commander-in-chief. But the careless insinuations of Hortense rankled; the two friends parted rather coldly when Mistress Tryon took her leave, and Margaret was left in rather a gloomy mood.

When her husband presently entered she, although she had been expecting him, rose up in much confusion, then sank into another chair, then rose up again.

"Benedict," she stammered, and her eyes were frightened.

He glanced quickly at her appealing face and his own paled. There was always this shadow over their great affection, the shadow of the difference in their beliefs, and each went about with the fear ever present in his heart that one day this shadow would grow and darken till it blotted one from the other and they groped in the blackness of estrangement. This fear was intense in Arnold's voice as he caught his wife's outstretched hands and gazed apprehensively into her loving eyes.

"I must speak to you," she said. "For days I have been meaning to — some words Hortense said have decided me."

"That foolish Hortense," he interrupted impatiently. "She thinks of nothing but her own pleasure. What has she been speaking of now?"

Margaret withdrew her hands from his grasp. "It is not only what Hortense said that troubles me," she answered. "It is what I have in my heart always."

He stood motionless, looking at her with a sad frown. He had long known that it must soon come to a discussion of this subject they had so long avoided, and he was half relieved, half pained, now the actual moment was upon him, for he had no doubt at all about what she was going to say.

He moved to the window, clasping his strong white hands behind his back, and stood so, looking at her in an attitude that emphasized the rather reckless grace of his figure, which was well set off by the blue uniform.

"Benedict," said Margaret, "you know what I am going to ask you, do you not?"

He drew his chestnut brows together in a deeper frown. "I think I know," he replied, "but I want to hear how you put it."

"I put it this way," she answered. "I ask you to join the loyalists. I want you to lay down your command."

He did not speak, and she, drawing courage from his troubled silence, continued in a firmer tone. "You are not pleased with your position. You have long found it irksome. Congress has found fault with you, your duties are arduous, your rewards slight, and you never had that great enthusiasm for the cause that makes these things nothing to a man. What reward did you get for nearly meeting death at Saratoga?"

"Washington," he answered, "has always been more than fair to me. He has always stood by me through everything."

"That is not sufficient reason for you to retain your command. I know he is your friend, but you will find other friends in the English ranks."

He looked at her sharply. "Ah, what shall I find in the English ranks? A bare pardon and a cold welcome. They do not want me. What service could I be to them?"

Their eyes met; then her glance dropped. "Benedict," she said, "I am not asking you to betray your trust, but to lay it down."

"Why do you say that?" he demanded abruptly.

Her glance rose and faced his bravely. "Because of what Hortense said. She seemed to think that her husband was meddling with Gates and Lee — even with you."

"That tale was told to General Washington. You know how much he believed of it. Lee and I are both in important commands," he answered.

"I know — yet the doubt just crossed my mind — that you might in some fit of anger — have written to Mr. Tryon."

"Women's fancies!" he interrupted impatiently.

Her beautiful eyes sought his, but his face was averted. She was not satisfied; on the contrary, she felt suddenly desperate; there was an urgent need to do something, to seize this moment.

With her whole soul she wanted her husband to come over to the side where all her interests lay, the side to which her family and her friends belonged, the side that stood to her for all that was noble in tradition and pleasant in association.

From the first she had seen that he was lukewarm in the rebel cause, and she had always hoped to completely detach him sooner or later. But she wanted this thing to be done openly and honorably. The dim possibility that he might betray his friend and his trust was worse than the possibility that he might always remain a rebel.

Yet she knew well enough that he could, from a worldly point of view, gain high terms from the British by playing the traitor, while if he joined them openly it would take all her influence to procure him more than a favorable reception. And the thought that he might be, even at this moment, struggling with this temptation, goaded her into wild speech. "Do not do it, Benedict," she said. "Whatever happens, do not do that!"

Benedict Arnold bit his lower lip and the blood leaped into his face. "What do you mean?" he asked hoarsely and harshly

"I know . . ." she said steadily. She took a step toward him. "Do not tamper with plots."

"Do you believe that I do?"

"No, no, a thousand times no!" she cried.

"Then why speak so?"

"Because I see the temptation . . ."

"Ah, the temptation!" he interrupted bitterly.

"Because I know that you have been treated ungratefully — and that you might . . ." She broke off and put her hands to her brow. She had never wanted words, strong, eloquent, powerful words, more, and she had never felt so utterly tongue tied.

"Will you not join the English?" was all she could say, and it sounded miserably crude and insufficient. He lifted his shoulders with an annoyed little laugh.

"You speak very calmly of very serious matters, Margaret. I have no intention of resigning my post in the American army."

"Because of General Washington?" she asked.

"No — because — oh, I do not know." His vexation deepened. "How can one put these things into words? Men do not change. I have chosen — do not let us talk of this again, Margaret."

"We must," she said earnestly.

He was silent; she cast about for worthy weapons, and, not finding any, proceeded to use a weapon that was not worthy. "Think of me," she said. "My position is — intolerable."

"Ah," he again flushed hotly, "you already regret that you have married a rebel?"

"No!" she answered vehemently, "not that — ever! Oh, my dear, you know it — have I not given up all the other things — for you? All that made my life is on the other side, Benedict, money, friends, position, parents, I forfeited them all — and I do not regret for one instant. But I want you to be one with my people."

She thought that she had impressed him, and, crossing the floor swiftly, she stood close before him with clasped hands and pleading eyes. "Benedict, rebels are always in the wrong."

"Who knows?" he muttered, with his face averted.

"Disloyalty cannot be right, dear."

Arnold made no answer.

She timidly laid her hand on the sleeve of the American uniform that she hated. "Come back to the old flag, the old allegiance," she said. "This cause you are serving is doomed to failure. What can they do against England? You must see that it is hopeless."

"It is an uphill fight," he admitted, "but Washington will never give in."

"Why should you stand by Mr. Washington in preference to me?" she demanded. "Why cannot you support *my* beliefs, *my* wishes?"

He suddenly stooped and kissed her forehead. "No, you ask too much, Margaret," he said gravely. "If you wish to go back to your people you must go alone."

"You know," she answered passionately, "that I would never do that."

He kissed her again and without another word went from the room.

Margaret Arnold was filled with a restless sense of apprehension that she could not still.

"He never *said* he was no traitor!" she murmured fearfully to herself.

CHAPTER III
WHITE PLAINS

It seemed as if it would prove as arduous a task to keep together the camp at White Plains as the camp at Valley Forge.

Disputes, discontent among the officers, suffering and hardship among the men, laxity and unreasonableness in Congress, were what the commander-in-chief had to daily contend with. Added to this was the disappointment caused by the withdrawal of the French fleet under Comte D'Estaing, who, after promising a juncture with Sullivan at Newport, had sailed away at sight of the British under Lord Howe and, being scattered by a storm, had dragged to Boston for repairs, leaving Sullivan to be crushingly defeated by the English, who fell on him as soon as his ally had deserted him.

This was a great blow to Washington, who had reasonably expected much from the French alliance, but an even deeper source of vexation to him than the unstable quality of his allies was the growing discontent of Arnold, and the protracted disputes that general was having with the authorities in Philadelphia on account of his loyalist wife and loyalist friends.

General Charles Lee had been disgraced after the Battle of Monmouth for his senseless orders to retreat that had nearly caused the Americans to be severely defeated, and rumor persisted that this behavior had been neither cowardice nor stupidity but treachery, and it was hinted that Benedict Arnold would behave in the same way had he an opportunity. Washington did not believe in the treachery of Lee, though he had thundered fiercely at that general's incompetence, and he did not for a second consider the charges against Benedict Arnold, who was at once his personal friend and one of his most trusted officers. But he was powerless to protect Arnold, whose high temper bitterly resented the charges brought against him, and for nearly a year the miserable dispute in Philadelphia dragged on, ending in Arnold being brought before a Committee appointed by Congress and charged on several trivial counts, from which he was vindicated, being, however, court-martialed and reproved for two petty technical offenses.

The commander-in-chief was ordered to administer a public reprimand. He did so reluctantly, for his sympathies were all with the offender, and he worded the official rebuke he had to deliver in a fashion that gracefully did honor to the reproved general rather than disgraced him — but in his heart he feared that Arnold had been struck to the heart, and struck bitterly, and that it was more the sickness of passionate pride sore wounded that ailed him than the weakness from his old Saratoga wound.

Vexed and roused by these unworthy disputes, Washington thought it time to disclose the knowledge he had long had of the plot against him among some of his officers. He did not doubt that Arnold had been the victim of some such, or perhaps the same, intrigue.

What finally decided him to speak was the fact that General Gates, against his advice, had been appointed in the place of General Lincoln, who had been defeated by Cornwallis and Clinton, who were ravaging the South.

Washington thought he saw in this appointment proof of Gates' influence with Congress, and, still smarting from the injustice done Arnold, he resolved to let the plotters know that he was aware of their conspiracy.

But Gates was only the tool, he was well aware. The real danger, the real menace, was the man who had always hated him, the one time suitor of Martha Custis, the Irish adventurer Conway.

As soon as he heard that Conway's puppet, Gates, was appointed to protect his beloved South, Washington resolved that Conway should leave the army. Accordingly, one day in June, in that year of disaster and fear, 1780, soon after Lincoln's defeat at Charleston and immediately before Gates left for the South, he and Conway received orders to wait on the commander-in-chief.

They obeyed without any apprehension. They had been secure so long that they felt absolutely safe.

Washington received them courteously in the farmhouse that was his headquarters at White Plains, but as soon as his servant, Billy, had closed the door he turned on them with the quiet deadliness that had shaken Lee at the battle of Monmouth and said, "General Conway, I demand your resignation."

If his own sword had leaped from his side and struck him Conway could not have been more astonished. He had no word to say.

Gates, the Englishman, was more master of himself. He had less to fear, and he was of a better breed. "This is rather abrupt, Sir," he said.

General Washington stood up, a head above them both, and his tired, brilliant eyes went from one face to another. "I wish as few words about it as possible," he returned. "I believe, General Gates, that you have chosen General Conway as one of your aides-de-camp in the South. You will choose another."

Gates was as pale as his pomaded side curls, but he stood his ground. "May I ask your reasons, Sir?" he demanded.

Washington looked at him through narrowed eyes. He was thinking of him in the old days at Monongahela as one of the slim, young officers who had helped carry Braddock's huddled form across the river.

"It is a pity," he said dryly, but not unkindly; "you might have made something of yourself, General Gates — something better than a puppet."

A deep red sprang into the thin cheeks of Horatio Gates. He put his hand softly on his basket swordhilt, then took it away with a deep sigh and fixed his eyes on Conway, who leaned against the wall like a drunken man.

"Have I your resignation?" asked the commander-in-chief.

Conway lifted his face that was distorted and mottled darkly; his eyes were bloodshot and his lips had a strained look.

"No, you have not!" he answered, and his tone quivered with the long hate, malice, and envy that he had borne this man.

Fire sparkled in General Washington's gray eyes. He threw back his head a little. "Then I shall lay before Congress the information I have concerning you," he said.

Gates gave a quick exclamation, and Washington turned to him swiftly. "Did you think that I did not know?" he asked. "If I was as simple as that, General Gates, I should not have been able to hold an army together during all these weary campaigns."

Conway put his hands to his throat and struggled with his Michelin cravat as if it choked him.

"I will deal with Congress, not with you, Sir," he said insolently.

"I have no doubt," was the steady answer," that you have friends in Congress, but I hold proofs of your conduct that would mean a court-martial for you were they disclosed. No Congress would be able to save you."

Conway's suffused face worked uncontrollably. "Do you threaten me?" he asked brazenly.

"Threaten you? Any time these two years I could have had you hanged for mutiny."

"Why did you hold your hand?"

"Because I wished to spare the American army the disgrace."

"You have no proofs."

"I have absolute proofs."

"You always hated me!"

"I despised you — always."

"You think to frighten me into resigning!"

"I think that you will resign, General Conway."

"Never!"

"Ah!" Washington, slightly pale, glanced at Gates. "You will resign before the expedition starts for the South."

Gates, alert and still very white, remained silent, waiting to discover how much the commander-in-chief knew.

"No!" answered Conway.

Washington put his hand in his pocket and drew out a wad of papers. "About six months ago," he said, "you were the prime mover in a conspiracy to displace me and make General Gates commander-in-chief. In this plot Gates, Lee, and you were concerned, but there was an inner plot for which you alone were responsible. The object of it was to deliver me, for a certain sum of money, into the hands of Mr. Richard Tryon, son of the late Governor of New York."

Conway's flushed face faded to a ghastly hue. Again he tugged at his neck band.

"I never knew of this!" cried Gates in great agitation.

"I believe, General Gates," said the commander coldly, "that you did not." Conway's eyes raved to the packet Washington held. "These are letters in your writing sent me by Mr. Tryon's secretary, who betrayed his master. They contain full details of the plan by which I was to be enticed into the British lines. These details enabled me to defeat them."

Conway breathed hard. With an instinctive desire to escape he backed toward the door.

"Now will you resign?" demanded General Washington.

"What of the others," asked Conway in a husky voice. "Your friend Arnold was in this."

Washington slightly flushed under the eyes. "You will keep your tongue off my friends!" he cried. "I *know* General Arnold's innocence as I *know* your guilt!"

"I was unaware of this," stammered Gates. "I should never have consented to tampering with the British."

Washington turned on him with a proud air. "Do you believe, General Gates, that I should submit to your appointment in the South if I believed that you were such as Conway?"

Horatio Gates bowed. "I thank you," he said. "I am quite at your mercy. You have been very magnanimous and you must do as you please with me, Sir."

Faint with the effort of making this speech, he caught hold of the back of a chair to support himself, and stood with his head hanging down.

Conway flared into savage bitterness at this behavior on the part of the man who had been his dupe.

"It is monstrous fine for you to talk," he said, "but you are in this as deep as I — General Gates."

"No! I am not!" the Englishman interrupted hotly.

Washington, with his eyes on Conway, interposed between them. "I know how deep General Gates has been," he said coldly; "his offenses are against me and I can overlook them. But your offenses are against America and these I will no longer tolerate." He paused a moment, then added in a flashing tone, "Your sword, General Conway."

Livid and shivering with rage, the Irishman tugged his weapon from the scabbard. "You think I am the only one?" he sneered. "Look to Benedict Arnold!"

Washington did not answer; his face was vivid with contempt. "Deny that his name is mentioned in those papers!" cried Conway, pointing to the packet Washington still held in his right hand.

"I have no wish to answer," said the commander-in-chief. "Your sword, Sir."

Conway cast it on the ground.

Washington did not lower his eyes; with the toe of his riding boot he moved the weapon aside. "Now go!" he commanded.

Conway lurched toward the door, dabbing his mouth with his handkerchief. "Look to Benedict Arnold!" he repeated vindictively.

Washington turned his back on him; the door opened, shut heavily and the traitor was gone.

There was a moment's pause of silence; then the commander-in-chief spoke to General Gates. "I have nothing more to say. Now that General Conway has resigned, this matter will never again be mentioned by me."

Horatio Gates lifted his head and answered with an effort. "Believe," he said faintly, "that I have never tampered with the enemy, that I did not know how far Conway had gone."

"You have already, General Gates, had my assurances on that point. I hope that you will be fortunate in the South," replied Washington.

"And as to these accusations against General Arnold — I must say that . . ." stammered Gates.

"It is unnecessary to tell me that. I trust Benedict Arnold absolutely," smiled the commander-in-chief. "You may believe it when I tell you that he has asked for the command of West Point and that I have given it to him."

General Gates glanced at him swiftly. West Point was the key to the whole American position.

"You are very generous," he murmured.

A few minutes afterward, when he was outside the commander-in-chief's headquarters, he paused, with his hand to his side, and looked over the camp. "I wonder," he said to himself in a kind of sick amaze, "if they are paying Arnold better than they did Lee? West Point! How is it possible?"

CHAPTER IV
JOSHUA SMITH'S HOUSE

Well within the lines of the American sentries and on the verge of a wood that sloped down to the banks of the Hudson, close to Stony Point, stood the humble house of a man named Joshua Smith, who was secretly in the pay of the English.

The warm September dawn had just broken, when two men with their hats over their eyes and wrapped in traveling cloaks issued from this wood and, approaching the house, demanded admission.

On the exchange of a password this was granted, and Smith, who had himself come to the door and who was alone in the house, conducted them to an upper chamber which commanded a view of the Hudson.

But when they had reached this room Joshua Smith did not at once depart, but stood in the doorway with a lantern in his hand (for the light was yet feeble), looking curiously at the two men.

He who was the slighter and appeared the younger threw back his cloak, showing the scarlet and white uniform of a British officer.

"I am an English officer," he said, "on business of Sir Henry Clinton's." He pointed to the window, beyond which the dawn glimmered. "I came on the vessel you will see on the river."

"Yes, I have marked it," returned Smith.

"We were conducting our business in the wood, when the sailors who rowed me ashore opined that it would be unwise to row back in daylight, so I bid them go and remained. Will you row me out to yonder ship when this gentleman and I have finished?"

The fellow looked shrewdly from one to another. "Not before nightfall," he said. "Do you know that you are in the American lines and within range of two of the American river batteries?"

"Well, at nightfall, then," replied the officer rather impatiently. "Meanwhile we can stay here? You will be well paid, you know." As he spoke he took off his hat, revealing a young and charming face.

"You can stay," returned Smith, "but if I make no mistake this business of yours is dangerous."

"Not to you," returned the officer. "You will be safe enough."

The man looked doubtful, but left without a word, and as the door closed behind him the second of the two strangers, who till now had remained motionless by the window, with his face sunk in his cloak, gave a sigh of relief and stepped forward.

"That fellow is cautious, Major André," he said.

"A spy needs to be," returned the other pleasantly, "but he will serve us — I make no doubt."

So saying, Major André, adjutant-general to Sir Henry Clinton, and one of the most charming and popular officers in the British Army, unhooked his mantle, for the air was warm, and seated himself on one of the low willow-bottomed chairs.

The other officer removed his hat, and as he turned his head and glanced with a startled expression toward the open window he disclosed the pale, haughty features and chestnut locks of General Benedict Arnold. "I thought that I heard something," he remarked.

"Nothing" returned Major André; "it is as still as heaven."

Certainly the complete silence of the dawn seemed only broken by the steady chatter of the waking birds in the woods.

"I feel as if there was a portent in the air," said Arnold softly.

"A portent of our success, I hope," answered Major André lightly. "With the capture of West Point the rebellion will end, I think."

"Surely nothing can fail now," said Arnold. "Listen again. I will pretend to repair the boom across the Hudson and will replace the middle of the chain by a rope one of your ships can easily break . . ."

"That is an excellent suggestion, General Arnold!" interrupted the Englishman. "I may take it, of course, that you will so place the troops that they will be useless — that is, defending positions that we shall not attack?"

"Yes."

"Would it be possible for you to weaken the fort by sending away some of the garrison on one excuse or another?"

Arnold reflected. "Not, I am afraid, without rousing the suspicions of General Washington," he replied.

"Ah, he is a vigilant commander?"

"Yes."

"Yet he has let himself be duped more than once," remarked André dryly. "I suppose he never believed that Lee supplied us with a written account of his plans for last year's campaign?"

"No, any more than when I asked for the command of West Point he suspected that I meant to deliver it to the enemy for a sum of money and an English generalship," returned Arnold, with a ghastly smile.

André looked at him curiously; Arnold caught the glance and added, "I suppose that you wonder at me, Major André?"

"It is not my business to wonder at anything," was the answer. "I am a soldier under orders."

"I have been ill-treated by Congress, yes, treated like a dog!" cried Arnold, "and I am avenging myself. For the pain I must cause General Washington I am sorry, for he believed in me through everything."

"Credulity is a failing," remarked André calmly.

"A noble failing."

"Still, a failing, and one for which General Washington must pay."

"Yes, he will pay," said Arnold grimly. "Even he will not be able to keep the war together after this — I would that it had been another man that I had had to betray." He was gloomily silent, for a thousand memories of the delicate consideration, the kindness, the trust of the General who had called him friend stung and tortured him fiercely.

And he had been gallant and fine himself. He had once been as upright, honorable, ardent in the cause of liberty as Washington himself, and that made his shame and degradation the deeper now.

Major André regarded him impatiently. It was not the Englishman's business to trouble about the scruples of conscience of this valuable tool. His only anxiety was lest the tool should fail. Deep in his heart he felt the scorn that an honorable soldier cannot help feeling toward a traitor. He remembered Sir Henry Clinton's amazement when he had first heard that the American officer who was dealing with him under an assumed name was no other than the brilliant Arnold.

"Arnold!" the British commander exclaimed. "It cannot be Arnold!"

And Major André, looking at the proud, graceful figure and fine face, felt something of the same astonishment. But it was not his business to show it.

He was himself on a perilous business within the enemy's lines, and his one object was to obtain the plans of West Point from Arnold, to arrange all details of the betrayal with him and to regain the war sloop, *The Vulture*, that waited for him in the Hudson, and return to New York with his task (which was one that he had never cared for from the first) completed. Therefore, he broke in upon Arnold's bitter reverie.

"Have you the plans of West Point with you, General Arnold?" he asked.

The dawn filled the room. In the pearl-colored light of it, the two men looked pale and wan as they gazed at each other.

Arnold took a packet of papers from the breast of his coat and handed them over in silence; the lace ruffles touched as the men's hands met; Arnold was shaking perceptibly.

André opened the package and spread the contents over his knee.

"You will find everything there," said Arnold in a low voice, "including passports for yourself for land or water in the name of John Anderson."

André considered a minute, then said, "There is no chance that Washington will leave Hartford before we gain West Point?"

"Are you afraid of him?" asked Arnold, with a terrible smile on his pale lips.

"Frankly — yes."

"I do not think that he will leave Hartford — he has no reason to. His design is to effect a joint movement with General Rochambeau. He ever relies too much on the French."

André could have added that the American commander relied too much on his own best friends, but he held his tongue and glanced over the passports and other documents before he put them inside the breast of his scarlet uniform. Then he rose. "There is nothing more to discuss, I think," he said.

"No," answered Arnold heavily. "No . . ." He was about to add more when a thunderous sound suddenly disturbed the placid stillness of the morning — the sound of cannon.

Arnold turned to André; for a second the two stood rigid; then both turned to the window.

Beyond the gold and crimson belt of autumn wood flowed the river on which waited the little British sloop that had brought André from New York, and as the two conspirators gazed from the window they saw that one of the American riverside batteries had perceived her and was opening fire, for cannon continued to boom and clouds of smoke threaded with scarlet flame obscured the opposite banks of the Hudson.

Arnold gave a sound like a great sigh and clapped his hand to his heart. André went very white and kept his eyes fixed on *The Vulture*, which was his only means of returning to New York.

The sound of the cannonading continued till the wood quivered in all the branches of its trees and the house shook.

"Why does she not return their fire?" muttered Arnold.

André did not answer. The possibility of getting within range of the American guns had not occurred to him; if he had considered it he would never have come so far up the river, but would have made an appointment with Arnold nearer to New York. He began to perceive that this recklessness had put him in a dangerous position, for he was within the American lines and his escort was under American fire. The smoke hung heavily over the river that was glimmering in the early September sunlight, but through it André could see the masts of *The Vulture*. She was dropping down the river.

"She is moving!" exclaimed André, horrified." He clutched his companion's arm and they leaned out of the window, gazing aghast at the British sloop of war. She was certainly rapidly falling back before the shore battery's guns.

Arnold gave a wild laugh. "What shall we do now?" he demanded.

But André, after the first shock, recovered his composure. He remembered that the captain of *The Vulture* had orders from Sir Henry Clinton not to return to New York without him; and he reassured himself with the thought that *The Vulture* would only get out of range of the guns and that she would wait for him lower down the Hudson.

"Smith can row me out after nightfall," he said coolly. And he preserved his calm even when he saw the ship disappear out of sight around a bend in the river.

"She will wait for you?" asked Arnold in an agitated voice.

"I have no fear of her forsaking me."

"But to reach her you will have to cross the fire of the batteries."

"They will not see an open boat after dark."

The guns, having accomplished their purpose, were now silent, and the smoke rose from wood and river and drifted slowly in wreaths away into the sky; the air was foul with the smell of powder, and the frightened birds were silent.

The two officers left the window. "You will remain till nightfall?" asked Arnold.

"I fear I shall not get this fellow to row me out before. If he would I would risk it."

"Better wait — they will be on the outlook at the batteries now — your uniform is a target."

"It is a safeguard," answered André. "While I wear it I am no spy."

He recalled the advice given him by Sir Henry Clinton before he left New York — not to disguise himself, not to enter the American lines, and not to carry papers.

The last two warnings he had disregarded, since he was well within the American outposts and had accepted from Arnold papers that contained absolute proof of the plot in every detail.

But he resolved to retain his British uniform knowing well enough the fate of a spy.

"I must stay no longer," said Arnold, "or my absence will cause comment."

"You have a horse here?"

"Yes — left with Smith before I came to meet you in the wood."

"Does Smith know you?"

"No!"

"But he will ask no questions?"

"Be content, Major André; he will ask no questions."

The Englishman held out his hand. "Then, goodbye, General Arnold, and may we meet under the British flag."

"Godspeed, and be careful — remember you carry the fate of West Point, perhaps the fate of the war, in your pocket."

"I shall be aboard *The Vulture* tonight and in New York by tomorrow's dawn."

At the head of the mean, dark, little stairs they parted; André to return to the room to wait with what patience he might till night fell and Smith would row him out to the sloop, and Arnold to return to his headquarters at the Robinson House, opposite West Point.

CHAPTER V
THE TRAITOR

A merry breakfast was in progress at the Robinson House; several officers and their ladies were the guests of General Arnold and his wife, and the headquarters of the Commander of West Point rung with the laughter and merriment of good spirits, for lately affairs had begun to look better for the Americans and there was every confidence that as Washington had held Clinton in check so long, and as there seemed no chance of the British breaking the American lines, this year might prove finally successful for their cause.

General Arnold himself was merriest of all; his spirits that had lately seemed downcast, were soaring; he seemed to have regained all his natural animation that he had largely lost since the bitter Philadelphia days.

His wife was rejoiced to see him so; never since that interview in Philadelphia had the subject of his leaving the American service been alluded to between them, but Margaret was almost content, even though she had given up the dream of one day seeing her husband united to her people, serving her ideals and following her flag, for she saw him trusted and honored in his present employ and she had forever banished the fear that had once tortured her — the fear that he would revenge himself by treachery for the treatment he had received at the hands of Congress.

She admitted now that this fear was unworthy, and she was ashamed that it had ever been allowed to touch her, and in her relief at the lifting of this cloud, her pride in the deference paid her husband, her joy in his constant affection, Margaret Arnold had been very happy for the last few months.

She was very happy now as she sat by Benedict Arnold's side at the head of her table in the pleasant diningroom of the Robinson House, that was filled with the warm honey-colored sunshine of a late September morning.

And in her rose-sprigged muslin, white lace fichu, with her unpowdered locks confined by a simple ribbon, she was as entrancing a vision as she had ever been when she graced the ballrooms of New York or Philadelphia in silk and brocade.

"I have surrendered! I have hauled my colors down!" she cried to an officer who reproached her laughingly with being at heart still a loyalist, "and you must call me a rebel, if you will!"

As she spoke the door opened and the colored servant showed in a couple of young officers, the foremost of whom was Alexander Hamilton. Arnold glanced up swiftly; for a moment his face was distorted; then he rose in his place as the young men advanced and calmly held out his hand.

"General Arnold," said Hamilton, sweeping of his hat to the ladies, "the commander-in-chief is on his way to break his fast with this good company, being at present across the river, or crossing. I am his herald."

"I was not expecting this honor," answered Arnold quietly. "I did not know that General Washington had any intention of immediately leaving Hartford."

"He found it no use delaying any longer with General Rochambeau, who is by no means ready, it seems, for an assault on the enemy."

So saying, Hamilton and his companion took the places that had been set for them amid smiling welcomes from the others, in which Margaret Arnold laughingly joined.

"If we had known, we would all have waited for General Washington," she declared.

"Madam," answered Hamilton, "he begged me to say that the company were on no account to derange themselves, as he did not know the exact hour of his arrival. He has stopped with General Knox to inspect some fortifications at West Point."

Arnold heard these words with intense anxiety, though he preserved an indifferent demeanor. If Washington delayed his coming, then the British attack, which was to take place today, would come off before the commander-in-chief had time to discover the broken chain across the river and the defenseless condition of the fort. If he should arrive immediately and at once start a tour of inspection he might easily observe the treachery afoot.

Yet Arnold scarcely feared this; he believed that he would find it easy enough to put excuses in the way of a tour of inspection being taken today. He joined in the conversation with all his old graceful ease. One of the company expressed a wish for a speedy peace.

"Peace!" cried Arnold. "Should we not all find peace dull after this?"

"Ah, General Arnold," answered Hamilton gravely, "but we fight for an object, and when that object is attained peace must follow — a triumphant peace." At this point a servant entered the room and whispered to Arnold that a dispatch bearer had ridden up from an outpost near Tarrytown with a message from Colonel Jameson, the commander there.

"Bring him in," answered the general indifferently.

Then he smiled at Hamilton and resumed the interrupted conversation.

"A triumphant peace without doubt," he remarked, "but I fear that there are many arduous campaigns ahead of us before we compel the English . . ."

The dispatch bearer entered, and, saluting, offered Arnold the message from Colonel Jameson.

Pausing in his speech, Arnold tore open the envelope and glanced at the letter. His wife, chancing to glance at him, thought she saw an extraordinary look come over his face, as if he had been struck suddenly dead, and all his pulses had stopped together on a given signal. But the next instant he had folded the paper carelessly up and put it in his pocket as he continued his interrupted sentence.

"As I was saying," he said, "I think the English will be a long while before they recognize the independence of the colonies."

"Not so long, I think," answered Hamilton staunchly, "if we have many more campaigns like the last."

"That is the proper spirit, Major Hamilton," laughed Arnold. "And now I must beg the indulgence of all of you. I have been summoned to West Point, but shall be back directly — I hope with General Washington."

Margaret felt her whole body grow suddenly cold. She had caught the servant's whisper that the dispatch was from an outpost near Tarrytown, not from West Point, from Colonel Jameson, not General Washington.

While the guests who had been expecting the commander-in-chief every moment were expressing their regret at the departure of their host, he, rising carelessly, bade them all a smiling *au revoir* and left the room with a light step.

Horrible doubts and dreads clutched at Margaret's heart; old terrors that she had thought dead revived; she could not endure the suspense. "I must ask Benedict if we are to wait for him or not," she said, commanding herself to speak lightly. "Or if I shall not serve another meal for General Washington."

Everyone was absorbed in listening to Hamilton's account of Washington's last interview with General Rochambeau, and none of them noticed her agitation as she rose and left them.

As soon as the door was closed behind her she ran upstairs to her bedroom. Her husband stood by a bureau, emptying the contents of the drawers into a dispatch case; his back was toward her as she entered.

"Benedict," she said, closing the door behind her.

He turned a face so distorted that at first she thought it was some stranger.

She stifled a horrible cry and staggered to the bed. "What has happened?" she muttered.

"What should have happened?" he answered.

"That dispatch — was from Tarrytown — why did you not say so?"

He was unbuttoning his uniform; his unstrapped sword lay on the floor already.

"Find me another coat, quick!" he commanded.

She tottered to the wardrobe and mechanically fumbled with the clothes that hung there.

He came up to her and impatiently snatched a black ridingale from her cold hands.

"What has happened?" she repeated desperately.

He did not answer; he was pulling on the black coat, changing his hair ribbon and shaking his rolled curls into disorder.

Margaret dropped on her knees on the floor and turned over his heavy uniform; she unbuttoned the front pocket and drew out the dispatch with numb fingers. She spread it out on the floor and read with glaring eyes:

> Sept. 24th, 1780
> To GENERAL ARNOLD, at West Point.
>
> Sir:
> *A man calling himself John Anderson has been arrested carrying documents of an extraordinary nature in his shoes. These have been despatched to the commander-in-chief at Hartford.*
>
> COLONEL JAMESON.

"Who is this?" asked Margaret. "What do you know of this?"

She had not the strength to rise from her knees, but remained huddled in her muslin skirts, her hands clasped and her eyes fixed on her husband who never paused in his frantic preparations for disguise and flight.

As she spoke he turned to her, thrusting money and papers into the pocket of his cloak.

"John Anderson is Major André," he said, "and I am a lost man!"

"Major André!" she echoed wildly, thinking of the charming young soldier who had so often been her partner in minuet and cotilion during those festive seasons in New York and Philadelphia.

Arnold stooped and lifted her to her feet. "Margaret," he said, "my life ends when Washington sees those papers, unless I am within the British lines — do not faint — listen to me — I must drop down the river to find *The Vulture*, that is waiting for André . . ."

"Stop!" she interrupted hoarsely. "Stop — tell me what you have done — I must know."

He shook her fiercely. "Come to your senses if you do not wish to be the means of my death. Washington may this moment be at the door!"

"Why will you not face him?" she cried.

"I have sold West Point to Clinton — those papers Jameson holds are the proof of it. Do you understand now? Do you understand?"

She shuddered from head to foot, and, though his grasp of her on either arm was the only thing that held her upright, she tried to strain away from his touch.

"You are a traitor!" she said "You, Benedict Arnold! Let me go — you sold your trust for money — oh, I have gone mad — you dishonored — after all I said!"

"Do you want to see me hanged?" he demanded. "Let me go!"

She wrenched herself free of him and caught hold of the bedpost.

"Have *you* forsaken me?" he cried.

She moistened her lips. "What do you want me to do?" she asked.

He picked up the dispatch from the floor and thrust it into his pocket. "You must beguile Washington when he arrives. Tell him I am at West Point. The papers have gone to Hartford. He must have missed them, but they will follow him here. Meanwhile I might reach *The Vulture*, do you understand. Do you understand?"

She nodded.

"Have you any money?" he demanded. "I shall need to bribe the men who row me."

"There are my jewels," she said dully.

"Ah, yes — fetch them — make haste."

She staggered into the next room, her dressing-room, and, pulling a key from her bosom, opened a casket that stood on the table and drew out the strings of diamonds and pearls, the bracelets of rubies and gold that had adorned her in her joyous days in Philadelphia.

"Make haste!" came her husband's desperate voice.

Walking heavily, she returned, her hands full of the sparkling jewels. He took them from her and bestowed them in his pockets, while she stood lifeless, colorless, and motionless before him.

"God bless you, Margaret!" he cried, and would have taken her in his arms, but she repulsed him.

"Goodbye," she said.

"No more than that? It is your people I have served!"

Margaret swayed on her feet. "It is my people who will despise you, now and always."

"Have you no other farewell?"

"How can a dead thing reason, Benedict? And you have slain me as you have slain your own honor."

"Do you take it this way?" he cried, catching hold of her arm.

"Save your life," she answered him, "for you have lost everything else in the world."

"Will you wish me good fortune?" he asked wildly.

Her eyes flashed in her pallid set face. "Thank the love I once had that I do not curse you," she said.

She dragged her arm from his and slipped, half unconscious, on the floor at his feet.

He picked her up and laid her on the bed. He would have kissed her a desperate farewell, but she hid her face from him in the pillow. With a bitter sob in his throat he turned away, fled the house by the back and, getting in, bade the men row their swiftest down the river.

For some moments Margaret lay motionless on the bed; then she sat up and put her hands to her head. Mechanically she glanced at the little gilt clock.

There was no time to be lost; the Commander-in-chief must be here soon.

She rose, picked up her husband's uniform (he had taken his sword, she noted), concealed it in the wardrobe, entered the dressing-room, locked the spoiled and disarranged jewel case and went downstairs. As she reached the entrance passage General Washington, followed by Knox, entered, laughing, and asking for breakfast.

"Ah, General Washington," said Mistress Arnold, "my husband has just gone to the fort at West Point. You must have passed and missed each other on the river."

CHAPTER VI
THE TRAITOR'S WIFE

The bewildered commander-in-chief turned back to the riverside; there the news he had heard at the Robinson House was confirmed; for General Arnold's barge was gone.

Therefore, there could be little doubt that Arnold had indeed gone to West Point fort; yet who could have sent him the message summoning him so abruptly from the rendezvous with the commander-in-chief? When Washington reached West Point and found that General Arnold was not there, and that all the officers denied having sent him a message, his confusion and amazement increased.

Thinking that there must have been a mistake and that Arnold had only left his residence on some trifling errand, the commander-in-chief returned immediately to the Robinson House.

The officers and their ladies had scattered. Mistress Arnold was alone in the breakfast room.

"Madam," said Washington, "your husband is not at West Point." She raised her eyebrows and answered serenely, "Then I must have misunderstood — I thought he said that he was called to the fort — he left the room carelessly, so I believed that it was nothing of great moment."

"No, I suppose not. Yet it is curious where he can have been called so suddenly."

Mistress Arnold moved to the window and opened the casement on the garden full of autumn scents and flowers.

"I suppose he went to one of the outposts," she said.

"That is strange, Madam, when he was any moment expecting me."

"Perhaps the summons was urgent."

Washington knit his brows. "We will imagine it must have been," he answered rather briefly. Had any man other than his favorite Arnold disappeared like this without leaving a message of explanation, he would have been angry.

He took a turn about the room; Mistress Arnold stood motionless, staring out of the window.

"Where is the man who brought the message?" asked the commander-in-chief suddenly.

She glanced at him over her shoulder. "I — do not know."

His powerful gray eyes rested a moment on her face. "Mistress Arnold — you look ill."

"Oh, I am very well — but a little — tired." Washington went to the bell rope. "May I command your servants, Madam?"

"Of course."

She sank into the deep window seat, her hands crossed in her lap . . . (How far down the river was he by now — how far?)

"He will surely be back any moment," she said. "Pray do not incommode yourself, General Washington . . ."

But he had already rung the bell.

"I am wondering who sent that message," he answered.

When the servant entered he requested that the man who had recently brought a dispatch to General Arnold might be sent for.

"I am surprised he did not leave a message for me," he remarked, and glanced intently at the pale lady in the window seat.

She met his gaze bravely, and smiled. "I only know what I have told you, Sir."

He looked at the clock. "General Arnold has been absent over an hour."

(An hour — how far could they, rowing desperately, get in an hour? Where was *The Vulture*? Had they reached it? Oh, the unutterable torture of this suspense!)

"Is it so long?" she asked lightly.

To her infinite relief a little bell rang.

"That is your breakfast, General Washington; I ordered it to be served in the little room, which is more pleasant — General Knox has had his."

She rose and invited him to follow her; he marked with some surprise her charming manner; this loyalist wife of Arnold's had always before been very cold to him; he thought that she was afraid of his anger at her husband's absence and he was touched by her effort to mollify him; his native courtesy and gentleness moved him to say, "I am delighted to accept your hospitality, Mistress Arnold — and I have no doubt that General Arnold will have returned by the time I have finished my breakfast."

She accompanied him into the next room, and when he, tired, hungry, and inwardly vexed at his friend's behavior, seated himself with a sigh before the well-appointed table, she employed herself in waiting upon him.

After a while the soldier who had brought the message entered.

Mrs. Arnold put down the jug of milk she held; her hands were shaking so that she knew that she must spill the contents if she did not.

(What did this man know? What would he say?)

"Ah," said the commander-in-chief pleasantly, "you brought a dispatch just now to General Arnold, did you not?"

"Yes, Sir."

"Where are you from?"

"The outpost near Tarrytown."

"What commander?"

"Colonel Jameson, Sir."

"Colonel Jameson sent a message to General Arnold?"

"Yes, Sir."

"Requesting his presence?"

"I do not know, Sir."

Washington leaned back in his chair; his eyes narrowed. "Has there been an attack on Tarrytown?" he asked sharply.

"No, Sir."

"Nor anything unusual?"

"No, Sir — unless it was the capture of a man yesterday that they took to be a spy."

"What did Colonel Jameson do with him?"

"He was sending him to General Arnold, Sir — then the order was countermanded. I met him being brought back."

"An Englishman?" flashed Washington.

"They said so, Sir. Young he was and of the gentry, but dressed in rough clothes. They say that he had papers in his boots."

Washington dismissed the soldier at this; when they were alone again he turned to Margaret. "It is this matter that has called your husband away Madam. Doubtless he found the capture of this spy important. Still I do not understand why the prisoner was not sent here, nor why General Arnold did not wait to see me."

"Do you think that he has gone to Tarrytown?"

"It is most likely."

"Should you follow him?"

"No, I will wait a while." And he proceeded to calmly finish his breakfast.

(How he trusts him — he will never believe — can I believe it myself? Is he safe now with the British? What shall I do with the rest of my life?)

As these thoughts raced through her mind Margaret Arnold sat at the other side of the table, gazing at the magnificent figure in the blue, yellow-braided coat that represented the judge of life or death over Benedict Arnold unless the delay was prolonged.

But suppose *The Vulture* was far down the river or had even already reached New York, what delay would serve then?

The exhausted men would drop at their oars — and the pursuers would overtake the drifting boat or the fugitive wandering on the banks of the Hudson.

She rose, feeling that if she sat still much longer she would shriek aloud her intolerable secret; as she got to her feet the door opened and Hamilton entered.

"Has General Arnold returned?" asked Washington at once.

"No, Sir. It is a dispatch rider from Colonel Jameson who has ridden to Hartford to find you — we must have passed him, belike he took a different road. He has dashed up from Hartford here — these are his papers, Sir."

And Hamilton laid a large packet on the white cloth among Margaret Arnold's fine glass and frail painted china.

The commander-in-chief took up the dispatch eagerly. "Now we shall get the key to this business at Tarrytown," he said, breaking the seal. "Hamilton, see to the messenger; he has had a stiff ride." Hamilton left the room; Washington was busy opening the package; Margaret crept to the door and locked it; there was no bell and the window looked on to the back, where few people passed, and was a considerable height from the ground; she had reckoned on these things when she had ordered the commander-in-chief's breakfast to be laid in this room. With the key of the door in her hand, she approached the table. "Well, what is the news?" she asked quietly.

Washington was glancing over Jameson's letter. "This captured man seems to be a British officer in disguise. He was endeavoring to reach *The Vulture*, an English sloop of war, that sailed up the Hudson as far as Stony Point, from whence the river batteries opened fire on her and caused her to retreat," he answered, rapidly summarizing the contents of the letter. "This spy, finding no one to row him back, was making his way on foot when he was captured near Tarrytown by some Americans, who took him to Jameson. These papers were found in his shoes . . ."

Washington laid down the letter and turned over the enclosed contents. Margaret stood quite still, watching him.

"Why?" he said. "Why . . ."

He frowned and paused, rapidly turning over the documents, plans of West Point fort, information as to the American movements, passports for land and water, a written scheme to cut the chain across the Hudson, an account of how the American troops would be posted at West Point to enable the British to easily capture the position in their assault planned for the 25th of September . . .

Washington dropped the papers among the breakfast things; he was so pale it seemed as if he must faint. All these papers were written and signed by Benedict Arnold.

He gave one heart-broken sob, "Whom can I trust now?" and staggered to his feet.

Margaret Arnold stepped back and flung herself across the door.

"Arnold!" muttered Washington. "Arnold!"

He picked up the papers; there was no need to read them carefully; one fact shrieked from them. Arnold had sold West Point to the British.

The stricken General's eyes turned to the woman. "So you brought him to this," he said passionately. "You have a fine triumph to boast of, Madam, in the British camp! I never trusted you — why could he not have married a fine woman?"

She was as white and tense as he. "Before heaven, I never knew of this before this morning. I often urged him to stand true or openly leave you. Spare hard words to me, General Washington, for I am smitten to the heart."

He retorted fiercely, "Do you think that I believe you? You have been beguiling me even now while he escapes!"

"Yes, he is my husband."

"And your partner in treachery. Oh, I was soft to allow loyalist women in my camps."

She set her back more firmly against the door as he approached, towering in his wrath. "Stand out of my way," he said.

"No — I am giving him a chance."

"Where has he gone?"

"I will not tell you."

For answer he caught her by the shoulders and swung her from the door. When he found it locked he gave a great cry of fury, and so wrenched at the handle that she thought he would tear it open by sheer force.

"The assault was to be today!" he cried. "And I must repair the preparations of this traitor."

Margaret paused by the window; she had the key ready to cast out among the thick bushes below. "Will you be merciful?" she asked hoarsely.

"No," he answered in a terrible voice. "He hangs, had he been my own brother!" This sent her to her knees in shrieking hysterics.

"No! No!" she screamed, dragging herself across the floor toward him. "You will have pity on me! I never wronged you! I never knew! You would not let him be hanged! You loved him once!"

"The key!" he said, "the key!"

Futile as she knew her wretched attempt at delay to be (for what, after all, could it be but a few moments gained!) she still persisted in it, swaying to and fro on her knees, the key clutched against her bosom while her wild, piteous eyes were fixed on General Washington.

She would not consciously hand over the key that would open the door for the alarm to be given, that would set a pursuing party on her husband's track.

"I must inspect the fort at once," said Washington, in a level tone; he struck on the door, but no one heard him; he went to the window and looked out, but there was no one in sight; it seemed as if this woman's device might cause serious delay, for every second, no, every moment, was precious.

He turned to take the key by force from the crouching woman on the floor, and she, divining his purpose from his swift movement toward her, sprang up to hurl it from the window.

As she was about to do so a low boom echoed through the still warm air and vibrated in the chamber.

"The British!" cried Washington.

Margaret sprang from the window, holding out the key toward him.

"Take it — undo his evil — do not let West Point be lost through him . . . Oh, heart! heart!"

Her voice trailed off incoherently; she sank across a chair as Washington took the key from her hand.

She heard him dash from the room and his shouted orders to Knox and Hamilton.

"He will save West Point," she said, and put her hands before her eyes, "but God Himself cannot save the honor of Benedict Arnold!"

She heard the rattle of an artillery team galloping past the window, and the joyous shout of the man to his horses, and at the thought that anyone could still be happy in this horrible world, she gave a wild laugh, then slipped unconscious to the floor.

CHAPTER VII
THREE WIVES

"Monsieur, you must speak to him for me; in the name of the country to which we both belong and which I have never seen, I implore you to have pity on me and speak to Mr. Washington for my husband's life." With this desperate appeal, Hortense Tryon slipped from her tired horse and leaned against the wooden palisade that surrounded the little farm that formed General Rochambeau's headquarters at Ardsley.

The young Frenchman whom she addressed looked at her gravely and with a kind of troubled pity. "Go back to your home, Madame," he said. "I will send an escort with you."

"I have no home," she answered. "All, all is gone, lost. And I have ridden desperately and alone to get here in time. Tell me, is not General Washington here?"

"Yes," said the Marquis de Lafayette, "but I can scarce trouble him with these matters. He is consulting with General Rochambeau the next move against Cornwallis."

The frail and weary little lady turned and hid her face against the brown side of her patient horse, and bitter sobs of despair shook her body.

No one seeing her now would have known her for the blithe and frivolous creature who had danced and reveled so thoughtlessly during the first epoch of the war.

She had changed with circumstance; and circumstances were different indeed to what they had been. Since the Battle of King's Mountain the tide had turned; Washington was practically master of the continent, and the English under Cornwallis were with difficulty holding their own at Yorktown.

This change was reflected in the daughter-in-law of the former governor of New York, who, instead of an imperious flattered little beauty with a scornful word for the "rebels," was now a distracted woman who had lost everything and whose husband was in the hands of the enemy as a spy.

"Ride back to New York, Madame," urged the Marquis. "If nothing could save John André, what can save Richard Tryon?"

She raised her tear-stained, disfigured face. "Will he be hanged?" she gasped.

"Ah, Madame," he answered, "why did he allow Clinton to use him as a spy?"

Hortense took no notice of this. "I must see Mr. Washington," she clamored. "I *must* — he knows me well; why, Monsieur, he took me from my dead parents' side when I was a child — he was my guardian — do you think that he would refuse to see me now?"

"Poor child!" murmured the Marquis. He looked at her tenderly; her delicate features and pale blonde hair reminded him of the ladies of his own land; after all, her history had been a sad one, he reflected, and if she had the misfortune to be the wife of a spy, she was only to be pitied, not blamed, and admired for the constancy of her affection.

"Mistress Washington will see you, perchance," he said. "She and my wife arrived here yesterday." Hortense gave a grateful cry.

"She will have pity on me, I know," she murmured brokenly.

With steps unequal from fatigue, and her head bowed with shame and distress, the unfortunate wife of Richard Tryon followed her conductor into the thatched house that was surrounded with sweet fragrant bushes and late flowers.

In a small room with a diamond paned window, paneled in oak and furnished with the comfort and simplicity of a substantial farmhouse, sat Martha Washington, sewing a great flag, when Hortense and her guide entered upon her. Her dark gown, her bright hair, her fichu of lawn were outlined against the bright square of the window, and the colors of the flag, red, white, and blue, showed brilliantly even in the dull room.

She looked up as the two entered and stared a moment, not knowing the travel-stained figure in the black cloak.

But as Hortense, snatching off her tricorn hat and revealing her silver pale hair, stumbled forward, Mistress Washington rose, catching the flag to her bosom.

"Hortense!" she cried.

Mistress Tryon hid her face in her hands and broke into hysterical sobs.

Monsieur de Lafayette explained. "Monsieur Tryon was captured spying in the American lines. He has been court-martialed and — and condemned to — Major André's fate."

"I never knew of this," exclaimed Martha, in great agitation.

"No, Madame, General Washington thought it would distress you — and he will blame me for speaking of it, but this poor lady is so anxious to make the endeavor to save her husband I could not find it in my heart to refuse her."

Martha flung the flag over the chair and, going up to Hortense, caught her to her bosom. "Dear child," she said, "do not weep — control yourself — something must be done, something *shall* be done."

In that moment she forgot everything: Hortense's forgetfulness of early benefits, her indifference, her ingratitude, her frivolity, her open espousal of the loyalist side, and only knew that the once blithe creature, stripped of all her vanities, had come in her misery for pity and comfort.

"Monsieur," she said to the Marquis, "is my husband now with General Rochambeau?"

"He was lately, Madame."

"When he is free beg him to give me a few moments of his time."

He kissed her fair hand with respectful tenderness and withdrew.

Hortense drew away. "I have no right to come to you now," she said hoarsely. "How did I ever earn your love?" She sank down on the settle by the window; indeed she was too weak to any longer stand upright.

"Will Mr. Washington see me?" she asked desperately. "Will he listen to me?"

"The commander-in-chief," corrected Martha gently, "has ever a pitiful heart."

"If he will give me his life," said Hortense, endeavoring to steady her trembling lips, "we will leave for England at once — we will no more trouble him."

"America," answered Martha gently, "belongs to the Americans now, and you are better in your husband's country." She picked up the flag and shook out its silken folds; white stars showed lustrous on a deep blue ground and red bars on white.

"The arms of Mr. Washington!" cried Hortense, who had known them well in the old Mount Vernon days.

"Yes, his arms, and the new flag of the new nation," answered Martha proudly. "One of the standards of the world now."

"Alas," murmured Hortense, gazing at this symbol of the youngest nation that had struggled into vigorous being despite the sword and fire of the old world. "We are all undone! — and I submit, I desire to save nothing but Dick's life."

The door opened, and she sprang to her feet, thinking that it was the dreaded commander-in-chief. Martha turned, too, with the same thought.

But it was a woman who entered, a woman so still and cold in bearing and expression that the other two stood motionless, staring at her. She wore a dress of black velvet and a black beaver; in her gloved hands was a riding crop.

Her face, heavily shrouded by her hat, showed of a dead white, as if all health and color had been forever swept from it by some fierce illness; her figure was very erect and thin, and her eyes gleamed with a sparkle like the fire of fever. Martha was the first to recognize in this figure the wife of Benedict Arnold, now a general in the British Army and fighting against the Americans in the South.

"You!" she exclaimed, in accents of contempt, and a hot flush of anger stained her cheek.

Margaret Arnold did not wince nor change the bitter calm of her expression.

"I thought that you were in the South," said Hortense feebly.

Margaret flashed her one glance, then returned her gaze to the wife of the commander-in-chief. "Your contempt is undeserved," she said, in a low voice. "I know that I bear my husband's shame. But you, who know me, might believe that I was not his accomplice."

Martha put her hand on the flag that lay across the chair before her, as if the touch of it gave her strength. "What brings you here?" she asked.

"I wish to see your husband."

"He will not care to see you, Madam; spare him the pain of meeting the wife of the man whose name never passes his lips."

Margaret, never lowering her eyes, answered in a steady voice, "I am on my way to join my husband. I go with a dead heart. You will both understand what life is going to be for me, when I tell you I no longer care for him. But I am his wife. At first I could not bring myself to see him again, but now I am going. He has no friends, no honor, no respect and he needs me. Either of you would do the same. We shall go to England."

Both the other women were silent.

Margaret continued, "I have come a long, difficult journey from New York," she said; "I have been two months on the road. And now I have reached the South. I feel like one nearing the gates of Purgatory."

"Why did you come here?" asked Martha. "What can you have to say to us or we to you?"

"Two days ago we met a man from Yorktown," answered Margaret Arnold. "He had been wounded in some wayside skirmish and soon after he reached us he died. He told me that he was an American spy (he took me for a rebel, too), and before he died he entrusted me with his information." She paused. "I will give this to General Washington," she added, at last, "as some amends for — West Point." The two women stood utterly silent; when the door opened all three started. It was the commander-in-chief who entered.

He looked straight at the pale lady in the black; and stood arrested a few paces inside the door. In the stillness she spoke. "Sir, your spy sent to Yorktown will never return. But take this news. Now De Grasse is in Chesapeake Bay, Cornwallis will endeavor to escape by hurling himself forward to the South."

"Why do you tell me this?" asked the commander-in-chief.

"As some amends," she answered. "Perhaps, through pride, as I wish you to believe that my hands are clean of last year's work."

"And for this object you would hurt your own people?"

"I have no people," she answered wildly. "What do I care now about the war? I have given you the news I was entrusted with by your man."

"I knew it," said Washington quietly. "I have this moment given Monsieur de Lafayette orders to block the English in this design. Yet I thank your loyalty none the less."

"I have always been loyal to you since I married one of your generals, Sir."

Thoughts of their last meeting darkened his face. "Where are you bound?" he asked.

"To the South."

"To — him?"

"Yes."

"Ah!"

They looked straightly at each other; the blood slowly mounting to her face and throat. "I was innocent," she said.

"Madam, I believe it."

"Thank you."

She came slowly to the door and he opened it for her, bowing as she passed him.

When the door closed on her he gave a little sigh. "She is too good for Benedict Arnold," he said, and it was the last time he ever mentioned the name of the man he had once loved.

Hortense rose, trembling, from the deep window seat. "You have been merciful to her," she said; "will you be merciful to me?"

His eyes narrowed at sight of her piteous face. "Oh, Dick Tryon's wife," he said slowly.

"Hortense," she sobbed, "Hortense, who owes you so much."

He glanced thoughtfully at his wife, who stood by the silken folds of the flag.

"Listen to her," said Martha softly. "She will go to England with her husband — for the sake of the old days, listen . . ."

He was silent, thinking of the winter's day when he had found the child asleep beside the dying man in the cold wigwam — thinking of the day he had returned to Williamsburg to ask Martha Custis to look after this child, and she had parted the curtains and stood before him in a lavender blue gown.

Hortense was searching his face with desperate expectancy.

Martha gently touched the lace ruffles at his wrist. "Save Richard Tryon," she whispered sweetly.

He gave a little sigh as if he shook off memories and, turning to a little black desk that stood in a corner, he scrawled a few lines on a bit of paper that he handed, still wet, to Hortense.

"This is your husband's life," he said simply. "Take it to Major Hamilton."

Her hand shook so that she could scarcely grasp the paper, her knees relaxed beneath her, and she sank across the flag-covered chair, sobbing incoherent gratitude in a wild reaction of relief.

Martha raised her and wiped her eyes. "Go to your Dick," she said; "the officer without will conduct you to Major Hamilton."

She started up wildly. "Yes . . . yes . . . I must go to him."

She broke from Martha's kindly grasp and hurried from the room.

Washington looked after her with a slight smile. "There is a butterfly with broken wings," he remarked.

He came up to his wife and fingered the flag beside her.

They looked into each other's eyes. "Is it nearly finished, dear heart?"

"Nearly finished."

"And the war — is nearly finished, too, Martha."

"Yorktown will fall, Cornwallis will surrender?"

"Yes" — his eyes shone — "when that flag is completed, Martha, it will fly over the last British stronghold on American soil."

CHAPTER VIII
"THE WORLD TURNED UPSIDE DOWN"

Lord Cornwallis was cornered; De Grasse had driven back the English fleet that had sailed from New York to his rescue, and Washington had closed up round him; Lafayette held the approach to the South; the two rivers were in the hands of the enemy, and Chesapeake Bay was full of French warships.

At last "check!" had been cried in the long game of war — and cried by the man who, eight years ago, had appeared to have not the least chance of success.

Cornwallis knew that his surrender would be the end of Britain's attempts to hold America, and he made several desperate and heroic efforts to escape. A fearful hurricane foiled his wild endeavor to withdraw by water, and a fierce attempt to break through the lines of the enemy encircling him only resulted in his being repulsed and driven back into the fort that was crumbling to pieces under the fire of the French and American batteries.

Yorktown itself was battered to the ground beneath a cannonade that continued day and night; the fire of the guns was incessant, and the English flag that waved above the fort was tattered to a mere rag. At last the redoubts were carried by assaults led by Hamilton and Deux Ponts, and their own guns were turned against the English who still gave no sign of surrender. The commander-in-chief was scarcely ever out of the saddle; he organized and supervised every detail of the bombardment, and his eyes were ever turning to the tumbling defenses of Yorktown for the signal of surrender.

But Cornwallis was slow in succumbing. For three days after his redoubts had been captured, he resisted the terrific cannonade that silenced his own guns and shook his fortifications to pieces round him. Then, on October 17th, Washington, riding through the thick, foul smoke close under the walls of the fort, heard the thin rattle of a drum coming in the pauses of the cannon.

He looked up instinctively to the broken ramparts above him, and saw two figures on the wall of crumbling masonry, standing clear against the sky line.

One was a drummer boy in a scarlet coat and white sugar-loaf hat, beating a sad little rat-tat on a big drum strapped before him.

The other was an officer, bareheaded, who waved a lace handkerchief at the end of a cane.

Washington's heart gave a great leap as he saw the patch of white fluttering on the ramparts of Yorktown. He instantly gave orders that the bombardment was to cease.

An American officer rode up to the fort, and the Englishman with the flag was blindfolded and conducted to where Washington waited on horseback amid the French and American batteries.

The Englishman, guided by an American either side, was brought to the commander-in-chief's stirrup. As he was halted, he saluted.

"You come from Lord Cornwallis?" asked Washington.

The messenger turned in the direction of the voice. "Yes, Sir. My lord is willing to surrender Yorktown if you will permit twenty-four hours' truce to arrange terms."

Washington answered at once. "I will allow two hours."

To this the Englishman agreed with a promptitude that showed that the staunch Cornwallis was still only endeavoring to make the best of a hopeless position.

Washington outlined his terms, and the British officer returned to Yorktown with them.

By nightfall the details were finally agreed upon and, while Sir Henry Clinton was still hastening to the Chesapeake with help for the besieged, Lord Cornwallis and eight thousand men became American prisoners of war.

The news blazed across America; from all the thirteen states rose the shouts of thanksgiving, and on every lip was the name of George Washington.

On October 19th the English marched from their entrenchments through double lines of French and Americans, and laid down their arms. It was a warm, sunny, golden morning and sweet breezes blew above the ruined city and battered fort.

Washington, sitting erect on his splendid horse, felt his task in the main completed as he watched the British columns swinging by.

They were playing an old English air; Washington knew the name of it; he had heard his brother Lawrence whistle it in the old days at Mount Vernon.

"The World Turned Upside Down," it was called, and Washington thought it was the world turned upside down indeed to many of these officers who had danced in New York while he starved on the Delaware, who had toasted the "end of the rebellion" while he was flying across the frozen plains of New Jersey, and now were laying their arms at his feet. He sat motionless, the quaint little melody ringing in his ears, the scarlet line of the British before his eyes, and in his heart the one word — "America" — "America!"

Lord Cornwallis was sick and left the fort privately, being unable to sit a horse.

One of his aides-de-camp, General O'Hara, carried my lord's sword; with the bare weapon glittering in his hand, he rode up to the commander-in-chief and presented it, saluting.

Washington motioned to one of his staff, General Lincoln, who had once been my lord's prisoner, to take the sword.

That officer touched it, for a second taking the hilt in his hand, then, saluting his side, he returned it. General O'Hara rode on with the other British officers; he looked back at the handsome figure of the American commander. Beyond him was the shattered outline of Yorktown, and on the ramparts of the fort the new flag, the stars and bars, struggled against the breeze. General O'Hara, thinking of the tattered Union flag hauled down, paled a little, but recovered himself with the good humor of his race.

"Gentlemen," he said to those who rode about him. "I salute the new flag — and — Mr. Washington!"

THE END

The William & Mary Trilogy
by Marjorie Bowen

The life of William III, Prince of Orange, Stadtholder of the United Netherlands, and King of England (with Queen Mary II) is one of the most fascinating in all of history. Both the author and the publisher of this book have been interested in this subject for many years. Although the story as told in this book is partly fictional, all the main events are faithful to history.

F. Pronk wrote in *The Messenger* about Volume 1: The author is well-known for her well-researched fiction based on the lives of famous historical characters. The religious convictions of the main characters are portrayed with authenticity and integrity. This book is sure to enrich one's understanding of Protestant Holland and will hold the reader spellbound.

D.J. Engelsma wrote in *The Standard Bearer* about Volume 1: This is great reading for all ages, high school and older. *I Will Maintain* is well written historical fiction with a solid, significant, moving historical base . . . No small part of the appeal and worth of the book is the lively account of the important history of one of the world's greatest nations, the Dutch. This history was bound up with the Reformed faith and had implications for the exercise of Protestantism throughout Europe. Christian high schools could profitably assign the book, indeed, the whole trilogy, for history or literature classes.

C. Farenhorst wrote in *Christian Renewal* about Volume 1: An excellent tool for assimilating historical knowledge without being pained in the process, *I Will Maintain* is a very good read. Take it along on your holidays. Its sequel *Defender of the Faith*, is much looked forward to.

Time: 1670 - 1702 **Age: 14-99**

Volume 1 - *I Will Maintain*
ISBN 0-921100-42-6 **Can.$17.95 U.S.$15.90**

Volume 2 - *Defender of the Faith*
ISBN 0-921100-43-4 **Can.$15.95 U.S.$13.90**

Volume 3 - *For God and the King*
ISBN 0-921100-44-2 **Can.$17.95 U.S.$15.90**

William III and the Revolution of 1688
and *Gustavus Adolphus II*
2 Historical Essays by Marjorie Bowen.

F.G. Oosterhoff in *Reformed Perspective*: I recommend this book without any hesitation. The two biographies make excellent reading, and the times the essays describe are of considerable interest and importance in the history of our civilization. Moreover, although Bowen obviously is not one in faith with Gustavus Adolphus and William of Orange, her essays relate incidents that are testimonials to God's mercies in preserving His Church. Remembering these mercies, we may take courage for the present and for the future.

Time: 1672 - 1689 **Age: 14-99**
ISBN 0-921100-06-X **Can.$9.95 U.S.$7.95**

***Oliver Cromwell, The Governor of England* by Marjorie Bowen**

A historical novel in which the whole story of Cromwell's dealings with Parliament and the King is played out. It is written with dignity and conviction, and with the author's characteristic power of grasping the essential details needed to supply colour and atmosphere for the reader of the standard histories.

Time: 1645 - 1660 **Age: 14-99**
ISBN 0-921100-58-2 **Available D.V. in 1999**

William the Silent Series, Vol. 1 - *Prince and Heretic* by Marjorie Bowen

This fascinating story begins with William the Silent's marriage to Anne of Saxony and ends with his riding into exile after his first armed clash with Philip of Spain. The author develops her novel with an art that is a potent blend of the historian's careful attention to detail and the novelist's skill in vivid character delineation. This book is doubly interested if one recognizes the fact that the first William of Orange was a forefather of the present day Dutch and English royal families, and of the last emperor of Germany. It is hard to tell which of the 2 famous Williams (Father William the Silent & Great-grandson William III) was most important in the history of the Western World.

Time: 1551 - 1568 **Age: 14-99**
ISBN 0-921100-56-6 **Available D.V. in 2000**

William the Silent Series, Vol. 2 - *William by the Grace of God*
by Marjorie Bowen

The William of this stirring historical novel is William, Prince of Orange, better known to history as *William the Silent*, who led the successful revolt of the Netherlands against the bloody tyranny of Alva and Philip of Spain. Miss Bowen (1888 - 1952), who had no contemporary equal in the art of creating historical atmosphere, has drawn her hero with dignity and charm and made live again the heroes and statesmen who created, after years of suffering and struggle, the Dutch Republic.
— Adapted from an advertisement in one of Bowen's books published around 1926.

Time: 1568 - 1584 **Age: 14-99**
ISBN 0-921100-57-4 **Available D.V. in 2001**

Although William was assassinated in the end of this book, the abovementioned add goes on to say, "Third Novel of this Series to follow."
The intention may have been to write about William's sons Maurice and Frederic Henry, but to our knowledge no third volume ever appeared.
The first edition of volume 2 was published by E.P. Dutton in New York in 1916. We have a copy of the second edition of 1917. If anyone is able to help us find the entire or part of the third volume, we (and many readers with us) would greatly appreciate obtaining a copy. Methuen & Co. Ltd in London, England also published many of Marjorie Bowen's books. They published volume 3 of the William & Mary Trilogy, [For] *God and the King* on September 28, 1911 and reprinted it twice in October of 1911. The Fourth Edition was published in April 1912; the Fifth Edition in November 1912; the Sixth Edition in October 1915; and the Seventh Edition in September 1922. *God and the King* was dedicated to Major-General F. De Bas of the Dutch Army, who translated her books into Dutch.

***A Stranger in a Strange Land* by Leonora Scholte**

John E. Marshall in *The Banner of Truth*: This is a delightful book. It tells the story of H.P. Scholte, a preacher in the Netherlands, who being persecuted for his faith in his own country, emigrated to the U.S.A., and there established a settlement in Pella, Iowa, in the midst of the vast undeveloped prairie. . . The greater part of the book is taken up in telling the stories of the immense hardships known after emigration. Interwoven with this story is an account of Scholte's marriage and family life. . . It is a most heartwarming and instructive story.

Time: 1825 - 1880 **Age: 14-99**
ISBN 0-921100-01-9 **Can.$7.95 U.S.$6.90**

The Seventh Earl by Grace Irwin

A dramatized biography on Anthony Ashley Cooper, the Seventh Earl of Shaftesbury, who is most widely remembered as a 19th-century British philanthropist and factory reformer. "This is Grace Irwin's strongest and most poignant book . . . I have been moved and enriched by my hours with *The Seventh Earl*," wrote V.R. Mollenkott.

Time: 1801 - 1885 **Age: 14-99**
ISBN 0-8028-6059-1 **Can.$11.95 U.S.$9.95**

***Captain, My Captain* by Deborah Meroff**

The true (fictionalized) story of Mary Patten's courage against overwhelmings odds at sea. By the author of *Coronation of Glory*.

Time: 1837 - 1861 **Age: 14-99**
ISBN 0-921100-79-5 Available D.V. Fall of 1997

***With Lee in Virginia*: A Story of the American Civil War by G.A. Henty**

Few great wars have been fought out by each side with greater intensity of conviction in the rightness of its cause or with more abundant personal heroism than the American civil war. Of this heroic clash of opposing convictions Mr. Henty has made admirable use in the story of a young Virginian planter, who, after bravely proving his sympathy with the slaves of brutal masters, serves with no less courage and enthusiasm under Lee and Jackson through the most exciting events of the struggle. He has many hairbreath escapes, is several times wounded, and twice taken prisoner; but his courage and readiness and, in two cases, the devotion of a black servant and of a runaway slave whom he had assisted bring him safely through all difficulties.

Time: 1864 A.D. **Age: 14-99**
ISBN 1-887159-09-6 **Can.$28.95 U.S.$19.99**

***Things We Couldn't Say* by Diet Eman & James Schaap**

The true story of a love stronger than Nazi persecution.

Dr. K. Sietsma, the author of *The Idea of Office* (a book that everyone should read), was not the only member of the Sietsma family who died in Dachau. His nephew Hein died in the same place. Dr. J. Faber wrote about Diet Eman's book (the fiancé of Hein): The striking aspect of this book is that it testifies to God's faithfulness . . . I heartily recommend it not only to my contemporaries among Dutch immigrants but also to their children and grandchildren. ["One of the best war-books I ever read!" R.A.J.]

Time: 1940 - 1945 **Age: 14-99**
ISBN 0802837638 **Can.$25.95 U.S.$19.95**

***A Mighty Fortress in the Storm* by Paulina M. Rustenburg Bootsma**

Fay S. Lapka in Christian Week: [This book] . . . is the fictionalized historical account of the actual village of Never Thought Of (literal translation of Nooitgedacht) in the Netherlands, and the efforts of the tiny, two-farm town to aid the resistance. This is a thoroughly interesting, at times warmly-amusing story, that will be enjoyed by adults. The photographs reproduced throughout the text add realism to the amazing story.

Time: 1940 - 1945 **Age: 14-99**
ISBN 0-921100-37-X **Can.$11.95 U.S.$10.90**

Israel's Hope and Expectation by Rudolf Van Reest

G. Nederveen in *Clarion*: This is one of the best novels I have read of late. I found it captivating and hard to put down. Here is a book that is not time-bound and therefore it will never be outdated.

The story takes place around the time of Jesus' birth. It is written by someone who has done his research about the times between the Old and New Testament period. The author informs you in an easy style about the period of the Maccabees. . . Van Reest is a good storyteller. His love for the Bible and biblical times is evident from the start. He shows a good knowledge of the customs and mannerisms in Israel. Many fine details add to the quality of the book. You will be enriched in your understanding of the ways in the Old Testament.

Time: Inter-Testament Period **Age: 15-99**
ISBN 0-921100-22-1 **Can.$19.95 U.S.$17.90**

Beric The Briton: A Story of the Roman Invasion by G.A. Henty

This story deals with the invasion of Britain by the Roman legionaries. Beric, who is a boy-chief of a British tribe, takes a prominent part in the insurrection under Boadicea; and after the defeat of that heroic queen he continues the struggle in the fen-country. Ultimately Beric is defeated and carried captive to Rome, where he is trained in the exercise of arms in a school of gladiators. Such is the skill which he there acquires that he succeeds in saving a Christian maid by slaying a lion in the arena, and is rewarded by being made librarian in the palace, and the personal protector of Nero. Finally he escapes from this irksome service, organizes a band of outlaws in Calabria, defies the power of Rome, and at length returns to Britain, where he becomes a wise ruler of his own people.

Time: 62 A.D. **Age: 14-99**
ISBN 1-887159-06-1 **Can.$31.95 U.S.$21.99**

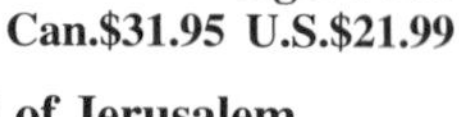

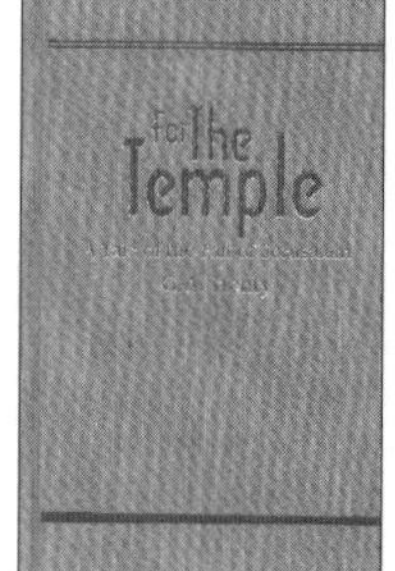

For The Temple: A Tale of the Fall of Jerusalem by G.A. Henty

Mr. Henty here weaves into the record of Josephus an admirable and attractive story. The troubles in the district of Tiberias, the march of the legions, the sieges of Jotapata, of Gamala, and of Jerusalem, form the impressive and carefully studied historic setting to the figure of the lad who passes from the vineyard to the service of Josephus, becomes the leader of a guerrilla band of patriots, fights bravely for the Temple, and after a brief term of slavery at Alexandria, returns to his Galilean home with the favour of Titus.

Time: 70 A.D. **Age: 14-99**
ISBN 1-887159-00-2 **Can.$27.55 U.S.$18.99**

Against the World - The Odyssey of Athanasius by Henry W. Coray

Muriel R. Lippencott in *The Christian Observer*: [it] . . . is a partially fictionalized profile of the life of Athanasius . . . who died in 373 AD. Much of the historical content is from the writing of reliable historians. Some parts of the book, while the product of the author's imagination, set forth accurately the spirit and the temper of the times, including the proceedings and vigorous debates that took place in Alexandria and Nicea. . . This is the story that Rev. Coray so brilliantly tells.

Time: 331 - 373 A.D. **Age: 16-99**
ISBN 0-921100-35-3 **Can.$8.95 U.S.$7.90**

The Shadow Series
by Piet Prins

One of the most exciting series of a master story teller about the German occupation of the Netherlands during the emotional time of the Second World War (1940-1945). K. Bruning in *Una Sancta* about Vol.4 - The Partisans, and Vol. 5 - Sabotage: . . . the country was occupied by the German military forces. The nation's freedom was destroyed by the foreign men in power. Violence, persecutions and executions were the order of the day, and the main target of the enemy was the destruction of the christian way of life. In that time the resistance movement of underground fighters became very active. People from all ages and levels joined in and tried to defend the Dutch Christian heritage as much as possible. The above mentioned books show us how older and younger people were involved in that dangerous struggle. It often was a life and death battle. Every page of these books is full of tension. The stories give an accurate and very vivid impression of that difficult and painful time. These books should also be in the hands of our young people. They are excellent instruments to understand the history of their own country and to learn the practical value of their own confession and Reformed way of life. What about as presents on birthdays?

Time: 1944 - 1945 **Age: 10-99**

Vol. 1 The Lonely Sentinel
ISBN 0-88815-781-9 Can.$7.95 U.S.$6.35
Vol. 2 Hideout in the Swamp
ISBN 0-88815-782-7 Can.$7.95 U.S.$6.35
Vol. 3 The Grim Reaper
ISBN 0-88815-783-5 Can.$6.95 U.S.$5.65
Vol. 4 The Partisans
ISBN 0-921100-07-8 Can.$7.95 U.S.$7.20
Vol. 5 Sabotage
ISBN 0-921100-08-6 Can.$7.95 U.S.$7.20

Who was Piet Prins (pen name for Pieter Jongeling 1909-1985)?

Mr. Jongeling was born in the northern part of the Netherlands and studied to become a teacher. He indeed did teach for some years, but soon became the international correspondent of a Dutch newspaper. In 1942 he was arrested by the Germans and sent to a concentration camp. After the allied victory in 1945 he returned to the Netherlands and became one of the most important journalists and politicians in the Netherlands. For many years he was the editor of a Reformed Christian daily newspaper, in which he wrote most of his children's books as serials under the name Piet Prins. The first thing many people read, when the newspaper arrived, was these serials. In 1963, Mr. Jongeling became member of the Dutch parliament for the Reformed Political Alliance. One commentator mused: "What makes Jongeling such a remarkable parliamentarian? That's simple. The man works like a horse! He is always fully informed. When Jongeling speaks, the house listens." Both as a journalist and a statesman, Pieter Jongeling knew himself bound by the inspired Word of God and as such his labour has born much fruit.

Stand By, Boys!
by K. Norel

This is a true story of things that happened when the waves of the North sea broke through the dike and flooded much of the Netherlands in 1953.

Time: 1953 **Age: 10-99**
Cat. Nr. BTP 2799 **Can.$ 6.95 U.S.$ 5.90**

William of Orange - The Silent Prince
by W.G. Van de Hulst

Whether you are old or young you will enjoy this biography on the life of William of Orange. Read it and give it as a birthday present to your children or grandchildren. A fascinating true story about one of the greatest princes who ever lived and already by his contemporaries justly compared to King David.

Time: 1533 - 1584 **Age: 7-99**
ISBN 0-921100-15-9 **Can.$8.95 U.S.$7.90**

Three Men Came To Heidelberg **and** ***Glorious Heretic*** **by Thea B. Van Halsema**

From the sixteenth-century Protestant Reformation came two outstanding statements of Faith: The Heidelberg Catechism (1563) and the Belgic Confession (1561). The stories behind these two historic documents are found in this small book. Frederick, a German prince, asked a preacher and a professor to meet at Heidelberg to write a statement of faith . . . The writer of the Belgic Confession was a hunted man most of his life. Originally he wrote the confession as an appeal to the King of Spain . . .

Time: 1560 - 1563 **Age: 12-99**
Cat. Nr. IP 1610 **Can.$7.95 U.S.$5.95**

Struggle for Freedom Series
by Piet Prins

David Engelsma in the *Standard Bearer*: This is reading for Reformed children, young people, and (if I am any indication) their parents. It is the story of 12-year-old Martin Meulenberg and his family during the Roman Catholic persecution of the Reformed Christians in the Netherlands about the year 1600. A peddlar, secretly distributing Reformed books from village to village, drops a copy of Guido de Brès' *True Christian Confession* — a booklet forbidden by the Roman Catholic authorities. An evil neighbor sees the book and informs . . .

Time: 1568 - 1572 **Age: 10-99**
Vol. 1 - *When The Morning Came* **ISBN 0-921100-12-4** **Can.$9.95 U.S.$8.90**
Vol. 2 - *Dispelling the Tyranny* **ISBN 0-921100-40-X** **Can.$9.95 U.S.$8.90**
Vol. 3 & 4 are still to be translated and published.

Salt in His Blood — The Life of Michael De Ruyter
by William R. Rang

The greatest Dutch Admiral is an example of Christian love and piety, and fascinating because of his many true adventures as a sailer-boy, captain, and pirate-hunter.

Time: 1607 - 1676 **Age: 10-99**
ISBN 0-921100-59-0 **Can.$10.95 U.S.$9.90**

Huguenot Garden **by Douglas M. Jones III**
A Children's Story of Faith

Huguenot Garden is a children's story of the daily and adventurous episodes in the lives of Renée and Albret Martineau, young twin sisters in a seventeenth-century, French Protestant family. The episodes follow the twins and the rest of the Martineau family as they work, worship, commune, and suffer persecution together. The story aims to portray the ideas and historical details common to Huguenot life in La Rochelle, France, 1685, a tragic year whose final quarter brought the full wrath of Louis XIV.

Time: 1685 **Age: 10-99**
ISBN 1-880692-21-X **Can.$10.95 U.S.$8.50**

When speaking about the Huguenots, one often hears the exclamation, "I am also a descendant of the Huguenots!" Considering the fact that thousands of Huguenots were dispersed over the whole world, especially to Canada, England, The Netherlands, Switzerland, South Africa, and the U.S.A., it is very likely that 30% of the North American population has some Huguenot blood running through their veins. Of the Protestants it may well be the majority that has some connection with those who were martyred and exiled for their faith. Eight generations back our forefathers number approximately 132. One of these ancestors may very well have been a Huguenot. But, aside from the family connection, all descendants of the Reformation, who maintain the Faith of the fathers, will realize the kinship we have with these brothers and sisters in Christ. This kinship, and the example of their faith, has moved Inheritance Publications to launch a series of books entitled:

Huguenot Inheritance Series

1 - *The Escape* by A. Van der Jagt
2 - *The Secret Mission* by A. Van der Jagt
3 - *How They Kept The Faith* by Grace Raymond
4 - *The Young Huguenots* by Edith S. Floyer [1997?]
5 - *Driven into Exile* by Charlotte Maria Tucker (A.L.O.E.) [1998?]
6 - *The Refugees (a Tale of two Continents)* by A. Conan Doyle [1999?]

Most titles in this series (except for # 1 & # 2) were published for the first time about one hundred years ago. It is our prayer that these books will be read by many people in thankful remembrance of those who were faithful unto death, for the glory of God, and as encouragement to live also in faithfulness and gratitude before our Heavenly Father.

Roelof & Theresa Janssen